Black Skies
RIVIERA

ISBN: 978-1-8380448-5-5 (eBook)
ISBN: 978-1838044862 (Paperback)

Cover design by: **Steamy Designs**
Photographer: **Wander Aguiar**
Model: **Andrew Biernat**
Editing by: **Light Hand Proofreading**
Proof by: **Amanda Marie Edits**
Formatting by: **Midnight Designs**

SINFULLY SEXY ROMANCE

To Sammy B,
This book wouldn't exist without you.
Thank you for pulling it back from the brink...

Blurb

From international bestselling author Catherine Wiltcher comes a brand new standalone mafia romance.

★ ★ ★ ★ ★

"A beautifully written gem of a story"
- USA Today Bestselling Author, Charmaine Pauls

She's a debt no sinner can pay...

They call this place the Billionaires' Playground.
I, Aiden Knight, staked my claim the minute I arrived.
Now my casino is the hottest church in town,
And vice is the only confession required.

Issa Dubova is the queen of cloudy diamonds:
An innocent.
A Bratva princess.
My new wife...

She's nothing more than revenge to me:
A pretty bargain for the names of the men who killed my father.

I never asked to see the shape of her heart.

I never asked for her to fill the blank spaces of mine...

A Note from the Author

Black Skies Riviera is my very loose interpretation of *The Count of Monte Cristo*. If you are familiar with the story, you will recognize nods to certain character names and circumstances.

Please note that Ielena/Issa Dubova's surname is spelled differently to her father's name—Dubov. This is deliberate. In Russian, adding an "a" or an "ova" to the family name means that the female "belongs" to that family.

…But not for much longer.

"Hatred is blind; rage carries you away;
and he who pours out vengeance runs the risk
of tasting a bitter draught."

— Alexandre Dumas

Prologue

AIDEN

Fourteen Years Ago...

There's a town in Sicily where the streets are paved with sin. Some say it's the place to go when you're hung, drawn, and desperate. For me, it's a gateway to the Underworld—my ferry crossing being a budget flight from London Heathrow. I landed at one p.m., and by two p.m. the Devil himself was requesting a meet and greet.

Tommaso Zaccaria.

Don of the Zaccaria family, and a single extortion away from becoming *Capo Dei Capi*, *boss of all bosses*, of the *Cosa Nostra.*

Or so says Wikipedia.

Four days ago, I knew nothing about the mafia. I was a punk kid of sixteen from Brixton who cared more about spending money than making it. Then life happened. A whole lot of life.

Murder.

Pain.

Vengeance.

Three shit-smeared fists grabbed a hold of my heart, forcing me to grow up hard and fast.

Now I'm sitting opposite the most notorious crime boss in the world in a back room of a run-down *trattoria*, next to a sweet-smelling stack of Sicilian lemons. There's a faded poster of the Italian 1990 World Cup soccer team taped to the wall above his head.

We're not alone. Two of his men are standing guard. Black sunglasses. Black weapons. By rights, I should be scared, but grief has gone and punched that emotion right out of me.

Zaccaria runs his finger over the crumpled note I traveled fifteen hundred kilometers to show him, smoothing out the creases and tracing the dark bloodstains. I count the seconds as he pores over the words—the silence painful and dragging.

Eight hundred and fifty-six…

He's younger than I expected: late fifties or thereabouts. He's not as kingly sadistic or as gentrified as Hollywood would make you believe, except when he's pointing his empty gray eyes at you like the twin barrels of a loaded gun. He looks like the skinny old uncle who everyone's afraid of. The one who never married, and who enters a room under a cloud of suspicion. There's no throne of bones for him either, just a cracked wooden chair with a missing spool that creaks whenever he shifts position.

Despite my age, I see him for what he is: a killer, an oppressor, a wide deceiver. His disguise is the rattling of a trap door beneath your feet, right before his hangman pulls the lever.

"How old are you now?" he barks suddenly, his heavy accent adding extra indolence to his words and making all the dust particles scatter.

"*Now*?" I frown. "'Now' implies that we've met before, Mr.

Zaccaria."

"Haven't we?" He aims those dead gray eyes at their target—namely, my face—and holds firm.

Somewhere in my head I hear the click of a safety.

"Sixteen."

"You seem older."

"Past the age of consent, but it's a bitch to get a drink around here."

Even after everything I'm still a cocky little shit.

A ghost of a smile quirks his lips. "That's something we shall have to rectify." He casts his gaze to his men and a bottle of Limoncello and a couple of glasses are placed on the table between us. "Your father was a good man," he declares, pouring out two generous shots. "A loyal man, who will be mourned."

"I have no goddamn idea how he was connected to you, though."

My expletive produces more of his sinister smile.

What? They don't curse in the mafia?

Without asking for his approval, I take the glass closest to me and tip the contents down my throat. Regardless of what I just said, I've done more drinking in the last week than I have in a lifetime.

"Jacob Knight did me a favor a long time ago," he murmurs, "and a favor for me is a favor for life."

"Does that favor carry on down the family tree?" I pour myself another. Extra-large. "Because four nights ago, Mister Big-Shot Mobster, someone murdered my parents, and the only fucking clue I have for any of it is that note in your hand."

"*Ach.* Your generation throw curses around like blunt knives," he says with a wince. "You'll learn, soon enough, that with age comes refinement."

"And with youth comes perception." I pour myself a third. "The minute you heard about that note you sent a happy hello to my roach motel. It tells me that my father, a broke car mechanic from South Shields, meant more to you than the rest of your favor whores."

Zaccaria chuckles. "You are fearless, but you are reckless. Tell me, what really brings you to Sicily?"

"Justice."

He cocks a graying eyebrow at me. "Would you care to be more specific?"

"I want the names of the men who killed my family."

"And what makes you think I'd know?" He takes a casual sip of his Limoncello. Just a sip, mind you. He's practicing the refinement thing he mentioned.

"My father had *that note* stuffed into his mouth the night he died. It doesn't take a genius to figure it out."

I watch him glance at it again. "Are you rich? Because this kind of justice comes with a price that few are willing to pay."

I lean forward over the table with three shots worth of thirty-percent proof firing up my veins. "Try me."

But for all my bravado, my instincts aren't forewarning. This face-to-face will either solve my riddle or leave me pushing up daisies with all the other corpses in this town.

The tension builds and strains before Zaccaria relaxes back into his chair. I've impressed him. I'm guessing he doesn't have many grief-stricken, ballsy-as-fuck, sixteen-year-old kids up in his face very often.

"Have you heard of *La Società Villefort*?" He delivers the name with a respectful flourish, as if it's some kind of Illuminati bastard child.

"What do *you* think?" I cock my own eyebrow back at him.

"Where I come from, we have a cafe called Dick's Chips and a nightclub called The Fridge."

"Careful," he warns, drumming his fingers lightly on the table. "I'm indulging your disrespect because of your loss, but my reserves are not infinite."

I force a swallow down. "What's this got to do with my father?"

"I believe the man who ordered the hit is under the protection of *La Società Villefort*. And that same protection will have filtered down to the soldiers who carried out the deed. If that is the case, you may never have the justice you seek."

"You're the boss of the Zaccaria family," I grit out. "Codes and rules don't apply."

"*La Società Villefort* would disagree. They're an international organization, established to safeguard politicians, the rich, the supremely powerful... Once you are under their protection, there isn't a law or a grudge that can touch you."

"There must be a way—"

"There is one." I watch the muscles flexing in his hollowed-out cheeks as a hard decision is considered. "Until now, I've resisted affiliation with *Villefort*. I am old fashioned," he adds with a shrug. "I source my protection from loyalty and fear. But for Jacob." His fingers move to the note again and his expression tightens. "For Jacob, I would be willing to infiltrate it. I will find the men responsible for this crime."

Relief has me pouring out a fourth shot and raising it in toast. "I want to pull the trigger myself," I say, trying to sound like a hard-ass when the most I've ever butchered is road-kill. "I want them dead by Christmas."

Zaccaria laughs—a full, rasping tenor, as if his own depravity has somehow forced its way inside and claimed squatters rights. "I wasn't being coy when I inquired about your wealth, Mr. Knight. It is not money I seek for this. It is servitude. *Your* servitude. You will be an associate to *La Famiglia* for as long as it takes me to source these names. From now on, you work for me."

The decision is easy, as far as I'm concerned. London is tainted, and I was drifting into a life of petty crime anyway.

"How long will this 'servitude' last?"

"It takes fourteen years for approval to *La Società Villefort*. I expect the same from you."

"Fourteen *years*?" I bang my shot glass down on the table in shock.

"*Villefort* is a retirement insurance policy for a particular… *generation*, which excludes me at this time. As corrupt men grow older, they grow weaker. They make mistakes—mistakes that can cost them a life's work, reputation, and fortune. There are no wrongs that *Villefort* cannot put right. Murders go unsolved. Illegal bank accounts remain hidden. Tax evasion becomes a game."

"Fourteen years," I whistle again. "How much is membersh—"

"An amount that a smart young man like yourself will earn for me one day. First, you will receive a proper education, and then I will teach you how to gut a man like a fish." He flashes his white teeth at me. "Revenge is a dish best served cold… It is a long game. It sits on the table marinating in violence until you'd do anything to get a taste. The skills I will teach you over the next fourteen years will bring about your satisfaction. Your soul will be stained, but your black heart will be full. You will want for nothing more in life than this."

I try to stand up, but shock, age, and alcohol pitch me

sideways. I ignore the laughter echoing all around me as I steady myself against the wall.

"Tell me something, Mr. Zaccaria," I slur. "What the hell did my father do to earn this kind of gratitude from you?"

The don's expression sobers and his men's laughter follows suit. "The greatest gift that a father can ever receive," he replies smoothly. "He saved my son's life."

Chapter One

ISSA

Fourteen Years Later...

"*All women become like their mothers. That is their tragedy. No man does. That's his.*"

I shut the slim book with a decisive thwack, and slide it back into my purse.

Not me.

Never me.

This isn't a statement of fact from Oscar Wilde. It's my motivation to prove him wrong.

I may not know the names of all the presidents who have walked the corridors of the Élysée Palace, or why macarons from Paris—*only from Paris*—ignite in your mouth like mini explosions, but I know I'd rather die than become like my mother.

"More Sancerre, *mademoiselle*?" The waitress pauses by my table on her way to the bar and I catch her glancing at my fingers. They're clenched around the stem of my glass so tightly the whites of my knuckles are showing.

"*Non, merci.*" I smile up at her, loosening my grip.

"Are you sure?" She arches a knowing eyebrow.

"*Oui,*" I say more firmly. *If I'm absent from my father's house for much longer, there'll be hell to pay.*

"As you wish." She drifts away and I glance at my watch.

Ten minutes.

Ten more solitary minutes to inhale a sonnet and exhale the dirt.

This time it's a Karina turn of phrase, a quirky burst of a thing, because that's what my sister is to me—the bright curve of a smile whenever I'm sad or act too serious.

I miss her. I forgive her. Even though she's left me standing on the edge of something that's black and terrifying.

Drink your wine, Issa.

Exhale.

It's been four weeks since we last spoke, but she's forever catching in the filter of my mind. Like the time she said she hated men who snapped their fingers for service in restaurants. Like the guy in his fifties at the next table in the beachfront bar, the one who's leaning back in his chair with his fat legs crossed awkwardly to the side as if they're all set to spring apart at any moment.

Lifting my Sancerre to my mouth, I sip and study. The pain in my chest is a thousand sharp, stabby knives today, and I'm grateful for the distraction. He's American, as far as I can tell. The creases in his cream linen suit match the lines gathering at the corners of his Wayfarers, and his wine carafe is sitting empty like a threat in front of him. He looks like a washed-up movie producer on the tipping point of some ugly PR scandal.

Snap, snap. "Can I get some service over here, please?"

Can I get a life transplant?

I bought the illusion my parents sold me for twenty-two years, even when it was tainted with ignorance and decaying with neglect.

From the outside, life looked perfect. Too perfect. That should have been my first clue, but what socially awkward young woman wants to turn down a shot at peer envy? My clothes were always stylish, my ponies thoroughbreds, and my language multi-cultural. I was taught to speak Russian, English, French, and Italian fluently—my education courtesy of the most exclusive schools in Paris—and I was carefully dissimulated from the realities of my father's business.

Until I watched him shoot a man dead on the front porch of our estate six months ago.

That's when the truth slipped and I caught a glimpse of my real cage.

Our security detail wasn't a hired firm for the rich and famous, they were stone-cold killers, loyal only to my father. He wasn't the esteemed Parisian businessman that he portrayed himself to be. He was their *Pakhan.*

After that, the blows kept coming.

His close confidante, Maxim Lebedev, a man who I considered close enough to be my godfather, was one of his *Brigadiers.* His business cohorts were *Two Spies* and *Derzhatel Obschaka.* The men at the fringes of our lives were nothing more than *Patsan* soldiers...

Worst of all, I learned that freedom is an unobtainable fantasy for Bratva women like us. Our wealth makes our fiction easier to swallow, but it doesn't take away the taste. Last month, I was dreaming of a job at *The Louvre.* Today, I've arrived in Cannes to marry a man I don't even know the name of, and my future? It's just another commodity for my father to barter and trade.

I refuse to let this define me, though.

My end game is too important.

She's too important.

Snap, snap.

The edge of the bar's terrace blends seamlessly with a rainbow mile of golden sand and bathing suits. I don't remember Cannes being this beautiful the last time I visited. Beautiful people, yes, but not with the same vibe and texture—from the plush greens of the palm trees lining *La Croisette* to the white-bullet leanness of the vessels harbored in the nearby *Vieux Port de Cannes*. It's the paradox of life, laid out before me like a perfect, billion-euro picnic. You notice so much more when uncertainty is punching holes in your existence.

Beyond the beach, the Mediterranean is a shimmering blue ribbon mixed with threads of silver and gold. The waves are calling to me as my fingers inch toward the charcoal pencil at the bottom of my purse next to my book. Not that I'll ever swim in them again. *In a few strokes I could capture the outline of that superyacht on the horizon.*

"Ielena."

My hand retracts guiltily as one of my father's men appears next to the table, turning my personal space into something dark and claustrophobic.

"I'm coming," I tell him in Russian, motioning to a glass that's three quarters drunk.

"Quicker. Your father is expecting you."

"Five more minutes." I hold his gaze, watching his scowl spread like poison.

"Three."

"Fine."

He stalks back through the busy bar and out to the waiting car.

Snap, snap. "For the last time, can I get some fucking service over here?"

A shocked hush descends over the terrace as all eyes swing from the angry American to the waitress.

"Of course, *monsieur.*" Smiling tightly, she pulls out her notebook and makes her way over. "Pardon me. I did not see you there."

Her English is as fluent as her lie, which is just as well because this man reeks of bad Hollywood.

"Get me a Ricard Pastis in a highball. Double-quick." He doesn't even look up from his cell as he barks out his order. He keeps scrolling through his messages as if he's searching for the Holy Grail in tiny black letters. Cambria font.

The waitress shifts her weight to her other foot, and I can hear her internal scream from here. "Would that be with a dash of grenadine, *monsieur?*"

"*Grenadine?*" He takes on her question like an uninvited challenge. "Why the fuck would I want something like that in my Ricard?"

"Because it's the traditional French way," I interrupt coolly, having heard enough. "It's called the Milk of Marseilles."

"And who the hell asked you, Miss Prissy Prosaic?" His top lip curls in scorn as he takes in my elegant white shift dress, my flawless make-up, the subtle diamond studs in my ears, and the neat chignon. It's the uniform I'm forced to wear to curb my individuality and to hide all my secrets. My father's men were careful to leave their frustration only on the parts of me that good girls never show. "Go back to whatever over-privileged money pit you crawled out from, and stay the hell out of my business."

A rush of warmth hits my cheeks. Before I have a chance to respond, an icy riposte beats me to it—with an accent that's a full wheel of British contempt.

"I suggest you take your own advice there, Anderson. Or perhaps you'd prefer my fist to make the decision for you? How much do you owe me again?"

The sunburn drains from the American's cheeks as he clocks the guy standing behind me. "Aiden Knight," he splutters, switching from rude to repentant in a heartbeat. "You're a long way from Monaco."

"It's a pleasant day and I fancied a drive." There's a pause. "Fist, Anderson," he reminds him smoothly. "And I want the half a million you owe me."

"You'll have it first thing tomorrow." Anderson stands so fast his chair falls backward with a clatter. "I was just, ah, leaving." He chucks a fifty-euro note onto the table and turns toward the exit like a sprinter focusing on the finish line.

"Aren't you forgetting something?" The man's voice has a tinge of amusement to it now.

"Right." He swings back to me so fast his Wayfarers slip down his nose. "Sorry. Bad day." Next, he turns to the waitress. "Here, have a tip." Another fifty euros gets tossed onto the table, and then he's gone, bouncing off tables in his haste to escape.

It's all because of the man I can't see, the one whose presence is furling around my body like an anaconda's embrace. He smells of danger, too. Of sinful memories that never fade. Of the kind of bastard who would reel a woman in and use her up before taking Juliet Capulet's dagger to her heart.

All this, and I haven't even seen his face yet.

"Everything okay, Nicolette?" I hear him say, slipping into flawless French. His shadow is bolder and more defined than it should be. It's burning up my shoulders and casting near black across the white tablecloth.

The waitress nods, scooping up the cash from the table with a grin. "Oui, Monsieur Knight. Your timing was perfect. As always."

"Glad someone's pleased to see me. And more wine for the *mademoiselle*."

Instinctively, I smack my palm across the top of my glass. "No, please, I—" I turn and stop, my protestations lost forever to the busy terrace.

Urbane.

Savage.

Beautiful.

The colors of him… *My God. The colors.*

It's not so much their vibrancy. It's their parity, and how they all meld together to make up a picture of male perfection.

His inky-black hair—short on the sides and long on the top—creates a flawless frame for a set of golden features as sharp as they are sensual. In contrast, his gaze is a stormy cerulean-blue ocean. A designer suit and a fitted black shirt deliver a hard sell for a body that's ripped and lean, and there's an enticing dash of dark hair at his open neckline.

"Do people normally act that way around you?" My words come rushing out as I forget my head, my manners, and everything else in between.

"You mean like frightened *lapin*?" His eyes gleam unpleasantly. "Only when I'm pointing my hunting gun at them. What are you drinking?" he asks, switching back to English again.

"It's not necess—"

"No arguments." His expression screams arrogance, and he

defies my wishes with a smirk. "My bar. My rules. Nicolette, another Sancerre, I believe." He nods at the hovering waitress.

"You own this place?" I say in surprise.

"Amongst others… Fuck it. I need a drink as well. It's been a hell of a day. Open a bottle of the Château Pavie, Nicolette," he shouts, pulling out the canvas chair next to me. *Without my permission, I might add.* "The 2001, not any of the later ones."

"Yes, *monsieur.*"

"May I suggest the 2015 instead?" I say quietly, feeling the need to dispute his choice, but not fully understanding why. "The hints of black cherries and oak are stronger on the palate."

"You know your Saint-Émilion?" His mouth quirks in surprise as he slowly folds his body into the chair, his movements in stark contrast to the sudden, sharp peak in my heart rate.

I don't have his full attention, though. Not even close. One minute he's gazing out at the beach, the next those cool blues are greeting old acquaintances on the terrace.

"So, what do I call the newest sommelier on the Riviera?" he says, nodding at someone else over my shoulder.

"Issa."

"*Issa?*" I adore my nickname. It's feminine and strong—a rose with thorns—but the scornful way he says it makes it sound silly and frivolous. "How disappointing."

"I'm not sure I follow."

His expression hardens. It's like he's seeing me for the first time, and not liking what he sees. "*Issa* is neither one thing nor the other. It's the *mudblood* of appellations… A chronic indecision." Nicolette places two glasses and a bottle down in front of us. "Issa," he adds, with another of his wicked smirks, "is a piss poor attempt by your parents at the whole naming thing."

I sit there gaping at him, too shocked to think of a comeback.

"So, tell me. Are you a *half-measure mademoiselle*, both in name and in life?" His gaze drops to my neat and unexciting dress with the same disinterest on his face as the American had.

And it stings.

It stings more than it should.

"Did you rescue me from one insult, just to give me another?" I sputter. The woman who never shows any emotion is sliding dangerously close to showing all of them at once.

"Don't kid yourself, I wasn't rescuing anyone." He clinks my untouched glass with his own and drinks deeply, catching the eye of someone else to my left. "You were an excuse to pick a fight with a man I don't like very much."

I blush again. "*An excuse?*"

"Yes, a decorative, if somewhat insipid excuse."

"Then why deign to sit with me if I'm so insipid?" I say tartly. "Never judge a book by its cover, Monsieur—"

"Knight."

I scoff. "Not from where I'm sitting."

"Not from where anybody's sitting, if I'm being honest." He grins wolfishly. "Knights defend virtue, which is a fucking waste of time if you ask me. Don't you agree, Miss…?"

"Doe," I say firmly, gathering my things together. "I don't feel like having my surname ridiculed as well." There's no way in hell I'm being ripped apart by some cruel Englishman who views me as nothing more than his afternoon's entertainment. "I'm leaving now, *monsieur*."

"So soon?"

He doesn't look in the least bit bothered by it.

"Yes, I didn't realize chivalry came with a twist of scorn." I then watch, incensed, as his eyes start to drift again. "You could at least give me your full attention when you're offending me!"

His head snaps back, eyebrows lifting. And then he laughs, a lush and dangerous sound that awakens parts of me it really shouldn't.

"Well, well, well, the blank canvas has a smear of paint, after all."

You have no idea.

"Why are you being so rude? I never asked you to sit here. I never asked for your wine or your disrespect."

"Why? Because I find your kind insufferable and I fancied the sport… Vive la revolution," he drawls. "Let them eat brioche. Am I right?"

"My *kind*?"

"Stupid rich, bored, empty, unemployable, unsalvageable."

All the things my mother is.

All the things I'll never be.

"If you'll excuse me," I say, tossing my napkin down. "I have a new fiancé waiting."

Wow. I must be desperate if I'm throwing that in his face.

"Then go." He dismisses me with a flick of his hand. "Run along to your half-measure billionaire husband-to-be, and make your equally half-measure children in your ghastly half-measure mansion by the sea."

My vision starts to swim as he unwittingly outlines the black hole I'm being sucked into.

"And your life is so perfect?" I say, blinking at him.

"At least my happiness doesn't hang on the success of Chanel's spring/summer collection."

There's a pause as I drown in his terrible, hurtful, *alluring* masculinity, and then I'm tipping the contents of his expensive bottle of wine all over his glossy black head and Armani suit.

"*Au revoir*, Monsieur Knight," I say, slamming the bottle

back down on the table as he leaps to his feet with a furious curse. "I may be a big joke to you; I may be something to mock and despise, but I can promise you this. I have colors that you will never know about, I have a core of steel running down the length of my spine and into my rich-girl Louboutins, and more importantly—" I grab my silk purse, and spin on said heels "— after today, I guarantee you will never think of me as boring again."

Chapter Two

AIDEN

Four Hours Earlier…

My kingdom sleeps.

Light streams through the stained-glass windows, stripping the blackjack tables of their sin and burnishing the golden tips of the static roulette wheels. The cries of the slot machines are jarring in their silence. Their parapets of neon lay dormant and dull.

I'm carving a path through this wasteland with my dead father's words playing on a loop inside my head, drumming beats and rhythm into my stride.

"Smart men are illusionists, son. We created the long game. We embrace patience for the prize, even if it burns like goddamn hell to do so."

For fourteen years, I've created and waited, and now I'm all but fucking done with patience.

Past the baccarats, the casino bar rises up from an ocean of crimson. It's the color that stains my life, my Rococo ceilings, my exclusive bank accounts…

"Morning," I murmur to Frankie, who is standing by the counter waiting for me, a strip of polished mahogany that sentries a champagne and whiskey collection worth a couple of million-plus.

"Aiden the Raven." He shoots me a crooked grin as we shake hands.

His massive six-foot-four frame is mostly comprised of side-eyes and sarcasm. We both hail from the same streets of London where survival isn't a birthright, it's the number of punches thrown on a battlefield. He followed me to Sicily when we were kids, and we've been keeping bad company ever since.

He handles the day-to-day running of this place, ensuring that the hosts, the supervisors, the dealers and the croupiers all live and die by our rules. He has other talents, too. Darker stuff. Easy trigger fingers type stuff. Twist a rough diamond in the palm of your hand and it'll blind you with all kinds of light.

"When's the last time you were up this early?" he asks.

"Back when my conscience was as clear as the Med." I gesture to the empty tumbler and the bottle of fifty-year-old Glenfiddich he's placed on the counter for me. "Is that an anesthetic or a Bloody Mary in disguise?"

"What the hell do you think?"

Ignoring his chuckle, I pour myself a generous double, knocking it back in one.

"Where is he?" I say, grimacing as the alcohol trails a fireball down to the parts of me that used to beat free of this bullshit. Back to a time, long ago, when I fought my battles with my fists, front and center. When I wasn't navigating this eight-million-meanings-in-a-chess-move Sicilian crapola.

"Private room off the atrium." Frankie reaches over the

counter for another glass.

For ten years, I was happy to keep my hands red-wet for Tommaso Zaccaria. I was the man who eliminated problems, and I brought in Frankie to help bury the bodies. Then I learned about *La Famiglia's* plans for international expansion on the French Riviera. An opportunity to turn the place into my own private playground? A license to print money?

Sign me the fuck up.

Zaccaria agreed, so for the last four years we've been using each other like backstreet whores. No conversation, just dirty action and a blank space for regret. I clean Italian money through my luxury casino, and in return he gives me a percentage that would make any gold-digger's eyes sting.

Now he's here uninvited. Invading my space... My kingdom. The man who never leaves Sicily these days is dishonoring me with his presence.

"Did he say what he's here for?"

Frankie's shrug is non-committal as he measures out a drink for himself. He knows what I'm angling at. He knows how badly the taste of revenge cancels out the single malt on my tongue. "He requested an audience, nothing more."

"Pissed?"

"Preoccupied."

"Interesting." I mull this over as a second Glenfiddich disappears down my throat. "So, the don himself, a bunch of his sons and his *consigliere* decided to have themselves a little fun on the Côte d'Azur." I opt for the simplest of explanations as I slide the tumbler away and turn toward the atrium.

"Aiden—"

"Stop." I clip the wings off his next words with a look. He should know better. *I'm the fucking Raven, remember?* I circle darkness. I feast on it. I grow stronger on it.

Never, ever, am I the victim of it.

I find Zaccaria in the dealer's chair at the head of the blackjack table, shuffling a deck of cards like a pro. Six of his clan are fanned out either side of him, three apiece. Some are leaning against the other tables. Some are slouched in their chairs, smoking gold tipped cigarettes and sharing another of my whiskeys. Straight swigs. No finesse. Their suits are as tailored as my own, but strip down the Armani and we're just a bunch of Fagin's crew underneath it all.

The number of men doesn't faze me, but their attack formation makes me pause. The don has positioned himself like a centerpiece general, but I'm the one who's firing first.

"We had a deal, Zaccaria." Sliding my hands into my pants' pockets, I stride up to the table, acting like the iceman has cometh and my last fuck to give just took a private jet out of Monaco. "I hope you've come to deliver."

He laughs, the sound as wicked and depraved as I remembered. "My, my, the young boy who ran away to Sicily all those years ago has done well for himself."

It goes both ways, old man. Still, I take the compliment with a nod, projecting the whims of a so-called gentleman, even though we both know it's bullshit. I did what he asked of me, and now I want what I'm owed.

"I'm cleaning your money more effectively than a Chinese laundry these days. We're fast approaching the two billion mark, and Interpol still doesn't have shit on us. That's two billion— neatly folded and pressed, and delivered to an account of your choosing."

"Yes, yes." He dismisses my words with a flick of his wrist, as if that figure was nothing more than a monetary inconsequence. "Your servitude to this organization has been noted."

"*Noted?*" My emphasis on the word is doused in disbelief. "Is that all I get for making you enough clean green to keep you in white truffle pizzas for the rest of your natural life?"

He hums and shuffles the cards again, but I'm smart enough to know when a soft sound is a prelude to a tough sell. He wants something else from me, but I'm damned if I know what.

"You will never be a made man, Knight," he states gruffly, as if it's some kind of personal tragedy to him. "You will never take the vow of *Omertà*. Still, I like to think that *noi siamo vecchi amici.*" *That we are old friends.* "That you will always be more than an associate to this great family."

And you will always be more than a mere Capodecina, I think, taking in the slicked-back gray hair and the trenches plowed deep into his skin like the graves he's dug for his enemies. He finally earned the title of *Capo Dei Capi* a few years ago. He's the boss of all the bosses now. All the clans of the *Cosa Nostra* bend the knee to him or they have them shattered.

Cruising to a stop in front of the blackjack table, I bite down on my patience and don't much like the taste of it. "You've known all along that my interest in your organization only cuts as deep as your connections."

He smirks and nods, splitting the deck into two equal piles. Plumes of smoke curdle the air all around me as he reveals the top four cards, each one representing a different suit:

King of spades.

Ace of diamonds.

Queen of hearts.

Jack of clubs.

He chuckles again. "Do you weight your cards, Knight? Are they always this rich in your presence?"

"I gamble with choices, not money." I finger the old lighter in my pocket, rolling the smooth steel between my forefinger and thumb. "Nothing more than a thousand euros ever leaves my wallet here."

"What about history? Do you gamble on that?" His next smirk strikes me like a lash from a cat o' nine.

"Are you questioning my loyalty?" I narrow my eyes at him. Once upon a time, he scared the shit out of me. Now I only scare myself. "What is this? A mafia interrogation or a real swell time?"

"This, Knight, is more of that servitude we discussed fourteen years ago."

Our gazes catch and I fire an unspoken question at him.

"All in good time, my friend." He offers me a sage, Brando-esque nod as life imitates art in all its stupid hubris. "You have a history; *we* have a history. Even these cards have one." Reluctantly, I follow his eyes down to the cut deck. "Some believe that the four suits represent the four classes of English Medieval society." He points to the king of spades. "Swords for the military." He moves his finger to the ace of diamonds. "Coins for the merchants." Another swipe left to the jack of clubs. "Batons for the peasants, and finally…" His digit comes to rest on the queen of hearts, tapping gently. "Chalices for those who *believe*."

"Are you suggesting I find God?" I say idly. "He and the cult of innocence are pariahs out here. This is where the good die young and the bad live forever."

"Not God, no." I watch him swing his fingers back to each

card in turn. He's taunting me with something that's still masked in black. "Tell me. Which of these four suits represents you best?"

"Suits being the operative word." I adjust my Windsor knot and smooth down the black tails of my necktie. "These days I own the most exclusive casino in Monte Carlo, so I'm staking my claim over all of them."

His wispy gray eyebrows turn down in disapproval. "Greedy?"

"Realist." I flash him a cocky grin and a ripple of amusement pierces the smoke. "Give me what I'm owed and I'll let you educate me some more."

"Sit." He gestures to the empty leather chair in front of him. "You're wrong. Three suits smile at you. The other mocks you."

"*Mocks*?" I take the chair with a scowl.

"You are an army of one, you were born into poverty, and now you're a nobleman for sin." He deals my life story with dangerous aplomb, pointing to each card in turn, before returning to the queen of hearts. "Your weakness will always be this… this *lack of faith*." I watch as he takes the card and rips it in two, tossing the pieces in my direction. "You are an associate out of duty only. You are an associate only because it gets you what you want."

"I was straight with you from the start, Zaccaria. You knew what I wanted." Leaning forward, I rest my forearms on the table. "You're giving me a headache with all the hush-hush. Spit out the reason why you're really here, and then I can go back to corrupting this place."

There's a long pause, and then he's sweeping his hand across the cards, forming a jagged white arc on the green felt. "Do you recall the day we first met?"

I'm transported back to a memory of a room with peeling

paint, infused with the rich earthy aroma of freshly roasted Italian coffee and sweet Limoncello.

"I remember a boy on a mission," I clip back. *And emotions I've long since buried.*

"You came to me for answers."

"You gave me fuck all in return."

He huffs out a disagreement. "I educated you. I taught you the discipline of *La Famiglia*. Don't forget, I was the one who set you up here—"

"Zaccaria—"

"Three months ago, I was sworn into *La Società Villefort*. I have the names you seek. I have your list."

The room falls silent.

"All of them?" The glide of my throat sounds like thunder.

"Both of them," he clarifies with a nod. "One hitman. One lookout."

"You're certain?"

"As certain as I am of my sons' devotion to me."

But not of mine.

His subtext is clear. Since I left Sicily, I'm not his fixer dog anymore. *Lack of faith, my arse. The old man's feeling neglected.*

"So? Where are they?" I fold my arms across my chest to disguise my hammering heart.

"I will honor our agreement, Knight, but there are new caveats."

"What fucking caveats?"

"I see your language is as colorful as ever." He glances at his eldest son, Luca. "This stretch of coastline is being eroded by war," he states briskly. "We are not the only big fish in a golden pond. *Le Milieu*—the French mob—Bratva... Especially Bratva. No crime is committed here without Russian or Italian involvement. Bloodshed is rife, yet why waste more lives when there is an abundance of opportunity for us all."

He's not telling me anything I don't already know. My ties with the Bratva cut off the circulation to my morals as effectively as my ties to the *Cosa Nostra* do. Their money filters through this place as well, and I go to great pains to ensure that neither one knows about my involvement with the other.

"There was an agreement," interrupts Luca, taking a lazy drag on his cigarette. Dark-eyed, Sinatra smooth, late twenties. We could almost be twins. "The first of its kind between Aleksandr Dubov, the *Semion Pakhan,* and my father. It was a way to bring peace to our organizations."

"What agreement?" *How the fuck did I not know about this?*

"His eldest daughter, Karina, and Luca were deemed the match to bring our two great families together." I watch Zaccaria's expression switch to that of a Tuscan thunderstorm.

"*Were?*" I gesture at Luca's bare ring finger. "Was her Russian pussy not up to standards?"

"Her double-crossing Russian pussy," he corrects with a glare. "A day before the wedding, the *baldracca* disappeared, bringing shame upon us all."

Not me. I'm immune to such sentiment.

"Big deal. So, you got jilted."

"Dubov has another daughter."

"There you go." I toss him a sympathetic grin. "Second time's a charm. Let's hope she's not the runt of the litter."

"Not me, *bastardo,*" he says, his fleshy lips curling into a smirk.

I can feel a plot twist coming on and I'm not going to like it.

"Karina is a disgrace," agrees his father. "She will be found and dealt with in due course. Meanwhile, Dubov has offered us

Ielena as a sweetener to help keep the deal alive."

Ielena?

"So which of your sons is the lucky man?" I glance at each of them in turn, only to be greeted by a wall of gloating.

"She will never be good enough for us." Zaccaria gathers up the cards into a messy pile. "Not now. Not ever. Instead, I have decided that *you* will marry her." He stops and flashes his teeth at me, like he did all those years ago—a camera flare on a done deal. "To have her betrothed to an associate, and not to a made man, will punish Dubov for his eldest daughter's indiscretion… And bring us favorable terms for the deal."

A bark of disbelief rumbles up from the center of my chest. "I have neither the time nor the inclination to take a wife. Find some other man to do your dirty work."

"You want the first name on your list?"

"My God, you're serious."

"Two caveats for the two names you seek. The first will be given to you as a wedding gift, and the second for information about the whereabouts of Ielena's sister—"

"So, I'm your fucking P.I., too?" I'm struggling to comprehend the maelstrom of shit he's just dumped on me.

The Italian frowns, deepening the trenches to bat caves. "Ielena is hiding something and I want to know what. Are we clear?"

"No, we're not fucking clear. What are you going to do to the next 'old friend' who cleans two billion for you? Cut off his dick and make him smoke it?"

"In seven days, I'll be back in Monte Carlo to finalize the deal with Dubov and I want you sitting at the table with me. The deal will benefit you, too. That's all the time I'm giving you to seduce the secrets out of your innocent new wife. Lie, steal, debase… Show me how much you still want your justice."

Is he kidding me? What have the last fourteen years been? A scratch and sniff commitment? At the same time, my free will is slipping down my spine like ice. This marriage is all that's standing between me and the only thing that matters.

"We have other ways to make people talk besides forced matrimony, Zaccaria," I snarl. "I should know. I'm damn good at it."

"Arranged matrimony," he counters smoothly. "Not forced."

That's a matter of opinion.

"Anything else?" My temper is crashing through the flashing red safety zone now. "The blood of my firstborn, perhaps?"

Zaccaria reaches into his jacket pocket and produces an Arturo Fuente cigar. He's celebrating, and so he should be. Turns out, I'm still his lapdog after all.

"Why me?" I grit out.

"Your lack of faith was…*concerning* me." He clips the end of his cigar with a stainless-steel cutter and brings a match to the stub. "The *Cosa Nostra* is demanding this show of loyalty. You've grown powerful outside the confines of *La Famiglia.*" *Puff. Puff.* "You're turning into a dangerous man, and dangerous men need to be taught humility once in a while."

"By gift-wrapping me and delivering me to the Russians? I'm amazed her father agreed to this."

"He is a proud man. Bratva obey their own codes of honor. He is also a man of vision, and Ielena is a sacrifice he is willing to make."

My fingers close around my father's old lighter again. It's a solid reminder of why I do what I do when shit gets hazy, and things are pretty out of focus right now.

"The marriage application will be lodged with the town hall

immediately. The intent will be posted, all hugely expedited of course. The ceremony will take place tomorrow afternoon."

"How do I know you're not lying?" I move fast, slamming my fist down on the blackjack table, and setting off a ricochet of shouts and cocked guns behind me. "How do I know this list isn't just a couple of random hits you want taken care of?"

"I gave you my word." He ices me with a glare. "You've waited and hoped and I'm here to deliver, with a few tweaks to the original agreement." He smiles, but it doesn't come close to affection. "I believe congratulations are in order."

I ram my fists into my pants' pockets again. "Is she here?"

"She arrives from Paris today. She's been born and raised in this country. She knows no other."

My fiancée.

My. Fucking. Fiancée.

This is a joke.

"I want that first name, Zaccaria. Before I even *think* about consummating this sham. Do you hear?" I pause as I exit the room to deliver my parting shot. "And if you think I'm partaking in any of your prehistoric first night mafia rituals—"

"I don't give a damn what you do with her." He rises to his feet as well, his movements stiff and deliberate and more in keeping with his age than the devil that he is. "This is not a traditional mafia betrothal. Send her back to Paris after you've used her up. Throw her over the side of your yacht. Her father won't intervene." His harsh laugh follows me out into my glass-domed atrium. "As far as we're concerned, the only useful things about Ielena Dubova are her sex and her secrets."

Chapter Three

AIDEN

Present...

"What the hell happened to you?" says Frankie as I erupt from the bar a dripping mess of fury. He's leaning against my Maserati, smoking a Marlboro Red, his expression of interest framed by silver trails of cigarette smoke.

"I had a disagreement with a bottle of Saint-Émilion. What do you think happened? And what the hell did I tell you about smoking?"

His eyebrows quirk in disbelief as I stand there, raking my fingers through my sopping wet hair and shaking off the excess.

"Tough vintage."

"Tough day. Jesus." I rip at my tie in disgust, yanking it down to half-mast. "I smell like Bill Gates' wine cellar. Where the hell did she go?"

"Who?" Frankie chucks his stub away and glances up and down the palm tree lined *Croisette*, but there are only fast cars and sunburned tourists littering the spotless asphalt.

"The uptight socialite. Dark-haired, easily offended…"

Dick-jerkingly stunning when giving me heated declamations.

Frankie shrugs. "Haven't seen her. Did Anderson cough up?"

"Not yet. I'm considering a debt extension."

"He owes the casino half a mil, Aiden…"

"Bring the baseball bat out of retirement if it tickles your balls that much. He's staying at The Mandrake. Penthouse suite." With that, I stalk over to the car with red wine trickling down between my shoulder blades. There are two schools of thought when you're born piss-poor like us. If money ever comes your way, you count the pennies like him, or you hold it to ransom like me.

"I'm not splitting it with you if I do."

"Oh, fuck off."

"Was she cute?"

"As cute as a used syringe on a kiddie beach," I say, wrenching the driver's door open.

I've been walking around like a lit fuse ever since Zaccaria's happy little casino stopover this morning. I was planning on detonating it all over that weasel, Anderson, and then I clocked the Paris Hilton clone sitting at the next table—her manners as neatly folded up as her napkin. A beautiful waste of space, whiling the hours away in the company of rich strangers, just because she could.

Something about her slid right under my skin like broken glass. The world is a spinning sphere of prejudice. I've had to fight for everything. I've fist-pumped one deadly sin after another to cement my place, while people like Issa have had it handed to them on a silver platter by a snooty English butler in coat tails.

She never stood a chance.

Turns out, neither did my suit.

"It's not like you to crash and burn," I hear Frankie say. "Maybe it's the universe telling you to quit sharking about with a new fiancée in your pocket." He aims it low with his trademark grin, landing a bulls-eye on the one thing I'm trying hard not to think about.

"If we ignore that particular shitshow, *it* might go away."

"*It?*" He strides around to the passenger door, shooting me a dirty look over the clean black lines of my two-hundred-thou car. "Your fiancée has a name, Aiden."

Ielena.

Ielena.

I-don't-want-to-be-married-to-ya.

Burt Bacharach should make a song about it.

"*It* is a means to an end. Nothing more," I tell him. "I don't intend to kiss, finger, suck or fuck Ielena Dubova beyond what is necessary. Even talking is off limits. I'm planning to hang her next to my Warhol so she can have meaningful conversations with that instead."

"And her secrets?"

"Mine before the week is through. I'm going to give my little virgin sacrifice a wedding night she'll never forget."

"You're acting like a dickhead, Raven," he warns.

"That's because I am a dickhead, but I'm also filthy rich and handsome as hell so I can get away with it. What's your excuse?"

"I'm the dickhead's best friend."

"You're more than that, we're blood brothers. Now get in the car." I slide into the driver's seat and press the ignition switch. "I need to wash the tantrums of a sulky teenager out of my hair."

Frankie shakes his head and swings in beside me.

I let the engine purr for a few beats. "You coming back to

The Cristo?"

"Nope, drop me off at the casino on the way. We open up in two hours and Deputy Dawg from the Gambling Commission is hounding me for the latest gaming ops reports."

"Stuff another thousand down his throat." I pull away from the curb and join a line of Porsches and Ferraris heading south. "That'll cut off the air supply to his curiosity. You'd think after four years the guy would take a hint."

"Word on the street is he just bought an apartment in Fontvieille with cash. I reckon he's developing a taste for your 'hints'"

"Then buy him another, and hopefully he'll piss off for good."

Frankie chuckles and it's a pleasant break from his disapproval. "You planning on buying everyone off, Raven?"

"It's worked so far."

"Except for your Russian bride. Cash ain't talking over her."

I hit the brakes at the lights too sharply. "What the hell did I just tell you?" Propping the crook of my elbow against the door, I run a hand across my jaw. "Call Morrel about the passport and guns. Have the set-up ready. As soon as I have the name, I'm taking a trip."

"A honeymoon without the bride?" He pulls out his cigarettes.

"As long as I get the wedding gift, I'm good with that." I snatch the unlit Marlboro Red from his lips and crush it in my palm of my hand. "You know what they say... That shit'll kill you."

"Says the man up to his nuts in Bratva and mafia." He fixes his lips with another cigarette just to wind me up.

"Says the man who *works* for the man up to his nuts in

Bratva and mafia," I respond dryly, ignoring the provocation.

We're in this together. It's the pact we made. As for the cigarette, I know he won't be lighting it anytime soon. I'm not the brutal killer I was four years ago, but bad memories die slowly. He knows what lurks beneath the spit and polish, and I'll always have his respect for that.

Silence falls as I consider the clusterfuck of the last couple of hours. I may be collared and leashed, but I still have bite. Zaccaria kept my revenge under lock and key for fourteen years. He turned it into his own personal servitude, and now it's time to set myself free.

It's an hour's drive from Cannes to Monte Carlo, but my Maserati shaves off fifteen minutes on the *Moyenne Corniche*. I don't even glance at the coastal views as I navigate the meandering road with the pedal to the floor, racing up behind snap happy tourists in their Fiat Panda rentals, and messing up their pictures.

I'm suspicious of beauty. I indulge occasionally, but I keep it at arm's length. There's always an ulterior motive beneath the gloss, like a layer of razor blades waiting to make me bleed for it.

Frankie's busy in the passenger seat. He's tapping figures into a spreadsheet on his iPad, barely shifting as I take the hairpins at sixty. As for me, I'm stinking up the cream leather interior with sour grapes—both tangibly and figuratively. I had a quick fuck and a strong drink in mind for tomorrow. Now, I have a marriage to contend with and it's messing with my focus. I feel caged, bitter, and played, but it's time to focus on the bigger picture.

Two men were instrumental in the murder of my parents.

Two men will pay for that with their lives.

After dropping Frankie off, I head for *Port Hercules*, calling ahead to ensure that one of my deck crew is waiting for me by the outer port.

Exiting the car, I chuck the keys at them and make my way along the quayside to where my sixty-meter superyacht, *The Cristo*, is berthed. I have an impressive property portfolio, but I never reside in any of them. Static walls are provincial. I prefer an ever-changing horizon outside my windows, not a blank expression. I require easy access in all areas of my life, and that goes for an easy exit, too.

I bought *The Cristo* the day I made my first hundred million. She was the sexiest thing I'd ever seen, with killer curves and sweet graphics.

Open her legs and she's even prettier.

Seven staterooms, a double height atrium in the main saloon, and a Jacuzzi… She also comes with an eight-person crew, all of whom I personally handpicked.

"Afternoon, Felix," I say, striding past one of them, ignoring his puzzled glance at my appearance. Felix is close to fifty, a hundred relations removed from the queen, and has a loyal gray manner as mild as his appearance.

"Welcome back, Mr. Knight." No one speaks cut glass like him.

"Fix me a Glenfiddich. I'll take it on the lower deck once I've had a shower."

"Certainly, sir. Would this be before or after you receive your guest?"

I stop and turn. "What guest?"

Felix blinks. "A Mr. Maxim Lebedev is waiting for you on the upper deck, sir. He's been waiting there for some time."

I bet he has.

"Change of plans. Bring my drink there," I say, heading straight for the outer staircase as a sea breeze races across the deck, wicking more red wine from my hair.

I find the Russian on the cream leather couch that hugs the stern. He's wearing black wraparounds to accessorize his smug expression and one ankle is thrown carelessly over a knee. To show he means business there's a gun resting on the table in front of him and an extra-long drink in his hand.

Mid-forties, he'd be a good-looking guy if the left side of his face didn't resemble the jaws of a meat grinder. There are rumors of a fire. Rumors of his *Pakhan's* displeasure… Whatever went down in the past, he wears his scars like a churned-up battlefield.

"What happened to you?" he says, irritating me right away on two accounts. Firstly, he's not bothering to stand and greet me, and secondly, his smoky accent is a reminder I'll be waking up next to a female version of that in less than twenty-four hours.

"To truly enjoy a vintage these days, first you have to fucking wear it." I reach down for the gun and check the clip.

Fully loaded.

"Is that a new Riviera custom?" he enquires slyly.

For his part, he doesn't flinch. We don't trust each other, but we don't fear each other either. I don't fear anyone except the ghost of missed opportunity.

"Cut the crap, Maxim." I toss the gun back down on the table. "Why didn't you tell me about the marriage of convenience between the *Semion* and the *Cosa Nostra*? We had an understanding, you lying piece of shit. You keep me on the inside with Bratva, and I let you cut your deals inside my casino."

Maxim is Dubov's *Brigadier*, even though they have a fucked-up, complicated relationship that no one's allowed to ask him about. The Riviera may be one of Dubov's cells, but he prefers to do business from Paris, except when his youngest daughter is about to get 'confettied' in every sense of the word. Maxim was moved down here four years ago to oversee shit. All my Bratva dealings thus far have been with him directly.

"Because I knew Karina would never go through with it." He takes a sip of his drink and then pokes at the ice with his straw, invoking all the casual arrogance of a man proven right. "I've known her since she was a little girl, Aiden. She doesn't follow the rules. She bends them to fit the shape of her ambitions." He bares his teeth and hisses out a string of Russian curses. "She was never going to stand by and accept that Italian *vyblyadok* into her bed."

"Holding out for another, was she?" I say pointedly.

Maxim curses again, almost wistfully so. "That girl is not for marriage."

"Unlike her dear sister."

"Aren't you going to sit down, Aiden? You're making me nervous."

"Nope." The bite of this conversation is akin to us swinging our dicks at each other, and I'm enjoying the psychological advantage of mine being level with his face. "I'm guessing you already know what's happening at four p.m. tomorrow afternoon?"

He removes his sunglasses and tosses them down next to his gun. "I assure you that Ielena will be equally...*upset* about the man she is being forced to marry. You are an associate to both Bratva and the *Cosa Nostra*, Aiden. You have no clear allegiance. You are a spinning needle compass who finds only himself. As such, you are a dangerous man."

"That's the second time someone's called me that today."

"Ielena's life is already over. This marriage will taint her forever."

"If you're trying to insult me, may I suggest crashing my Maserati instead?" Felix appears next to me and hands me my drink. "Keep them coming," I urge in an undertone. "I'm jumping headfirst into a whiskey bottle for the rest of the evening."

"Yes, sir."

"Aleksandr is unhappy with the match, too," warns Maxim.

"He's still bending over and taking it up the ass, though."

"As are you," he says, dropping the goddamn mic on me. "He respects you, but he doesn't like you, Aiden. Like most of us here on the Riviera."

"I'm not here to be liked. I'm here to make money." I knock back the whiskey and start craving another. "I take it there'll be no touching speeches after the ceremony?"

"Aleksandr will not be attending. Neither will Zaccaria. He is already back in Sicily, and I understand he will only be returning for the deal discussions next week. This is a transaction, not a fairytale, and it should be treated as such."

"He really is tossing his daughter to the big bad wolf. If I were a better man, I'd feel sorry for her."

"No need for that level of condescension." Maxim shoots me a fleshy grin. "At twenty-two, Ielena is an innocent in many ways, but you may find yourself pleasantly…challenged by her."

"Does she have a core of steel running down her spine and into her rich-girl shoes?" I say, drawing on a very recent wine-soaked memory. *Why can't I get that teenage diva out of my head?*

His expression drops. "Why did Zaccaria choose you to be her groom?"

"Why not?" I retort, refusing to play ball with the man who

failed to pass to me in the first instance.

"Because there are other mafia associates on the Riviera. Men who are more malleable to the idea of an arranged marriage to Ielena Dubova." There's a pause, and then the sound of more ice crunching. "I know you, Aiden. You wouldn't have taken this lying down. If there was a get-out-of-jail-free card, you would have stuffed it down Zaccaria's throat and fired a bullet home to make it stick."

"Maybe I'm in the market for a wife." Relenting, I collapse onto the couch next to him with a gratified sigh.

"Zaccaria makes his decisions like a *Pakhan*. He's careful. Everything has a reason and a consequence. You're a chess piece being manipulated into the wrong position." Maxim glares at me. "Dubov wants to know what sway he has over you."

"Maybe she's a prize for years of loyal service."

"I think not."

"I don't give a fuck what you think," I say, losing my cool. "Now get the hell off my yacht so I can go take a shower."

"As you wish." He rises to his feet, sliding his gun under the back of his shirt. "This marriage changes nothing about our agreement. We will still operate inside your casino for the percentage that we agreed."

"Like hell you will." I watch him restore his sunglasses, resisting the urge to grind them into his eye sockets. "What about my 'welcome to the family' bonus?" I lean back into the couch, resting both elbows next to my head, projecting like a king reclaiming his throne. "Tell Dubov I expect him to reconsider."

"What exactly are you bargaining with here? Ielena's welfare? Is she to be punished if he doesn't agree?"

"Would he care?"

The sudden direction of this conversation is piquing my

interest. It usually takes ten minutes of a face-to-face to get to the point with Maxim. A quick glance at my watch tells me nine minutes fifty have already passed.

"Go take your shower, Aiden." With a grunt, he turns to leave, his non-answer giving me all the answers I need. Dubov wouldn't give two shits if I beat his daughter up.

But Maxim would.

Why?

"Shall I save you a seat at the ceremony?" I call out after him. "Even business transactions need witnesses."

"I'll send a whore in my place." He barely breaks his stride as he tosses this over his shoulder at me. "It'll be more in keeping with the wedding theme."

He's right. This time tomorrow, Ielena and I will both be royally fucked by a bitch called matrimony.

"I'm not planning on hurting her, Maxim." *Not physically anyway.*

He stops and turns. Whipping his sunglasses off again, his remaining good eye spears me to the couch. "Do I have your word on that?"

"I want my golden handshake first," I say, neglecting to tell him that it's dependent on how quickly she gives up her sister. It's bad enough being beholden to one criminal organization.

He spits out a Russian curse, something about dogs and dicks.

"This inner conflict is a real stain on your bad guy persona, Maxim," I tut, threading a light accusation through my words. "Has my pretty little Russian virgin been deflowered already?"

"Give me your word, *mudak*," he snarls, his face a mangled mask of fury.

But my senses are primed for blood, and right now I can

smell a ton of it. "Dubov doesn't give a fuck about her, does he? So if you want my cast-iron guarantee…" I leave the sentence idling in threat.

"*Mudak*," he spits again.

"Do you need me to spell it out for you? M–O–R–E M–O–N–"

"You have no idea how lucky you are, Aiden. These girls… Issa…"

"Issa?" A second sea chill races across the deck, laying siege to the black and white stripe parasol above my head, but rattling the locks of my composure more. "Why the hell did you just call her that?"

Maxim pauses. "It is Ielena's nickname. She's had it since she was a child."

Holy.

Shit.

"Is she here?" I demand, ignoring the odd sensation in my chest.

He nods. "She's in Cannes. At Dubov's estate. She arrived from Paris an hour ago."

"Did you see her before you came here?"

"Yes, briefly."

A killer smirk tugs at the corners of my mouth. "Was she, by any chance, wearing a plain white dress in anticipation of tomorrow?"

Maxim doesn't answer. He doesn't need to. I caught the surprised jerk of his head all by myself.

Issa, Issa. You poured the wrong bottle over the wrong bastard on this Riviera.

I'm still laughing as he disembarks from *The Cristo*.

Chapter Four

ISSA

H ave you ever noticed how the mesh bits in lace look like the intersecting bars of a prison cell?

I did. Five minutes ago. As I was sat on the edge of a strange bed in a strange room, in a strange wedding dress, with a strange perfume smothering my senses like a designer rag.

My fingers won't stop playing with the delicate trim on the high-neck bodice. It's as if I'm trying to find a weakness in the yarn so I can plan my escape, even though I know that's not an option. We have a plan—Maxim, Karina, and I—and it doesn't involve distraction or deviation of any kind.

The dress is beautiful.

Beautifully oppressive.

It's a Dorian Gray mirror gone askew. The material is stupidly fussy and over-detailed, and it makes me look about twenty years older than I am. Still, at least it covers up the bruises and the worst thing—

"Come, Ielena. The car is waiting for you."

Marie enters the room clapping briskly, as if the sound will unchain my heavy heart from the bed and propel me to my feet. Her face is a painted mask of encouragement, but it reminds me of a *colombina* I bought in Venice once. The initial dazzle concealed the flaws. The cracks in the porcelain grew wider and more obvious as the truth clawed its way to the surface.

That was another day I learned that nothing is what it seems.

Marie's claps grow louder in my ears. "Up! Up, lazy girl! What are you waiting for?"

A knight on a white horse?

A miracle?

Reluctantly, I stand for her inspection. I'm not sure when or how Marie first entered my father's life, but her presence is more front-and-center than my mother's these days.

I loathe her.

She's brittle and calculating, and our relationship is a ping-pong match of mutual hostility. Unfortunately, since Karina disappeared, Marie's winning most of the shots. She's subtle about it, though. Her words are well-fed piranhas. They'll take tiny bites here and there, leaving me stung and permanently unsettled.

She stops in front of me, a smoky swirl of coral-pink chiffon, and I brace myself for more teeth.

"Oh dear." She casts a critical eye over my wedding dress. "Oh dear, oh dear... Still, it's the best I could do at such short notice. You have no idea the strings I had to pull to get you something suitable in time."

If she expects me to thank her for it, I'd rather choke on the lace.

Her assessment moves up to my face and she tuts out

even more disapproval. "Good grief. Your make-up is abysmal. Antoinette!" Her maid appears in the doorway like a dutiful pet. "She needs less rouge on her cheeks. And that red lipstick is wrong. She looks like a whore, not a virgin bride."

There goes my one shot at individuality today.

Is this really happening? Has it really only been twenty-four hours since my father announced that I was to marry a man I'd never even met? A one-minute, formally worded deposition slotted in between his business meetings. He takes longer to peruse menus in restaurants.

He took longer to request his men to beat me.

"Dressing table," barks Marie, giving me a not so gentle shove in that direction.

Gritting my teeth, I allow myself to be "de-whored," by Antoinette. On the plus side, marriage means leaving Marie behind. Even she wouldn't dare disrespect the wife of Luca Zaccaria.

"I don't see why we're bothering with this charade," she mutters, driving an extra pin into the base of my chignon and scraping my scalp on purpose.

"What do you mean?" I catch her eye in the mirror, instantly wary of the cruel green glint that I find there. "This is what my father expects of me."

I'm rewarded with a cold smile for my curiosity. "I meant why go to so much trouble to look the part when the ceremony room will be empty."

"But Signor Zaccaria's family will be in attendance." I've read all about mafia families and the eight billion aunts, uncles, and associated offspring who get wheeled out for occasions such as these. Kind of like a Bratva wedding when a sibling's disgrace hasn't double-booked the venue.

Her eyes widen for a beat, and then the chill in her smile drops a couple of hundred degrees. "What makes you think you're marrying into *La Famiglia*, child? What makes you think you're good enough for one of Zaccaria's precious sons? Your sister has polluted you, like she's polluted your father's reputation, and today you will pay the price for her disgrace."

My stomach lurches. She's right. My father never actually *confirmed* who my groom was.

I assumed.

I just assumed.

Oh my God. It has *to be the Italian.*

"Who am I supposed to be marrying?" I whisper.

She shrugs, as if the detail is insignificant. "You'll find out soon enough."

"I don't believe you! He wouldn't do this! Where's Papa?" I rise to my feet, but her bony fingers clamp around my upper arm to stop me.

"Sit down, stupid girl." I wince as her grip tightens, her coral pink nails digging crescents into my skin. "Your father has no desire to see you. He left for Paris an hour ago."

My mouth snaps shut when I realize I'm gaping at her. "But he's walking me down the aisle. I'm playing the role of the good Bratva daughter for him. The least he can do is guide me through the scene."

"Be quiet!" Her mask cracks, just like my *colombina* did, but this time spite comes pouring out. "The only things accompanying you to that altar, child, are shame and solitude. You are all alone in this world now, Ielena. Your sister has deserted you, and your stupid mother is soaking your memory in gin."

"Let go of me, Marie!"

"*All alone*," she mouths back.

Shrugging her off, I sit back down at the dressing table. My hands are shaking as Antoinette pats away the last of the red Chanel before smoothing on a dash of Vaseline, and then painting my lips a pale mauve.

Even that seems wrong. I need a shot of color confidence to bring my fair skin and frozen expression back from the brink, not something that'll fade me out even more.

I'm only a half-measure, remember?

An image from yesterday slams into my mind, one with raging battlements of contempt in his eyes.

Aiden Knight.

The man I couldn't stop thinking about all of last night. The beautiful, cruel memory that tempted my fingers between my thighs at the break of dawn.

What was it he said about me again?

"Stupid rich, bored, empty, unemployable, unsalvageable."

If only he knew... I'm so much more than he'll ever give me credit for. Sometimes the ugliest of lies are wrapped up in the meekest of packages.

I hear Karina's voice is in my head suddenly, telling me to hold on to my rainbow, no matter what. We made promises to each other the night she left. The kind you cross your hearts with, schoolgirl style, and keep until you *die, die, die.*

"Are you finished?" I catch Marie's eye in the mirror and hold it. Screw her. Screw my father. They could marry me off to a beggar on the street and I'd still find a way to paint my world gold.

She rolls her eyes and nods.

"Good," I say, firing back a ping-pong shot of my own.

I was right to feel that sense of satisfaction earlier. I'm not some little girl she can push around anymore. My new groom may not be Luca Zaccaria, but my father's choice for me would have been tactical. He'll be a man of standing in the Sicilian mafia. *He'll be enough.*

"Good?" she mocks. "You won't be saying that in an hour's time."

"Aren't you going to wish me luck?"

Without waiting for an answer, I rise to my feet and sashay from the room as elegantly as my badly fitted shoes—*thanks again, Marie*—will allow.

Heart pounding, I make my way down the elegant marble staircase, feeling like Scarlett O'Hara in *Gone With The Wind*, but with the whole world, not Rhett Butler, declaring that they don't give a damn about me anymore.

I reach the lobby to find the tall, stoic figure of my father's *Brigadier* waiting for me. There's another man standing there, too. He has his back turned, his black-suited shoulders blocking out most of the light from a nearby window. I'm so relieved to see Maxim I barely glance at him.

"You're here!" I take the last couple of steps too fast and nearly lose my footing.

He turns at my voice—eyes hooded, expression bleak. "Issa." He catches me with one arm as pain ricochets through my body, but I manage to silence my whimpers in time. "Careful, *zvezda moya*." He sets me right before sweeping his gaze downward. "Why, you look beautiful."

"You're the sweetest liar." I step back, embarrassed by my lack of poise. What's worse, there's a masculine scent in the air that's aiding and abetting that emotion, whipping up memories I'd rather forget. "Marie chose the dress, so you can draw your own conclusions from that."

"Tsch, Issa," he chides. "She chose well."

"Liar, twice over," I say with a shy smile.

"She's right, it's hideous," drawls a deep voice in perfect Russian. "But it's nothing a bottle of Saint-Émilion couldn't fix."

Colors. All the damn colors.

The same man from the bar and my late-night fantasies is smirking down at me, his cerulean-blue oceans churning with the same derision. My lungs flutter and lose function as I finally place the scent in the air.

"You," I gasp out.

"Me," he says flatly.

"Wh-what are you doing here?"

"My presence was requested, so it's a good thing I had another suit to wear."

My head swings to Maxim for answers, but the scars on his face offer me nothing, so I find it swinging back to *him*. It's magnetic. I couldn't stop it if I tried.

"Monsieur Knight," I say, pulling myself together. "How lovely it is to see you again."

He barks out a rough laugh. "You could strip paint with the acid in your voice, princess. Your insincerity is corrosive."

"Who knew a gentleman could be so vulgar," I counter quietly.

"Who knew you had the brains to come to that conclusion all by yourself."

"Have you two met before?" Maxim looks confused, trapped here in our simmering crossfire.

Aiden Knight cocks his handsome head and grins at me, but his eyes are like chips of ice. "Let's just say we had a difference of opinion over some home truths and a bottle of red yesterday."

Instantly, my heart is a drum and bass beat inside my chest.

I hate how British men have the whole archetypal bastard thing down to a fine art. His accent is a poisoned arrow with a fin-shaped fletching of contempt.

He's dressed in black Armani again today, though he's swapped the black dress shirt for white.

Colors. *Colors.* He wears them like a warning.

His necktie is a brilliant crimson, the same red as the lipstick I chose for myself until Marie instructed Antoinette to scrub it off. He's stolen it. *How dare he!* I find myself hating him more for that than I do for his insults.

"Is it true Papa left for Paris an hour ago?"

I mean to direct it at Maxim, but I can't seem to tear my gaze away from my nemesis. He's coolness personified, with the kind of hard arrogance that hazardous men exude

"Why? Are you worried he took his credit card with him?"

"That's enough, Knight," growls Maxim.

I blush right to my roots as my father's confidante proceeds to curse in both French *and* Russian at my English invasion. It's a bi-language of reproach, but Knight just shrugs it off. Clearly, his ninety-nine problems don't include Bratva *Brigadiers* who would be more than happy to use his head as target practice.

Is this man completely impenetrable or just plain indifferent?

"Jesus, you talk a lot of shit, Maxim," he says in a bored voice, cutting him off mid-flow. "If you're quite finished, her chariot awaits."

Her?

I watch him stalk through the open front door, down the stone steps, and into one of the waiting Escalades without so much as a backward glance at me.

Who *is* this vile, rude, arrogant man?

I meet Maxim's heavy stare with unspoken questions in

my eyes. Without answering, he takes my hand and presses something into the center of my palm.

"England," he murmurs, so quietly I have to strain to catch it.

She made it.

Thank God.

"Marie told me I'm not betrothed to Luca Zaccaria anymore," I say, failing to keep the panic out of my voice.

"No, *zvezda moya*, but he's still connected. We must proceed as planned. Infiltrate and wait. I will be in touch as soon as I can with the next stage of their plan."

"Then who?"

"Issa—"

"Please, Maxim," I beg. "You know what's at stake. Who the hell am I marrying today?"

He curses and swipes a hand across his jaw, as if he's disinfecting his next words for an unclean revelation. I then watch in mounting, escalating, soul-crushing horror as his gaze shifts to the vehicles outside. Or rather, to one in particular...

Please.

God.

No.

Chapter Five

AIDEN

How the hell does she do it?

How does she take my self-control and shove a meat hook through it?

Yesterday, I'd viewed Ielena Dubova as a mild splinter: sharp on impact, but easy enough to spurn with a shot of neat whiskey. Today, she's a festering wound. One I couldn't ignore even if I drank my own bar dry. Suffice it to say, I'm not laughing like a goddamn hyena any longer.

I don't need this distraction. She's a disposable part of a fourteen-year plan, nothing more. So why am I grinding the driveway gravel beneath the heels of my black Oxfords? Why, when I enter the car, do I slam the door so violently the whole Escalade shakes?

I was planning on behaving this afternoon. At Frankie's bequest, I'd agreed not to act like my usual, insensitive arsehole self, at least until the ceremony was over. Then she appeared at the top of the stairs in that monstrosity of a dress and bang went every resolution from here to kingdom come. She should have just stapled hundred-euro bills all over it, and called it what it was: Vulgar Couture with a shitty lace trim.

It was the classic falling domino, anti-elitist effect. After that, everything about her pissed me off.

First, it was the affectionate way she'd flung her arms around Maxim, gazing up at him like he was a loaded ATM. Side note: it made me want to rip the rest of his ugly face off, and I still haven't figured out why. Next, it was her reaction to yours truly. I can't remember the last time a woman looked at me as if I didn't have a dick dipped in gold and sparkles. When Issa Dubova looks at me, it's like my dick is a yeast infection waiting to happen.

Her delicate up-turned nose: infuriatingly cute.

Her creamy pale skin: nauseatingly flawless.

Her soft, brown eyes: disconcertingly direct.

Worst of all is her mouth—a mouth that I may or may not have envisaged in the shower last night doing more than just talking back to me. What the hell did they teach her at Swiss finishing school? Flower arranging, exiting cars without pussy flashing and habitual irritation?

The *mademoiselle* needs a reality check. I'm not the worst decision her daddy ever made. Luca would have broken her within a year. He's easy with his fists, and his dick sees more tunnel action than a high-speed SNL train. As for me, I'm choosier than you might think, and I've never raised my hand to a woman unless she's bent over my knee, panties around her ankles, and dripping all over my pants.

I bet her skin would look good pinking up like that.

Letting out a growl of frustration, I slam the back of my

head against the seat rest a couple of times to shake some sense into me.

The car door opens, streaming sunlight onto the back seat. Without a word, she slides in and carefully arranges the long hem of her dress around her feet. Positioning herself so far away from me she's practically wearing the window as an accessory. A side-eye confirms that there are glistening tears and snail tracks down her cheeks.

"Penny finally dropped, did it?" I feel a flash of annoyance again. "Or did Maxim share the good news?"

"Tell me why," she whispers, refusing to look at me. "Why does my father want me to marry *you*? You're not even Italian. You're British. I know about the Riviera deal with Tommaso Zaccaria, Monsieur Knight. What I *don't* know is how you fit into all this."

"Aiden," I murmur, my fingers seeking out the lighter in my pocket. "Trust me when I say you're not the only reluctant party here. Let's just get it over with, shall we? We have the rest of our lives to antagonize each other." I pause, trying not to gag as a sickly-sweet scent sticks in my throat. "Jesus Christ. Is that your perfume?"

She shakes her head. "This." She holds up her slim wrists like they're a reluctant apology. "My something borrowed."

"From what? The sewer? If you're that hot on tradition, borrow my aftershave. Better still, talk to the maids and splash yourself with bleach." I glance across at her, but she's still refusing to look at me. "Get back inside and wash it off."

Her perfect rosebud of a mouth tightens. "There isn't time."

"I decide that. Get inside. I'll deal with the rest of you in due course."

"You can't just order—"

"Care to take that bet?" I close the distance between us and hook a finger under her chin, forcing her to look at me. I can't stop staring at her fucking eyelashes, and how dark and thick they look all soaked in tears. There's a wildfire raging in her soft brown eyes and it's spreading all the way to the front of my pants. "You want to know more about me, princess, besides the figure on my dry-cleaning bill for yesterday's stunt? First lesson starts now." I drop her chin and lean across to shove the door open as she shrinks away from me. "When I say, 'Jump,' you zip the lip and ask, 'How high?' *Capisci?"*

"No, I don't understand," she argues. "I don't understand any of it. You're just a bar owner."

"Am I?" I say icily, neither confirming nor denying it. *Fucking gold-digger.* "Think you're better than me for living off Daddy's blood money, Ielena? Scared you'll be slumming it with me from hereon in?"

"Scared you'll be settling for half-measures?" Her nostrils flare in a way that tells me that the whole defiance thing is new to her. *Just don't make it a habit, sweetheart.* "As for the money, I couldn't give a damn about it."

"Says everyone who's never had to worry about their next meal. Still, I'm glad you brought that up, because I don't much feel like taking over your daddy's Amex mantel. Your allowance is going to be considerably smaller in this marriage than it was when you were swanking it up in Paris."

She looks at me like I'm Poseidon and I just stuck my trident in her heart. Even so, she's far too restrained to rip it out and stab me in the face with it.

"Like I said, I don't care about the money," she mutters defiantly. "I'll want for nothing if that's what it'll take to make this 'marriage' work."

"Keep on using those quotation marks, baby. This 'marriage' is me sealing a deal, nothing more." I lean over again, going in for the kill. "It's all for show. You know that, right? If I ever did this for real, rich bitches like yourself would be the very last in line." I'm vaguely aware at this point that I've gone and pushed my cuntishness to an all-time low.

"You're a bastard," she whispers, her anger playing havoc with her hard-fought poise.

"Yes, I am. Let's start at rock bottom with our opinions of each other. We'll take the express elevator down from there."

She flies from the car in a blur of white. I watch her stumble past a stony-faced Maxim and into the house.

"Fuck you, Zaccaria," I mutter, under my breath. "Fuck history, and fuck the two men who set this massacre in motion."

"Are you going for a record?" demands the Russian, peering in through the open door. "You've already pissed her off twice and we haven't even left the house yet. What happened to your word?"

"What happened to Dubov's family golden handshake?" I'm feeling that suffocating cloak of irritability yet again. "And what the hell are you doing here anyway? Where's the whore you promised me? I was looking forward to staring at something pretty instead of Ielena's frigid indifference."

Someone should give me a fucking medal for today because I'm on a roll.

Ielena doesn't do "pretty." She doesn't do "beautiful," either. To be honest, I don't know what the hell she is. At least she's delivering on her promise of never being boring. Meanwhile, Maxim looks ready to give me something else, namely the clenched fist hanging down by his side.

"Dubov wants me as a witness in his absence. Zaccaria's

requested a signed marriage certificate."

"Does your wife know you're crushing on your Pakhan's daughter?" I say idly, throwing a rock of accusation up in the air to see which truth it crushes.

Maxim's fist rises to waist height. "Are you questioning her purity?"

"I couldn't give a damn about her fucking purity. I'm not as obsessed with it as you lot are." *I want something far more precious from Ielena.*

A pale face slinks back into view, smelling a hell of a lot sweeter than she did a couple of minutes ago. Maxim reluctantly stands aside and I watch her climb back into the car and repeat the fancy rigmarole with her dress. The tears have gone. Instead, there's something steely and determined in their place that's pouring gasoline onto my crotch again.

I make my decision then and there.

"Take the other car and meet us in Monte Carlo," I tell him, pulling out my cell and dialing a number I know by heart.

Maxim frowns. At least I think it's a frown. It's hard to tell with that face. "The ceremony starts in two hours—"

"Give them a hundred and tell them to wait." I hold the device to my ear, counting out five peals of *test-my-patience.*

"Where are you taking her?"

"Maxim, this over-protective shtick is really starting to cramp your ugly style." Four more peals, and then a soft voice is heavy-petting my name.

"Tell me!" he thunders, banging his fist down on the Escalade's roof.

"Hold on a minute, Camille." I press the cell calmly to my chest to resume my new favorite pastime of Russian bear baiting. "In a couple of hours, Ielena Dubova will be under my body and over her virginity," I tell him, ignoring the horrified gasp next to me. "Until then, it's none of your fucking business."

Chapter Six

ISSA

The heavens open as we're driving out through the gates of the estate and onto the hilltop roads of La Californie. If I needed another omen about today's car-crash life experience, I'm receiving it loud and clear. The summer shower is as sharp as my future husband's tongue—pelting the windows with water bombs, flooding the panoramic views of the Bay of Cannes and the Esterel, and frosting up the inside of the glass.

I'm sitting, stone still, in my seat, my head bowed and a million dragonfly thoughts skimming my mind. We'd planned for Luca Zaccaria. Even one of the other sons would have been okay. More complicated, but workable. At least then I'd be in Sicily, in the orbit of the Devil himself, with a ring on my finger and an all-access pass. *Keep your friends close, your enemies closer, and your family so tight they're stealing your oxygen.*

Not Aiden Knight.

I didn't plan for him.

Not the man who makes me feel like the morning devastation after a force twelve hurricane. I can't seem to rebuild my defenses around him. Just when I think I have a new foundation laid, his vicious words tear it down again.

"I owe you, Camille. We'll see you in twenty."

Camille?

He calls out an address to the driver before ringing off from Camille with a husky French endearment that makes me want to puke. He returns his cell to his inside jacket pocket and adjusts his necktie with a practiced jerk.

I watch it all. Missing nothing. Studying him like I would the subject of my next still-life painting. There's something mesmeric about the way he moves. It's smooth and deliberate. It's like he has a grand plan too, and I'm just as much of an unwanted interlude.

"Stupid rich, bored, empty, unemployable, unsalvageable."

Aiden Knight doesn't know what's about to hit him.

"I take it the dress was a freebie along with the perfume?" His deep voice breaks the chokehold over our silence. "Didn't your Bratva Papa ever tell you it was rude to stare?"

Embarrassed, I jerk my head back to the window. "I hardly think you're an expert on decorum," I retort in Russian.

"Speak English when you're in my company."

"I said, I hardly think you're an expert on decorum," I mutter defiantly. I hate the way he swings his spotlight on me when I'm least expecting it.

I hate the jolt of electricity I feel when he does.

"You don't know the first fuck about me, so stop pretending otherwise."

I'll get to know as much as I have to.

Outside, the shower has stopped. The moody grays are

lighter, but they're still spoiling for a fight.

"I know that you like to mock what you don't understand, Monsieur Knight... Actually, don't answer that," I add swiftly. "We've done more than enough talking for one day."

"That'll make for an interesting exchange of vows." He pulls out his cell again and taps out a message as the spotlight swings away. I remember this from the bar. The man has the concentration skills of a slug. "Are you planning on using sign language for the 'I do's,' or shall I expect an email with the relevant text in bold?" When I don't reply, he blows out a breath. "Okay, princess, it's time to establish some give and take." Pivoting around to face me, he places the crook of his elbow next to my head, giving me the whole alpha intimidation act.

"What give and take?" I say, glaring back at him.

"I ask you a question, you answer it, and then you're allowed to ask me one in return. We'll call it the Wimbledon of conversations. Just keep the volleys to a minimum. I don't want a black eye on my wedding day."

"Is that a joke or an apology?"

"I have nothing to apologize for. This is me calling a temporary truce for the sake of my sanity. Let's start again, shall we? Did you borrow the dress?"

After a beat, I nod.

"Good. Then you don't mind me burning it."

"Is that a question or a statement?"

"Statement. I don't do rhetoric." There's another beat. "What about yesterday's outfit?"

"Is it mine?"

"Yes."

"I dress how I'm expected to dress," I say, sounding defensive. "And I believe that was two questions."

"So now you get two in return." His lips tilt, and I find I can't stop staring at *them* now. My five a.m. fantasy is flooding back to me in all its glorious, graphic detail.

"Tell me how you're involved with *La Famiglia* and my father?"

"Straight for the dessert?" He sounds amused. "Don't you want an appetizer first?"

"I have a sweet tooth, Monsieur Knight." I'm growing bolder under his scrutiny, like a sunflower absorbing light.

"Again, it's Aiden. And I'll keep that in mind." He drops his elbow and adjusts his silver cufflinks. It's another of those casual gestures that strums a beat between my legs. "At sixteen, I packed a bag, ran away to Sicily and joined the mafia circus. Four years ago, I diversified. I own the largest casino in Monte Carlo, plus a number of other businesses, including bars and hotels, along the French Riviera."

My mouth drops open in surprise.

He glances at it and a cold expression wins a hostile takeover of his features. "Counting the euro signs already, are we?"

"No, I…" I pause and frown at him. "Why do you always assume my main motivation in life is money?"

He chuckles darkly. "Take me for a bastard, Ielena, but never take me for a fool."

He has a dimple on his chin. How have I not noticed this before?

"I base my opinions about people on kindness and compassion, not assumptions."

"I base mine on whether they're after my life or my money," he responds dryly.

"Money," I intone, pouncing on the one thing his whole orbit seems to spin around. "From the sounds of it, you're more obsessed than you perceive me to be."

"That's because I earned mine the old-fashioned way." He shoots me a crooked smile. "Green takes on a whole different color when you mix it with crimson first."

"I never asked for a cent from my father."

"But you took it anyway."

"You say it like I had a choice!" *I've never had a choice about anything.* I glance down at his tie, which suddenly seems a lot closer than it did ten seconds ago. Blushing again, I shuffle back to my side of the car. "How are you a made man if you're not Italian?"

"What made you think I was one of those?"

"But—"

"There are a lot of questions being asked out of turn here, *princess.*" He practically spits his endearment at me, and it strikes me then that he's not as cool as he's making out.

"My name is Issa—"

"I'll call you what I like. *Half-measure*, remember?"

"By the sounds of it we're both making sacrifices for this marriage. You have to put up with my curiosity and I have to shoulder your insults."

"How sacrificial are we talking here?" Out of nowhere, he hits me with a loaded look that has me squirming in my seat.

"You can't be serious," I say, rolling my eyes.

"We can always go back to hating one another in the morning."

The fight seeps out of me like a deflated balloon. I've tried not to think too much about this part. His bed is an inevitability that scares me for a million different reasons. His edges are razor blades. He'll tear my innocence to shreds.

"Is 'consent' to be a dirty word between us?" I say quietly.

There's a long pause, no doubt for him revel in my defeat like the conquering antihero, and then he shocks me with a sliver of humanity. "Fuck the rules. Fuck what's expected of you. You'll come to me when you're good and ready." I search his face for traces of scorn as he closes the gap between us again. "Having said that, my lenience comes with a price."

I knew it. "What price?"

"I don't like others playing with my toys," he says huskily, forcing me to inhale every brutal inch of his masculinity. "If I find out you've been touching yourself on the sly, all bets are off." I open my mouth, but he presses a warm palm to it before I have a chance to respond. "If I hear you moaning through my walls as you play with your pussy, I'll break the door down and take you any way I see fit."

This time when I blush, my dark hair catches fire.

I shake his hand off angrily. This man doesn't have any humanity. He left it in a dumpster somewhere along the route of his life.

"Don't look at me like that," he chides, inching even closer until he's a beautifully cruel close-up—taunting me with the promise of a heart and a soul that will never be mine. *Not that I'd ever want such a polluted thing.* "Your body belongs to me now. The paperwork is a formality. Your consent will be playing catch up soon enough."

"Stupid rich, bored, empty, unemployable, unsalvageable," I say, spitting his own words back to him, my hand itching to do some harm to those slanted cheekbones. "You just reminded me, so ineloquently, of how much you dislike my kind."

"Who says I have to like you?" His gaze drops to my mouth. "It's marriage and sex, Ielena, not a prom date and a hot fumble with your college sweetheart. Feelings get parked at the door with me."

"My father must have been out of his mind to agree to this!"

"Justifications are like excuses, Ielena," he says patronizingly. "Everyone has them. Even him."

"I'll never forgive—" I stop then, slamming a mental full stop on a conversation that's crumbling into the sea like cliff erosion.

"Oh, quit with the dramatics." He backs off, sounding bored again. "I thought Bratva offspring were programmed to obey from birth. How old are you?"

"Twenty-two," I grit out. "And my chip malfunctioned the minute you started disrespecting me."

"Don't confuse disrespect with the truth."

"Then stop thinking of my femininity as a flaw."

"Oh, for fuck's sake," he hisses, his frustration finally bubbling over as the driver clears his throat.

"Monsieur Knight?"

"What?"

"We're here."

"Where's here?" I peer out of the window, grateful for the respite. We've been so busy chucking verbal hand grenades at one another neither of us noticed the car had stopped. "This isn't Monte Carlo."

"It's a necessary diversion into Cannes... Stay here," he adds to the driver.

Exiting first, he motions impatiently to me, before reaching inside and taking my wrist when I don't move quickly enough. He's not rough with his touch, but I smother a gasp as my hip brushes against the doorframe. My body is a sheet of flames today. The pain in my chest is only getting worse. I need to see a doctor, but I can't bring myself to ask a fiancé who hates me for help.

Somehow, I straighten up—a sore sapling to his mighty oak. He's a foot higher than me, even in my heels.

"Find an outfit," he says, dropping my hand. "Any outfit, and I'll buy it for you."

"Is this a trick?" I eye him warily. People are bustling past, casting puzzled glances at a bride and a groom who are anything but happy and content. "Gentlemen like you have a way of disguising ridicule in their words."

He laughs and slides his hands into his pants pockets, the threads in his crimson neck tie splashing blood across his white shirt. "I'm no gentleman, Ielena. You should have figured that out by now." He takes a step closer, burning me up under the spotlight of his gaze again as a couple of bodyguards appear from nowhere. "This is your wedding day. You should be the one choosing the dress, not your father's latest fuck-buddy."

A smile threatens my lips, but I squash it immediately. "There's a catch. I know there is."

"No catch. It's simple. That outfit is offending me, and I want it gone."

Liar. He's the type of man with a hidden agenda in all of his games. Still, I accept his offer with a nod because I hate the damn dress almost as much as he does.

Spinning on my heels, I move through the crowds with Aiden and his two bodyguards falling into step behind me. He doesn't move to touch me again. He doesn't speak. He's like the midday sun: both warming and familiar, yet liable to leave you with a vicious burn if you hang around him too long.

"Are you lost?" he drawls after a while.

I'm not.

In fact, I'm surprised at how easily the route is flooding

back to me. Happy memories love company. They leave you with the simplest of clues so that you can return to them with the least amount of effort. The time I spent here nine years ago was the best three weeks of my life.

Turning off the main road onto a narrow side street, I head for *Rue Meynadier*, letting out a gasp of joy when I see a familiar faded gray sign peeking out from behind the tourist boards.

She's still here. Even after all this time.

"Wrong turn, Ielena," I hear Aiden say. "The designer stores are back on *La Croisette*."

Ignoring him, I step into the cool of the narrow store, inhaling the vibrant colors like a drug. It's not a wedding dress establishment or a designer boutique, but this kind of familiarity is far more precious to me than money. In the last month I've lost everything good in my life. Right now, I'm clutching at my past to bring me back from the brink.

Aiden instructs his bodyguards to block the access, and then he follows me inside. "What the hell happened in here?" he exclaims, glancing around. "Looks like someone slipped this place an LSD tab and pressed the button on a warehouse rave."

"You said it was my choice."

"True, but I wasn't planning on wearing my sunglasses when we're exchanging rings."

"Small mercies. You might mistake me for someone you want to marry."

He opens his mouth to crush me with his reply when an elegant lady in her late forties emerges from the back of the store. Her face lights up like Bastille Day fireworks when she sees me standing there in my ridiculous wedding dress.

"Ielena!" she cries, rushing forward. "Come here, *ma chérie*, where have you been hiding all these years?"

"In Paris, mostly." Her soft embrace hurts my chest like hell, but I feel the warmth of it right down to the marrow of my bones. There's only one other person in the world who hugs like this, and I miss her more than words can say.

"You look so beautiful." She drops her voice to a whisper. "But why are you wearing *that*?"

"I don't want to be," I answer truthfully. "Help me, Eloise. I don't have much time."

This draws her back to me with a frown. "Anything for you. You know this. What do you need?"

Her kindness is without borders and it makes me want to cry. I can't remember when we last spoke, but people like Eloise don't keep tabs on friendship. They see them as seeds that continue to grow, even in the darkness.

I watch her gaze shift to the tall mountain of mockery standing behind me.

"I need a dress, Eloise. Something bright. Something that doesn't make me look like I'm drowning in lace and bad decisions."

Her arms tighten around me, and it's enough to make me love her even more. "I have just the thing." Releasing me, she aims her dazzle at my new raincloud again. "Welcome to my shop, *Monsieur*—"

"Knight," I say, slipping back into English and politesse. "Aiden, this is Eloise Dubois."

To his credit, he greets her warmly enough. In turn, I watch her smile dim from a ninety watt to a ten as she brushes her palm against his. If he notices her change in countenance, he doesn't comment.

"Interesting place you have here." He looks around at the cluttered shelves and rails that are bursting with psychedelic prints.

"*Merci.*" She catches my eye, brushing her palm against her hip as if she's brushing his wickedness away. "I find color to be an emotional blanket. It can offer us comfort when life seems dull and desperate." She shoots me a look.

This is bad.

She's the epitome of good manners and refinement. If her mask is slipping in Aiden's company, I really must have fallen down amongst the sinners.

"Whiskey makes me feel the same way."

"Then your 'profession' is an excellent choice, *monsieur.*" This time there's no disguising the caustic notes in her voice.

I need to know more. I need to know everything.

Grabbing a couple of Pucci-inspired silk dresses from the nearest rail, and not even bothering to check their sizes, I walk quickly toward the changing room at the back of the shop. Eloise flies in after me, ripping the curtain across so fast the sound of screeching metal makes us both wince.

"Turn around," she urges, and I do as she says, standing silently as she rips apart the delicate beaded buttons. Soon enough, the despised wedding dress is pooling at my feet.

"You know who he is, don't you?" I whisper.

She sighs. "Everyone on the Côte d'Azur knows who he is, Issa. What troubles your pretty soul, *ma chérie*? You don't come waltzing into my shop after all this time in the company of *Le Corbeau* unless your skies are falling down."

"*Le Corbeau*?"

"*Oui*, The Raven. Like the poem." She spins me around and takes my hand, rubbing soothing circles into the dip between my forefingers and thumb. "He is the man who cannot let go of his past."

"What poem? What past?" I search her face for answers in her gentle lines.

"He is an ocean of blood, *ma chérie.*"

"I know what he is, Eloise. He's mafia—"

"Mafia, Bratva… He works for them all. He works for none. He is the most dangerous man in these parts…" Her gaze drops to my nakedness, and her face crumples in horror at the mess of red and purple marking my skin. "Oh, *mon dieu.* What has happened to you?"

"My horse threw me." I slap my arm across my chest to conceal the worst of it, but I can tell from her expression that she doesn't believe me.

"Issa?"

"Aiden didn't do this."

"Then your father?"

"Please. I don't… I can't."

"Hush, *bebe.*" She pulls me into her soft arms again. "Forgive me for jumping to conclusions. *Le Corbeau's* past has many cracks that bleed into his present."

"How do you know all this?" I mutter into her hair.

"I have lived here for a long time, Issa. I have seen many men like Aiden come and go, but he is the most…" She stops and blows out a troubled breath. "If I have spoken out of turn—"

"You haven't, but I need to—"

"Not here," she says firmly.

"Then I'll find a way to come back. I promise." Breaking her embrace, I reach for the nearest dress. The print is a livid swirl of reds and pinks, and it's going to clash like hell with his crimson necktie.

Good.

Losing the hanger, I shimmy the silky material over my

head. By some miracle it fits perfectly, with the high neckline covering up the bruises.

Le Corbeau…

Broken pasts…

I shouldn't care about her revelations. I shouldn't care that they're pricking my interest and binding me closer to him than a ring and a false promise.

"Beautiful," murmurs Eloise, smiling her approval before it fades again. "Tell me, what business do you have with that man, child?"

"The business of weddings," I say tightly. "In a couple of hours, I'll be standing on the steps of the town hall as his wife."

Her face crumples in on itself like a soufflé. "No, *ma chérie!* You mustn't! I won't allow it!"

"I have no choice. My father arranged it."

"Karina?"

"She ran away." There's no malice when I say it, just pain and sadness.

"Oh, Issa." The tears in her voice make it thick, oozy, and dangerously contagious.

"Silver linings," I say, forcing some cheer into mine. "I'll be living on the Riviera now so I get to come visit my favorite store every day."

"If you need anything, *ma chérie.* Anything at all…" she trails off in resignation. She knows there's no way out of this for me. Not unless I run, too.

"Right now, I need your strength and I need your dress."

"Ielena." Aiden's deep, mocking cadence invades the changing cubicle. "How long does it take to change into a dress? Time to go."

I can feel Eloise's love filling the space between us again, making me feel a little less alone. She gives my hand a final squeeze, and then stands aside to let me pass, peeling back the curtain to reveal my fate.

He's idling by the cash register, the picture of brutal refinement and irritation. He glances down at my dress and says nothing. He just quirks a dark eyebrow and tosses some notes down on the counter.

"No, *monsieur*." Walking over and scooping up his money, I thrust it into his hard chest. "I'm paying for this, not you."

"What with?" he mocks. "*Air*? You have no purse on you, princess. Therefore, you have no money."

"I'll earn it." I turn to Eloise, who is hovering by the changing cubicle. "How many days of working here will it take to pay off this dress?"

Her eyes meet mine and she gives me a small smile of understanding. "At least two weeks, *mademoiselle*."

"Soon to be *madame*," he clips back. "And no wife of mine is working in a fucking store."

"Would you like milk and sugar with that cup of hypocrisy," I tell him sweetly. "You scorn me constantly for taking hand-outs from my father, but you won't let me earn it when the opportunity arises?"

The next few beats are wrapped in open hostility, and then he's pulling out his cell phone. "Camille," he barks. "Cancel our appointments with Gucci. We've found something else."

This time when he hangs up, there's no fruity endearment for her. I've backed him into a corner, and he's far from happy about it.

"One week." He snatches one of the hundred euro notes from my fingers and tosses it back down on the counter. "And here's a deposit, just in case you can't hack it, *half-measure*. I'm betting a thousand more of those notes you're a quitter, too."

It's a dirty compromise, but I'm willing to take it and clean it, and make it my own.

"I'll see you on Monday, Issa," trills Eloise as we exit the shop, and this time her voice is laced with admiration.

Aiden marches me back down the side streets to the waiting Escalade, his security guys straggling in our wake.

Stone cold reality is rushing up fast and curling around my toes. My mind is on overdrive. I'm thinking about all the stuff Eloise told me. I'm thinking about the dangerous game I'm playing. Most of all, I'm thinking about the cracks in the cobblestones, and how close I am to slipping in between them and losing Karina forever.

Chapter Seven

AIDEN

I hate surprises.

I'm using the term "hate" loosely here. If I could, I'd tie them to a chair and slowly dissect them, making them die a slow, agonizing death until all that's left is a ghost of a bad idea.

It started the day I discovered my mother slumped over the kitchen sink, with the faucet running as cold as her body—chained in death to the same place she spent most of her life, courtesy of a twelve-hour case of rigor mortis. It was superseded, five minutes later, when I slipped on a crimson pool in the hallway and came crashing down next to my father's severed head.

Completing the top three of the Worst Surprises Hall of Fame was yesterday's bombshell order to marry some Russian virgin because her sister messed up and her daddy's too greedy to tell Tommaso Zaccaria to go fuck himself.

The truth is, I'm wary of them. No good ever comes of anything that smacks of life deconstruction. And that's exactly what she is.

Ielena Dubova.

A five-foot sabotage. A ball-ache. *A surprise.*

I don't know if she chose the kitschy red and pink dress to spite me, or because she actually likes it, but three things become clear as I stand in an empty room saying empty vows to a woman who despises me. Correction: a woman whom I've gone *out of my way* to make sure despises me.

I don't like the way she manipulated herself a job.

I don't like the way I agreed to it.

I don't like the way my dick keeps twitching whenever she defies me.

More.

Damn

Surprises.

She's not so much of a half-measure anymore. She's a full-on disaster.

"Vous pouvez maintenant embrasser la mariée." You may now kiss the bride.

Without waiting for an embossed invitation, I take her delicate jaw between my hands and slam twenty-four hours of frustration down onto that perfect rosebud. I do it because the urge to claim that mouth is now too much to resist.

She tastes different to other women. Sweeter. Purer. The need to taint her with the rest of me is running rings around my self-control. Her mewls of resistance fuel the flame; her soft hands drumming against my chest make "consent" that filthy, dirty word she spoke of earlier. Even the whole virgin thing doesn't seem like such a drag anymore.

Is this her first kiss?

Fuck me.

I pull away sharply, keeping her jaw locked in my grasp, feeling the bloom of another of her epic blushes heating up my thumb pads. Her dark eyes are wide with shock. Her lips are wet and swollen. *If it was, I just gave her one hell of an introduction.*

"Madame Knight," I murmur, feeling her body go even more rigid at my words. "I do believe I'm looking forward to our wedding night, after all."

I say it partly to goad a reaction out of her, and partly to feel more heat in that blush, but I never get the chance. Jerking her head backward, she leaves my fingers suspended in mid-air.

"I preferred it when you called me all those other things. Taking your name is the worst kind of insult." I watch her cast a glance at the shadows where Maxim is lurking. "Are we done yet? I'd like to scrub this day from my skin."

"Not yet, sweetheart. The conclusion is coming right up."

Struggling to control my temper, I lead her into the side room to sign our lives away. She stumbles in her heels, clutching at my arm, even though I know it scalds her fingertips to do so. As for me, I need a whiskey. No, I need a whole damn bottle of the stuff. Too bad I have a plane to catch in a couple of hours and murder on my mind.

Clucking with impatience, I hover over the glass table like a bad mood, watching her scrawl her name in black ink next to mine. Her hand is shaking so badly she litters her signature with muttered apologies. Meanwhile, our two witnesses won't stop scowling at me. If looks could kill, Maxim would have happily lined me up against the Iron Curtain and not stopped firing until he was sure. Frankie's pissed at me because I told him I'd play nice again today, and that kiss was anything but.

Ignoring them both, I push Ielena out into the sunshine. The *Place de la Mairie* is spread out in front of us like a dark, gray lake. Our mutual hostility is peppered by the soft sound of flags flapping in the breeze overhead. I yank her to a stop at the bottom of the steps, restrained by the ghosts of tradition. This is what newlyweds are supposed to do, right? They stop and smile, and revel in their smugness.

Not us.

There's no one here to take pictures or throw confetti, and for the first time it dawns on me how messed up this is for her. Dubov and Zaccaria have taken a sepia tone photograph of Ielena's dreams, scribbled me in with devil horns and a goatee, and then set fire to the whole thing. She's Bratva, born and bred, and right now my spirited little Russian doll is caught between duty and survival.

"We're leaving." I go to guide her into the car, but she spins away from me like a leaf caught up in the breeze. Maxim has followed us out. I catch the desperate look she exchanges with him and my temper kicks up a gear. I don't like it. It tallies too easily with what I felt when I tasted her. "Get in the car, Ielena."

She hesitates. "Can I have a minute to say goodbye?"

"No."

For the first time, her perfect composure sheds its topmost layer. "How dare you dictate this to me!"

"I can dictate anything I want to you, Ielena. Don't make me ask again or you won't like the result."

She acquiesces with a glare, and then I'm slamming the door on her so hard the Escalade rocks like a pimped-up Cadillac. There aren't going to be many door hinges left around us at this rate.

"Tell Dubov his daughter is no longer a Dubova," I bark at a hovering Maxim.

He spits a curse at my feet, and then something equally

unpleasant in Russian.

"Careful, Maxim," I purr. "You're perilously close to pissing me off."

"Show some respect, Knight. She's your wife."

"In name only. What's the history between you two anyway?"

"Stop repeating yourself. She's my *Pakhan's* daughter, I've known her since she was a child." He takes a step closer, so close I can count the strips of scarred skin that a long-ago fire got a hold of. "You're acting like a jealous man, Aiden... I warned you she'd be more than a match for you."

A second later, I have my arm around his neck and I'm crushing his half-pizza face against the tinted window of my jet-black Escalade, violence bursting like fire crackers behind my eyes. "This is my one and only warning to you, Lebedev," I hiss, batting away his struggles and curses, and forcing him even harder into the glass. I was raised on whiskey and vengeance, and that makes me stronger than Superman when I need to be. "Stay away from my wife. Don't look at her. Don't even talk to her. You want me to honor our deal? Then do as I say." With that, I let go of him with a savage push, watching as he reels backward into a crowd of guidebook toting tourists, scattering them like frightened birds.

Straightening up, he reaches for his gun, but Frankie gets there first. The Russian eases up on the dramatics when he feels the steel of Frankie's Glock rammed against the base of his spine.

"Calm the fuck down, everyone." I lean against the hood of the vehicle like a slick bastard, heat still pooling in my fists. "If you keep on disgracing yourself at my wedding, Maxim, you won't be invited to the anniversary ball."

"Is that compass finally focusing in one direction, Knight?"

His taunts are unfounded. Ielena will never be anything more to me than a chore.

"Do you want me as your enemy, Lebedev?"

"You make an enemy of me, you make an enemy of all Bratva," he growls, shrugging Frankie off before he remembers himself. He yanks his shirt down and smooths his hair. "Dubov is returning to Monte Carlo the day before the deal meeting. He wants a face-to-face with you."

"Tell him that Ielena and I would be delighted to host him for dinner," I say, flashing him a brittle smile.

"Not her. Just you. Your casino. Wednesday. Ten p.m."

"I'll make sure the champagne's on ice."

Maxim glares at me, his one good eye unblinking and focused. "Careful, Aiden. The Riviera doesn't forgive mistakes."

"I *am* the fucking Riviera," I respond coldly. "And your presence at this wedding is no longer required."

He drives off soon after that, the tires on his Ferrari spinning like circular black blades.

"That could have been handled better," says Frankie, sliding his weapon back under his shirt as he wanders over to join me.

"I wasn't in the mood to be subtle. I'm still pissed he didn't give me a warning about this deliriously happy event."

"I wasn't talking about Maxim… What the hell arc you playing at, Raven?" He motions me onto the sidewalk and away from the car. "That wasn't a kiss, it was a wrecking ball. Call a truce with her or we both end up losing."

"Who died and made you an expert on marriage?"

His gray eyes turn to flint. "Do you want that second name or not? She's not going to tell you shit at this rate."

Sometimes I forget he's as invested in this as I am. We share the same vengeance. We share the same burden of grief.

My parents found him on the streets at eight years old and raised us as brothers until the day they died. We took that brotherhood and made it soul-deep.

"Leave her to me." I glance at the tinted windows. "She's my problem, not yours. Has Zaccaria been in touch?"

His expression loosens up a little. "Maybe I don't have as much faith in your unicorn dick as you do."

"Concentrate on your own dick and I'll concentrate on mine."

He laughs.

I'm relieved.

"The private jet is on standby at Nice Côte d'Azur Airport," he says. "The name came through while you were signing the register." He reaches into his back pocket and hands his cell to me.

"Lorenzo Gambino," I say, scanning the details.

"He was the lookout guy."

"Connections?"

"Quick trace points me in the direction of the Rossi *Famiglia.* They're a faction of the *'Ndrangheta* in New York. Give me a couple of hours and I'll know more. The syndicate originates in Naples, but they're small fry compared to the *Camorra.*"

"Fucking mafia." I rip at my red necktie and loosen the top button of my dress shirt. "They breed like flea-infested rats. How did Gambino find himself in London fourteen years ago?"

"The *'Ndrangheta* supply cocaine to most of Europe. Maybe your father—"

"Our father," I correct him tersely.

"Maybe he had some shady shit going down we didn't know about."

I shake my head. "He was a full-time mechanic and a part-time crook. There's no way he was dealing crack and smack on the down low. We lived on a council estate, not a lie. You remember the note… He was connected to Sicily, not Naples."

How did you do it, Zaccaria? How did you infiltrate La Società Villefort so profoundly in such a short space of time?

"That name is a pile of TNT. It's like he wants us to pick a fight with the *'Ndrangheta*," says Frankie, cutting to the chase as usual.

"What's the status of their relationship with the *Cosa Nostra*?"

"Strained. Ever since Zaccaria terminated Rossi's *Consigliere* outside a Brooklyn deli last year."

"Jesus." I run my hand across my jawline. "We kill his men, we escalate the conflict."

"Who gives a damn as long as we make the targets? Fourteen years, Aiden," he reminds me.

Frankie sees revenge in black and white, while I see gray tributaries running in all directions like streaks of war paint. Regardless, we're both on the same page as far as Gambino's concerned.

"I want his location."

"Zaccaria sent it through as an extra wedding gift. There's even a business address."

"It's too easy, Frankie." I ran my hand across my jaw. "Where?"

"Siena, Italy."

"Good time to visit."

"Good time to kill."

We both fall silent as another group of tourists shuffle past, and then I'm swinging back to the car with a familiar fire detonating in my veins. "I want twenty-four-hour surveillance on Ielena when I'm gone. Tap her phone, her laptop, everything. If she contacts her sister, or if her sister contacts her, I want it lighting up every listening and tracking device we possess. She doesn't go anywhere without you or the boys, and log into the security feeds in that shop on *Rue Meynadier*."

"You got it."

I grab his arm as he reaches for the passenger door. "And if Maxim Lebedev comes sniffing anywhere near *The Cristo* in the next day or so, you have my permission to put him down like a dog."

Chapter Eight

ISSA

The Devil has taken a hold of my new husband.

I'm forced to watch on, helplessly, as he drives Maxim's face into the car window and holds him there until his scarred skin turns a wicked shade of white.

"No!" I reach for the door handle to put a stop this lunacy, but the driver slams his hand down on the in-car locking mechanism. "Let me out!" I scream, tugging on it regardless.

"I can't do that, *madame*," comes a flat drawl, his eyes fixed straight ahead.

"Fuck you!"

It occurs to me that I've never actually said those words out loud before as I smash my palms against the bulletproof glass.

It's all for nothing.

Aiden can't hear me or see me. Not that he'd give a damn if he could. When he finally lets go of Maxim, my cheeks are wet with frustration. Best laid plans are being ripped apart before my eyes, and it's all because of *him*.

Five minutes later, he's sprawled out on the seat next to me, his long, hard body taking up all of his allotted space and more. He's loosened his necktie and a graze of stubble is beginning to darken his jawline, adding an extra layer to his danger. There's a storm in his calm and a shudder to his stillness. Whatever is going on inside him, it's filling up the vehicle and squeezing me out as we travel the streets of Monte Carlo toward my new home. There's no apology or explanation for what he's done, and I know better than to ask.

I'm still fumbling for the positives to keep hope alive when he takes a call on his cell. Fluent Spanish. *Is there any language this man doesn't speak?*

We're in a war that neither of us can win. He calls me a princess like it's a dirty word. He splashes my life with ridicule and shades me with humiliation. I call him a beautiful bastard, but really, he's a field of poppies in Normandy. Beneath his surface, he's littered with razor wire and dirty bombs. Oh, and kisses that shake my foundations… It's safe to say I didn't see *that* landmine coming.

Men like him aren't supposed to hate kiss like that, shooting sparks into places they have no business being. I felt it all, from the heat of his possession to the lust in his touch. They call him the Raven, but really, he's a wolf—a living, breathing predator dressed up in Armani, with lawlessness dripping from his jaws. And my father tossed me at his feet like the grains of rice he never tossed at me on my wedding day.

Positives, Issa. Positives.

Karina is safe. She's in England in a place where neither the Italians nor the Russians can find her yet. I may not have acquired Zaccaria as my last name, but whatever Aiden is to *La*

Famiglia, he means enough to be offered my hand in marriage.

"Here, I almost forgot." He hangs up and reaches into his inner jacket pocket, before flinging a gray jewelry box onto my lap with all the care and grace I've come to expect for him.

"What's that?" I prod at it like it's a six-inch cockroach.

"Your new best friend."

An annulment? Deliverance?

No such luck. It's a diamond engagement ring. The biggest, boldest most vulgar thing I've ever seen. Still, I was raised with manners, if not with love.

"Thank you," I say dutifully, slipping it over my slim knuckles so that it sits on top of my detested wedding ring. *Thanks for the spiked collar around my neck, and the dead weight inside my stomach.*

I'm tempted to rip it off and throw it at him like I've seen all those beautiful women in the movies do. Diamonds are comatose stones. I much prefer bursts of color that dance like flames with the slightest of movements. Some of the most beautiful pieces I own have a value that's a fraction of this monstrosity.

The car starts to slow.

"Welcome to your new home, princess."

"So soon?" Outside is an expanse of an ocean so blue it's almost purple. "But we're at *Port Hercule*."

He catches my eye and holds it. "Let's just say I like to keep my horizons within touching distance."

"You live on a *boat*?" I splutter.

"No, I don't live on a boat; I live on a fucking superyacht," he drawls in that caustic tone of his, taking my reaction and warping it into one of his ridiculous rich bitch assumptions again.

"Wait—"

"True colors, Ielena?" Stepping out of the car, he leans back in with a twisted smile on his face. "By God, I'm going to make you appreciate what you have in life if it kills me." *Is he for real?* "Time to go."

My eyes dart to the ocean again and a rash of fear breaks out on my bare skin. My mouth dries up and my heart starts crashing against my rib cage. I haven't been this close to water since—

"Is your arse attached to the seat, or is this a defiance thing again? Get. Out. *Now.* Ielena."

He says it in a way that has me scrabbling headfirst into a nightmare.

Blinking back the tears, I stand shivering on the quayside in my pink and red dress in the lazy, late afternoon heat. He's gesturing at one of the largest superyachts in the port a couple of berths along, something sleek and graphite and menacing looking. He's talking at me, telling me something pertinent about it. His lips are moving, but I don't hear the words. My chest is a closed citadel. My lungs are like two pieces of lead.

"Aiden," I rasp, but it's lost to the cries of the gulls overhead. My terror fixes on the slim slivers of ocean in between each vessel, like blue lines for an oceanic parking lot.

"Ielena?"

Am I swaying, or are the gentle waves crashing into me?

"Ielena?"

His voice keeps skimming the surface of my bubble of panic, but it's never enough to pierce it.

"Can't breathe," I croak as the world flashes and fades to shades of gray.

"Shit."

"What's wrong with her?" comes another voice.

"Panic attack."

I feel his hands on my shoulders. I try to jerk away, but my body has stopped communicating with my brain. I don't want him to see me like this.

And then I'm falling, falling and landing in arms that are both hard and gentle and cold and welcoming.

I wake to a ring of gold above me. It tugs me back to reality with a firm hand.

My eyelids flutter, and then settle. The gold circle becomes a band of spotlights. I blink again and a cream-colored ceiling comes in view. I'm lying shoeless, but fully clothed, on top of a king-sized bed with a sweeping view of the Riviera coastline above my toes. I watch it rise and fall in time with my chest for a beat or two, like the steady gait of a horse, *or a ship bobbing on the waves.*

Tides of panic rush in. I try to sit up, but my hands slip across the silky comforter and it turns into an undignified scrabble, the material of my dress pulling across my chest and making me whimper in pain.

"Easy," murmurs a voice.

Aiden is leaning against the far wall—a perfect silhouette of sin—with his hands in his pants' pockets. His white dress shirt is wide open at the collar and the crimson necktie has been yanked loose.

"I need to—"

"You need to rest," he says firmly, striding over to the bed and glaring me into submission. "You're safe here. All aboard my unsinkable, multi-million-euro superyacht."

"They said the same thing about the Titanic." I glance

toward the window again. "Did I faint? How did I—?"

"I carried you up the gangplank and over the threshold." The corners of his mouth start on that ever-ready smirk. "Turns out there are some wedding traditions that even I adhere to."

"We've left port." The words stick in my throat. "I can feel the vibrations of the engines."

"I have urgent business in Cannes and I was sick of road travel." He removes his jacket and tosses it across the end of the bed. It's the first time I've seen him in just a dress shirt and pants, and I'm temporarily distracted from the anarchy going on inside me. With his broad shoulders, solid muscularity, and black ink crawling out from underneath the cuff of one wrist, he looks like a fallen angel on a trajectory straight to hell.

"Wh-what do you think you're doing?" I say nervously as he goes to remove his necktie.

"Consummating our marriage." He laughs when he sees my face—a sound so devoid of his usual cynicism it's almost melodic in its bass. "Ielena, I've seen cheap whores more thrilled at that prospect than you. Relax. I said we'd do this at your pace." He leans down and swipes my lips with a rough finger, eliciting a soft gasp. "Is it the water you're scared of, or just me? Or maybe, princess, it's a little both."

"It's too early in our marriage to be sharing secrets." I wrench my head away and offer him a chaste cheek instead. The way my body reacts around him is trouble. I'm like a wave of iron filings whenever his raw magnetism passes over me.

His finger hooks under my chin and jerks me back again. "It's never too early for that," he says, his smirk slipping into something sinister.

"I don't feel like sharing anything with you, Aiden. Not after what you did to Maxim earlier."

"Not yet, but you will." He lets go and straightens up. "In the meantime, I'll celebrate the minor victories. You're not addressing me like a French politician anymore. That deserves a double on the rocks, at least."

"So you're not taking advantage of my compromised emotional state?" I almost sound disappointed.

I watch his gaze land hungrily on my chest. "I'll be taking advantage of everything if you don't quit the backchat."

"You promised you wouldn't force me!"

He laughs again. "A promise is a temporary structure that could crumble at any moment. Didn't your Bratva Papa ever teach you that?"

Does he mean it? Does he not? I can never tell with him.

"Shall we have another round of that conversational tennis, Ielena?"

"It's Issa, not Ielena. Not even my mother calls me that."

"Not until I say it is. Not until you've earned it. Not until all those pretty *half-measures* have become whole." He sits down on the edge of bed and the dip in the mattress sends me scooting to the other side. His masculinity is punching holes in my defenses again.

"So, you're telling me I'm lacking?"

"On the contrary, I'm beginning to see your potential. Take your clothes, for example." He glances down at my dress. The hem has rucked up to my thighs and I'm all legs and red nail polish. *I managed to sneak that one past you, Marie.* "In the span of two hours, your taste has improved dramatically."

"You like it?" I say in surprise.

"I do."

"Why?"

"Because it cracks open a window to your personality."

I take a moment to let his words scatter and settle. "Will you allow me to take that job, or was it a just ruse to get me out of Eloise's shop?"

"I said I would, didn't I? I'm a lot of things, baby, but when I give the go ahead, there's no open return policy." He trails a lazy gaze over my body again, lingering for a fraction too long on my bare legs. "Do you know the other thing I like about the dress?"

"No."

"It shows off your best assets." With that, he reaches across the bed and hauls me closer until we're barely a foot apart and I can see the faint silver trail of a scar running through his left eyebrow. "You, Ielena, formerly Dubova and now very much a Knight," he clarifies huskily, "are more than the uptight bitch I first mistook you for."

"Am I supposed to be grateful for your backhanded compliment?" I say, staring up at his wicked flawlessness. "I read somewhere that men who put women down only do it to compensate for something."

His gaze drops to my mouth and all the heat in my body rushes southward. "Nothing to compensate for down there, sweetheart. You're welcome to find out for yourself."

"I don't like your engagement ring," I blurt out, wrenching my wrist away.

"I find that more encouraging than you know."

"Why? Because I'm shattering your preconceived notions about me?"

"Shattering?" He gives me that wolfish grin, the one that stiffens my nipples to sensitive peaks. "You'll have to swing your hammer a hell of a lot harder to make a dent in that."

"Why do you live on a yacht? Are you rootless as well as

soulless?"

"Touché. What did I call you yesterday again?"

"Stupid rich, bored, empty, unemployable, unsalvageable." It's a vicious citation I've already learned by heart.

"Well, we can scrap the unemployable thing, for starters."

"I'm not bored, Aiden."

I'm scared. Shit scared. I'm scared of what the last four weeks have done to my heart. I'm scared I'll never be me *again, or whatever version I was before Karina left, back in a time when I had horses and friends and sweet oblivion. Most of all, I'm scared of the man I married today and his ability to crush me like a bug if he so desires, of his ability to crush all of us if he ever finds out the truth.* "Neither am I unsalvageable."

"What about empty?" He's moving in close again. "If you lie back and think of England, I could fill you up right now."

"Do you have to be so crude?" Will I ever stop blushing in his presence? I'm like a walking, talking beetroot around him.

"That wasn't crude, sweetheart, it was foreplay."

Now it's my turn to laugh. "Oh really? I may be inexperienced, but even I know that's a crappy line."

This is new. This banter between us… This lightness…

I like it.

I like it more than I should.

"Stop trying to make me hate you, Aiden."

He freezes for a split-second. It's a quiver of hesitation, but I catch it right before it tumbles into the ocean like a falling star. "Maybe it's better for us if you do."

"How can it be better? I've done nothing to deserve your misery, except to be born into a wealth and privilege I never asked for. I'm not here to cause trouble for you." I'm shocked at how easily that lie slips out with such certainty. "You say you own casinos? You see people with bad hands all the time. If you can find it in yourself to soften the edges of your attitude—"

"You'll what? You'll *fall in love* with me? We'll have a Hallmark marriage and a tribe of delinquents?" The moment has passed. He's killed it, and he's back to ridiculing me again. "Sorry, Ielena, that's not part of the deal." He rises from the bed, severing the fragile truce between us.

"Just so you know, *Aiden Knight*," I say, my temper flaring. "I'd rather jump into the Mediterranean than catch feelings for you."

"Hallelujah. We finally agree on something." He snatches up his jacket with a cold precision and an even colder expression on his face. "You think Luca Zaccaria was a better option than me, sweetheart? Do you like broken bones and hospital waiting rooms? You would have been seeing those on the regular with his diamonds on your finger."

His admission hits me like an earthquake.

I think of the note Maxim sneaked me earlier today, and then I think of gray skies and empty pebble beaches. Of a stark white cottage with blue shutters battened down against the incoming storm.

"Why did you attack Maxim?" I blurt out.

"He was moving in on my territory."

"I'm not territory. I'm a living, breathing person." *With shattered dreams and a fractured present.*

"Who says I was referring to you?"

He's lying. He runs his hand through his hair when he switches from bastard to manipulation mode.

"Which part of London do you come from?"

"The shit part," he says, checking his watch. "Why do you hate water so much?"

I pause. "I-I can't say."

"You started this, princess. Don't tease me with the goods if you're not planning on a same-day delivery."

There's a knock at the door. "Mr. Knight?"

"What is it?"

A gray-haired British gentleman in a crisp white uniform appears in the doorway. "The captain has asked me to let you know we're coming in to port, sir."

"Thank you, Felix." The guy disappears and Aiden makes to follow. "Cheer up, buttercup, I'm giving you the perfect wedding night."

"What do you mean?"

He fixes his jacket and slides his necktie into his pocket. "I'll be out of town until tomorrow."

My heart leaps, and then stumbles with a misstep I never saw coming. *Does he have a lover?*

"Well?" He pauses in the doorway, his cool gaze casting aspersions about my response. "Happy?"

Of course he has a lover. This man oozes sex. I can't expect him to be faithful to a new wife who refuses to sleep with him.

"Ecstatic," I mutter, refusing to look at him, drawing my knees up to my chest for a modicum of comfort, turning myself into a shaking red and pink stain on his white bedsheets. I've never felt so unwanted, which is quite an achievement considering my childhood was devoid of parental love.

"This is your own cabin. You'll find your clothes and belongings hanging in the closet. Despite what you might think, you are not a prisoner here. There's a speedboat waiting to take you to shore at any time. Go and buy yourself some more dresses." He pulls out a black wallet and I watch in horror as he tosses a thick wad of notes onto the bed. He's right. It's going to take more than a couple of taps from that hammer to change his opinion of me.

"Get out," I hiss.

"Ielena…"

"Will you leave a wad of cash on the bed for her, too?" I say, refusing to look at him. "I said, get out."

There's another pause, and then he erupts with the deepest, richest, most contemptuous laugh of all.

It's still resonating around the room long after he's gone.

Chapter Nine

AIDEN

The best time to drink an espresso in the *Piazza Del Campo* is between seven and eight a.m. Tourists have yet to swallow up the fishbone-patterned red bricks in front of the *Torre del Mangia*, and the day is only a promise of heat, not the red-hot burn of deliverance.

There's a café to the north-western corner that's mostly cast in shadow before the late-morning gelato rush. It's not an impressive place. The windows are cracked and the olive-green awning above my head is ripped and faded. There are far nicer tourist traps on the outskirts of the *Campo*, but with only a handful of chairs and tables outside, and most of them empty, it's a good place to sit and plot a man's execution.

Behind me, a couple of guys are constructing metal bleachers for next week's *Palio di Siena* horse race. Their crude jokes and hammer blows are keeping all the early risers entertained. Across the main thoroughfare, a souvenir vendor is setting up his stall of overpriced shit for the day. The sky is blue, the clouds are white, and my intentions are as black as my coffee.

It's a strange moment to be present in, standing on the cusp of achieving something I've wanted for so long. Somewhere in my head there's an aircraft coming in for landing, and it's the final, few, weightless seconds before touchdown. My target is less than twenty meters away. He's leaning over the handrails in front of the *Fonte Gaia*, the rectangular fountain in the heart of the *Campo*. Black T-shirt and blue jeans, he's young enough not to look like a sleazy dick in nightclubs, but not old enough for café bar retirement yet.

He's smoking a cigarette like a carefree asshole—like a man who didn't set my life on a course to Sicily fourteen years ago—sucking and blowing and tapping ash at the water. The early morning sun catches the tips of the ripples, and my mind flits to Ielena and the accusation in her soft brown eyes last night. Will they glisten with damage or harden with payback when she finds out that I'm abandoning her on her wedding night for something far more satisfying than pussy?

Fuck that. I don't feel guilt for anyone.

I'm finishing up the last dregs of my espresso when my cell rings.

"Frankie."

"Can you see him?" he says, cutting straight to chase.

"In sight. The info was good."

"Good." He blows out a breath in relief. He's feeling the beats of this moment back in France as well.

"I'll call you when it's done. I need a clean exit out of Italy in the next hour." I chuck a ten-euro note on the table and feel the solid press of my Glock against my stomach.

"I'll make the calls."

"One last thing. I want you to swing by *The Cristo* later."

"Why? I have the surveillance on her like you requested."

I glance toward the fountain again. She hates water and I've left her on a fucking boat. "Just check on her, okay? See if she needs anything."

There's a pause. "I thought you said 'It' was so irrelevant you were hanging 'It' next to your Warhol?"

He's angling at something I don't have the time nor the inclination to dwell on.

"Just sort the transport," I tell him. "And her name is Ielena."

Two smokes later, and Lorenzo Gambino is on the move. I track him across the *Campo* and through the narrow side streets, past the brown signposts for the *Duomo di Siena* and toward the small *pizzicheria* he owns. The front window of the store is typically overcrowded. There are hanging lines of cured meats and huge magnums of Chianti, but all I see is my father's severed head and a pool of crimson blood. Gambino paid for this place and its contents with two large payments that appeared in his bank account the day after my parents died.

Who ordered the hit on my parents and why?

Zaccaria hasn't volunteered that information, so it's up to me to connect the dots. I plan on extracting a few answers before I'm done.

The cobbles are beginning to swell with chatter. Delivery trucks are beeping to pass. I watch him enter his store from under the awning of a nearby *alimentari.* I wait for ten minutes, and then I'm crossing the street and entering myself. Flicking over the sign and sliding the bolt across, I catch the eye of the man behind the counter. He nods once, and then jerks his head in the direction of the back room. Money favors the avaricious. I offered this guy a hundred thousand bonus if he turned a blind eye to what's about to unfold, and he nearly bit my hand off for it.

He busies himself with his meat slicer as I pull out my Glock and twist on the black silencer. Once done, I brush past the counter and down a short flight of wooden steps. It leads to a cellar doubling as a small storeroom, and a quick scan tells me that the only exit is the route I just traveled.

The rat is cornered.

Gambino looks up as I enter, sees the gun and panics. He stumbles backward over a wooden stack of fresh lemons and oranges in his haste to put some distance between us and shit goes flying everywhere. Up close, he even looks like a rat, with his scrawny face and twitchy eyes.

"*Qualcuno mi salvi!*" *Someone save me!* he cries, picking up random pieces of fruit and throwing them at me. I duck easily. His aim is as pathetic as his existence. "You shouldn't be here! I'm protected by the *Villefort*!"

"Your protection just got revoked, sunshine."

"Did Rossi send you?"

"No one sent me, Gambino," I say, slipping into Italian. "It's just me and an unforgiving bitch called revenge."

Frankie was right. We're caught up in a mafia war and we're picking over rotting carcasses.

He pauses his assault and blinks rapidly. "You're British?" A misplaced sense of relief overcomes the rat-like features. "I love the British!" Instead of fruit, he starts lobbing culture references at me. "Big Ben! The River Thames! Ah, ah, the Queen!"

"You didn't love my father much," I say grimly. "Or what

you left of him."

"Who is—?"

"Jacob Knight."

I watch with a dark satisfaction as those same features descend into chaos. "No," he whispers. "No, no, no. You disappeared from England. They thought you were dead."

"I was." I raise my gun to shoulder-height. "But then I was resurrected as the goddamn antichrist... Why did you kill him, Gambino?"

"I didn't! I never laid a finger on him!" He's gibbering and pleading, and pissing his dignity all over the concrete floor.

"Don't hang your guilt on semantics, Gambino. I can make this quick or I can make you scream for your *mamma* at the top of your fucking lungs. That decision rests on the next words that fall from your mouth. Why did you do it?"

"I was in the car outside the whole time!"

"Wrong answer."

The first bullet makes a dull fleshy sound as it pierces his left thigh. Gambino goes crashing to the ground again, along with more crates of lemons and oranges. A sickly-sweet smell starts mixing up with all the piss, reminding me of a bargain struck for this very moment fourteen years ago.

His pleading and screaming are bouncing off the mildewed walls in an endless song.

"Shut up, Gambino. No one's coming to help you." I aim the muzzle at his right thigh, smelling metal and savoring victory. The moment is here. The aircraft is hitting the ground and it tastes like the greatest fuck I ever had. *Almost as good as my new wife tastes.* "Who ordered the hit?"

"Rossi." He sobs the name at me as he's wiping the sweat from his eyes, smearing blood all over himself like the sacrifice that he is. "I don't know the details. I was a *soldato*. I'd never seen the other man before in my life. I was given a time and a place, that's it!"

"Should have paid attention, dickhead."

Another dull thud from my gun unleashes more of those piercing screams. "I don't know anything else! I swear it! I swear it!"

"Why did you run?"

"I got scared." He's all-out crying like a fat kid who dropped his *gelato*. "There were rumors Rossi had violated some secret treaty between him and Tommaso Zaccaria by taking the Knights out—"

"Zaccaria knew exactly where you were," I snarl back. "He was the one who gave me your location."

"I don't know anything else, I swear! I'm a useless man. I'm not even worthy of your bullets!"

Near-death is the great revelator. Gambino's finally grasping what a deadbeat he's been all his life. As for me, you can only have so much of a good thing. This man isn't a *soldato*. He's not even the dried shit on a *soldato's* boot.

The basement floor is another crimson pool, reflecting shades of history back to me. Everything points to Rossi ordering the hit, so I want him to know I'm onto him. My mind flits to the window display of this *pizzicheria… That might be one way to get his attention.*

When I fire my third and final bullet right between Gambino's eyes, I hear my father's voice again.

"Wait and hope, son. Wait and hope."

One down.

One to go.

Chapter Ten

ISSA

I'm standing on the threshold of my new walk-in closet, frowning at all the clothes I brought with me from Paris. Sophisticated, stylish, with muted tones and expensive fabrics… They belong to another woman, to a good and obedient daughter who always did what she was told and never asked questions. When my father's men beat me, they must have beaten that part right out of me, too. How else can I explain my newly acquired acid tongue and serpentine-like reactions toward a certain British non-gentleman?

Still, the realization that I never have to wear a single linen or mocha item again brings the first smile to my lips since he bailed on our wedding night. A new wardrobe will be my disguise. One part of my life will be bursting with life and color, even if the rest of me is balancing on a knife's edge. Karina used to tease me and say I could see the slivers of light under the door of any dark situation.

Next to the closet there's a luxury en suite, lined with white and gray calacatta marble. Forcing myself to face my fears, I melt under the shower for a hot thirty seconds before washing my hair at supersonic speed and wincing as the hot water splashes over my raw and aching skin. I can't bring myself to look at the damage in the mirror. If I do, I'll see the true price of betrayal.

Afterward, I towel-dry my long dark hair and slip into white lingerie and the dress I bought yesterday. Choosing to keep my hair loose, I open up my valise and pull out a small sketchbook and my graphite pencils from the front pocket. It's the set that Karina gifted to me on my twenty-first birthday last year, and these days it's more precious than ever. The note that Maxim slipped into my hand yesterday is tucked away beneath the black velvet tray, and I'm feeling a sudden urge to draw white cottages with bright blue shutters, over and over until they become tangible.

Collapsing onto the bed, I sketch a couple of lines with a 2H, my fingers skimming across the blank cartridge paper until the bare bones of the picture inside my head materializes in front of me.

I work fast after that, creating fragile connections to a place I can only dream about visiting. I imagine her sitting in a shabby swing on a veranda with peeling tread boards and a tatty red and white check throw tucked around her legs. The neglect is immaterial when the things that count are there in spades—the smile on her face, and a sense of freedom so animated I want it to dance me round and round an imaginary ballroom until I've spun one for myself. It's there in the sea breeze rattling the tattered screen door, and in the waves creeping up the beach to greet her.

She loves roses, so I add trails over all four of the front windows. Plump pink buds with tangled olive-green stems come alive in shades of light gray graphite.

I work like this for hours, chasing the sun as it moves from one side of my window to the other. My hand keeps cramping up, and I'm reluctant to shake the stiffness out. I don't want to stop drawing. I can't break the connection, but I don't have a choice when there's a sharp rap at the door.

"Come in!"

"A little light lunch, *madame*?" Felix enters my cabin with a tray of fresh fruit, bread, and cheese. He places it on my nightstand and I watch him glance sideways at my sketchbook.

"Thank you," I say, turning my drawing face-down on the bed. *Awkward.*

Raising his eyebrows, he gestures to the window. "We're moored up on the edge of *Port Pierre Canto, madame.* Would you like to see for yourself?"

I make my way over and I'm momentarily spellbound. The view of the bay of Cannes is like a movie scene. The troughs and peaks of the Esterel Mountains have formed emerald halos around all the pretty white and tan buildings in its foothills.

"It's beautiful," I breathe.

"Quite." I catch him giving me strange look. "Mr. Knight informs me that you have a fear of water."

"Trust me to be stuck on a yacht, right? I seem to be okay behind glass panes and steel handrails, though."

"Are you seasick?"

"No, thank goodness." I'm learning to love the gentle rocking motion as passing waves lap against the side of the hull. There's a strange comfort to it, like the warm nook of a mother's arms.

"Perhaps *madame* would like a walk around the yacht later? It's a beautiful day outside."

Perhaps *madame* might. I haven't left my cabin since I arrived and I'm suddenly itching to feel the sun-drenched deck boards beneath my feet.

"Sounds good."

"Then I shall see you outside."

Once he's gone, I drag a brush through my nearly-dry hair, reflecting on the weirdness of our conversation. I've grown up with servants all my life, but I've never met anyone who gives me the creeps quite as much as he does.

Grabbing my sketchbook and pencils, I make my way down a corridor that leads to a large saloon area with bleached wood floors and smooth white columns. Beyond the double doors is an empty sundeck with a jet-black Jacuzzi surrounded on three sides by white couches and smart lines of monochrome parasols, all rippling in the breeze.

I step into the sunshine and fill my lungs with salty-sweet air, feeling the strength of the sea filter down through my body. Is his decision to live on this yacht all about that sense of freedom again? Is he as trapped by the consequences of life as I am?

Sinking down onto the nearest couch, I resume my drawing, pausing every so often to lift my face to the patch of sunlight that's fallen between a gap in the parasols. The solitary cottage becomes a hamlet of three, the horizon sprouts a line of fishing boats, and there's another person sitting next to Karina now who—

"Would you like a drink?"

Startled, I drop my pencil. It starts rolling toward the sinister black edges of the Jacuzzi. I manage to grab it just before it drops into the water, and then I'm backing away quickly, my stomach churning at the sight of the gleaming, sun-tipped ripples.

"*Pardon-moi*," I croak, clambering back onto the couch. "I

didn't hear you approach."

Felix looks as deadpan as ever. "I'm sorry I alarmed you, *madame*."

Madame.

Madame.

Madame.

I glance at my finger and realize I've left my ugly engagement ring in my en suite next to the faucet.

There's a polite cough. "Drink?"

"Oh, yes… Um. Juice, please."

"What kind of juice?"

"Orange."

"Certainly M—"

"And I'll have scotch," interrupts a second voice. This one is deeper and familiar, and bitingly British as well. "Single malt, on the rocks. The usual."

Felix nods at the newcomer and disappears into the saloon.

"I don't believe we've been formally introduced." The man strides over to me, removing his sunglasses, the sheer size of him making me shrink down further into the couch. He's huge in every sense of the word, filling out the chest and arms of his white dress shirt with solid, unyielding muscle. His short, dark hair is almost military in its neatness and precision, and his penetrating gaze is taking no prisoners.

He stops in front of me and my mannerly smile drops like a stone. He's the man from the wedding ceremony yesterday. The one Aiden insisted on as his witness, and who held a gun to Maxim on the steps of the Town Hall.

"You have me at a disadvantage, *monsieur*," I say tightly, refusing to stand and greet him. "You know my name, but I don't know yours."

A large hand appears in front of my face. "Frankie Adams. I work for your husband."

I take it, and then drop it as quickly as I can. "Monsieur Adams. It's a pleasure to meet you."

"Likewise, Mrs. Knight." He chuckles and takes a step back, tucking his sunglasses into the front of his shirt. "Aiden warned me you have an icy reverb. He told me not to piss you off. Said you have a talent for dishing out red wine punishments when we least expect it. Shall I ask Felix to hide the Saint-Émilion, just in case? Or should that be that *by* the case?" he adds with an easy grin.

"Why are you here, *monsieur*?" I say, flustered by his words.

"Aiden asked me to swing by and check on you."

You mean spy on me.

"That's kind of you, but as you can see…" I gesture to the empty, tranquil surroundings. "I'm perfectly fine."

"You sure about that? I was there when you freaked out yesterday."

"Then you have me at an even greater disadvantage," I say, glaring up at him.

"We all have fears, Mrs. Knight. Some of us just have better coping mechanisms for them than others."

"What are yours? Pointing a gun at a man's back?" It slips out before I can stop it.

"You saw that, huh?" He sighs and glances at the ocean. "In my defense, Maxim was acting like a dick."

"So was Aiden."

"I'm not denying that, either." His handsome face splits in two again, and I find my own lips twitching along. He's droll and caustic, but there's a tough amiability about him. He's the tallest tree in the forest, the one that bends with the hurricane, but never uproots.

I watch his heavy gaze fall on the sketchbook and open pencil set next to me. "Do you draw?"

I shrug to hide my blooming panic. "A little."

"Has Aiden seen them?"

My smile turns into the full force of winter, complete with a light dusting of snow and several pointy icicles. "I don't know my husband particularly well, *monsieur*, but what I do know of him suggests he'd be far from interested. Nothing about our situation...*or me* amuses him, as he's been quick to point out on numerous occasions. Besides, I don't think he's a hobby kind of a guy."

"You think you have the measure of him already?" His dark eyes start drilling holes into my face. "I can tell you now, lady, I've known Aiden a long time and there's more to him than you think." *Oh, I'm counting on it.* "May I see?" He bends down to pick up my sketchbook, but I whip it away and hug it protectively to my chest, forgetting about the ugly damage beneath my pretty dress.

His grin drops when he catches me wincing. "You okay?"

"I'm fine," I rasp, breathing shallowly through the pain. "I'm so sorry, but an artist never shares unless it's perfect."

"As you wish."

Felix arrives on the scene with a loaded tray. Frankie chooses to remain standing as drinks are sipped and awkward silences observed. Finally, my curiosity gets the better of me.

"What do you do for my husband, Monsieur Adams?"

"Frankie, please. I oversee his business interests."

"Including his casino?"

"Including his casino."

I eye his massive arm muscles again. "Forgive me for

saying so, *monsieur*, but you don't seem like the businessman or accountant type."

"Forgive me for saying so, *madame*," he responds dryly, "but your husband doesn't seem the law-abiding type."

My lips start twitching again. "I'm sorry. I wasn't trying to be rude."

"No offense taken." He's swinging his tumbler between his forefinger and thumb. It's never enough to slosh the remains of his whiskey over the sides, but it's enough to unsettle me. "I wasn't bullshitting you before. Aiden wants to know how you are, and—full disclosure? I can't recall the last time he asked me to check on a woman."

I choose not to dwell on that revelation. "Did you grow up together?"

"What makes you think that?"

"Because of your accents."

He laughs. "There are sixty-five million people in Britain. Don't go jumping to conclusions."

"I don't do that anymore," I say with a sigh. "I find I'm frequently disappointed. You seem close, that's all."

He stares at me for a moment. "Perceptive."

"Floundering." I look away with a shrug. "I was meant to be marrying a man called Luca Zaccaria. Instead, I'm sitting here married to a man I'd never even heard of before yesterday. I know nothing about Aiden's story or his background... I was made to believe I was a 'sign on a dotted line' bonus, and now I'm locked up on a yacht and chained to a man whose idea of a good time is to make me feel as unwelcome as possible." I take a sloppy sip of my orange juice to build up the courage to say my next words. "I want to know how Aiden's connected to the Zaccaria *Famiglia*."

"You and the rest of the Riviera."

I give him a look.

"They're business partners."

"What kind of business partners?"

"The casino kind."

"Have you spoken to him this morning?"

He hesitates. "Briefly."

"Did he have a good wedding night?" I can't stop my resentment from creeping in.

"Not particularly. He spent half of it on an aircraft."

"An *aircraft*?"

"May I offer you a piece of advice, Mrs. Knight?" He beckons to a hovering Felix and furnishes his tray with his now-empty tumbler. "I wouldn't pay too much attention to your husband's business dealings. You're a Bratva princess... You know how this works."

"In other words, spend his blood money like a good wife, look pretty, and keep my mouth shut." I glance down at my juice.

"The fact that you're even asking this makes you more than a trophy wife already. I'm merely suggesting you don't go buying any shovels. You won't like what you dig up."

"What could there possibly be to shock me?" I say, arching my brows at him. "Like you said, I'm a Bratva princess, born and bred."

"Mrs. Knight," he warns.

"Why do people call him The Raven?" I say, remembering Eloise's words.

"On that note, the defense rests his case." He unhooks his sunglasses from the front of his shirt. "Aiden'll be back in a couple of hours. Enjoy your drawing." His gaze slides toward my sketchpad again. "I'll see you around, no doubt."

"No doubt."

I watch him leave with a seed of determination growing inside me. By the time his white speedboat is racing away from *The Cristo*, it's a plan in full bloom. So far, I've been a good girl and played by Aiden's rules ninety-nine percent of the time. Tonight, that other one percent is coming out to play.

Back in my cabin, I track down Eloise's shop number on my cell, ignoring Aiden's messy stack of euros as the call connects. I'd love a new dress, but only if Eloise allows me a store credit extension.

Not just any dress, either.

It needs to be something as scarlet as the warning he'll never see coming, with a high neckline to hide the damage and a back cut low enough to sell lust and temptation.

He has a casino with secrets.

Secrets that are mine to sell.

Chapter Eleven

AIDEN

The moment my private jet lands at *Nice Cote d'Azur*, I set my sights on Monte Carlo. There are a couple of big-stakes players due at the casino tonight, and I personally like to meet and greet all those who add extra zeros to my bank account's bottom line.

The dusk is a bloody delight and befitting of the day. It's dripping down from the sky, mixing with the water and turning the ocean a pinkish hue. As the Escalade climbs higher and higher into the mountains, the rash of superyachts bobbing on the horizon look like pox on an iridescent skin. Somewhere down there *The Cristo* is playing host to a confused young woman who wants to find middle ground with a man who is hell-bent on churning it up.

My main focus now is obtaining the second name for my kill list, which leaves me five days to fuck the location of her sister out of Ielena. I promised I'd give her time, but I need to accelerate the process. It's Seduction 101 from now on.

I find Frankie in my office, helping himself to my whiskey. It's a sprawling, circular room with an overkill of soft black leather and tinted windows overlooking the main gaming floor. He barely looks up as I throw my bag down on the floor.

"Good flight?"

"Had worse."

"Here." He hands his whiskey to me, and pours himself another. "Your present in the window of Gambino's store was an inspired touch. Thought it was an 'eye for an eye,' not a 'head for a head.'"

I take a sip and smile grimly. "I left a calling card for Rossi. Gambino confirmed what we'd already suspected. He also spoke about some broken treaty between Rossi and Zaccaria before my bullets shut him up."

What else are you hiding from me, old man?

Revenge is as circular as this room. It never ends. There's always an order from an asshole who took an order from another. The bodies will keep piling up. The twister will spin faster until everything is consumed, and you either learn to let go or you keep on spiraling.

I'm never letting go, and I've made my peace with that.

"I saw Ielena earlier," I hear him say.

"Oh?"

He takes a thoughtful swig of his drink. "She's hiding something."

"Try stating the fucking obvious." I wander over to the windows to survey my domain. It's packed in here tonight. The crowds around each table are three-deep, and the slot machines are ringing with the sound of other people's money. Every inch of my crimson carpet is a shoe designer's wet dream.

Frankie follows me over. "Let me ask you something. Why was Zaccaria so certain she had info about Karina Dubova's disappearance?"

I shrug. "Sisters talk. Her father must have told him they were close."

"Did the Russians rough her up before they handed her over?"

"What gave you that idea?" I say sharply

"Just a hunch." He takes another sip of his whiskey. "Try to find out if you can. It might be a way into her affections. Manipulation isn't a one-way strect."

"Christ, Frankie," I exclaim. "You're more of an unprincipled shit than I am."

He laughs, but there's a forced note to it. "Tell me it wasn't the first thing to cross your mind when I mentioned it."

I can't, because it did: in crystal clear detail, with side notes and annotated diagrams. Still, that's not what's pissing me off the most. That trophy belongs to the thought of another man's hands causing her pain.

"Unicorn dick or not, I'll get the truth out of Ielena."

"Fine, but go easy on her heart." I swing around in surprise, *and we all know how much I hate those.* "She's just a kid, Aiden," he says evenly. "When all of this is over—when we've used her up and spat her out—she has to pick up the pieces of her life and start again. And without her sister, if Zaccaria gets his hands on her."

"*When* he gets his hands on her," I say, irritated by his words. "That's quite a dick swing you're having there, Frankie— from devious bastard to caring criminal in under sixty seconds flat. Are you forgetting your place, brother? I make the decisions, not you. If I say we offer her up as a pagan sacrifice, your job it to organize the chants, the daggers, and the robes. Understood?"

"Go fuck yourself, Raven," he says good-naturedly, dropping his glass down on the desk and heading for the door.

"What happened to black and white?" I shout after him. "You want this justice as much as I do. For fourteen years, it's been the beating heart of our whole operation."

He pauses in the doorway. Door open. Hand on the handle. Scowl in place. "Perhaps I'm thinking there's something in your shades of gray theory, after all. Don't delude yourself. This shit isn't sitting easy with you, either. Bad men are players. We kill, discard, and move on. Good girls aren't so clear-cut."

"She won't be a good girl by the time I've finished with her."

"Monsieur Knight?" The crinkled face of my personal assistant, Camille, appears next to Frankie's massive shoulder. She's looking every bit of her fifty-five years this evening. Not that she cares. She's here for the money, so I pay her double to make her blind. She knows everything that goes on in this place, but as long as I keep her in tri-yearly holidays to Tenerife, she's loyal as fuck.

"What is it?"

"I just took a call from your captain. Madame Knight requested *The Cristo* be brought back to berth in *Port Hercule* this afternoon."

"Why the hell did she do that?"

"She wouldn't say, but you can ask her yourself. She's on her way to the casino. She's expected in the next hour."

I catch Frankie's eye. Now there's a chess move we never anticipated.

Fucking surprises.

Camille shifts her weight from one foot to the other. "There's one other thing."

"Go on."

"Senator Sanders and his wife have just arrived. I asked Adele to show them into your favorite private gaming room."

"Fine." I finish up my drink. "I'm heading down there now. And stop voodooing me, Frankie… You're coming, too."

Rick Sanders is the kind of man you'd have no trouble envisioning in the White House one day, with his feet up on the Resolute Desk and a killer smirk for all the former presidents and their disapproving portrait faces. Even if he lost the vote in every state, he'd still charm his way in through the front door. He's smoother than churned butter, and he has the kinds of connections I can only dream about, from top Bratva *Pakhans* to Colombian drug lords. You mess with this guy and he'll conduct a vivisection on you with his wife's tweezers.

On the hush-hush he's a former coke dealer from Brooklyn, but that doesn't look too good on paper for the Bible Belt voters, so a couple of years ago he painted himself legit, taking over the reins of his wife's family shipping business and making a cool billion in the process. His wife, Nina, is just as connected. She's Alexander Petrov's daughter, a dead *Pakhan* whose spirit is still haunting the Moscow underground. It means she's as Bratva as my own dear wife, if not more so.

I like them both so I keep them in my inner circle, rolling out the red carpet whenever they're in town. To be fair, it's been a while since they last visited. Squeezing out kids and corrupting the United States Senate can distract you from the finer things in life.

This private room is the most exclusive one in my casino. A couple of days ago, Zaccaria was in here with his sons and *Consigliere* laying down the law. Tonight, it's my domain again, with a private bar serving the best liquor in the house, a luxury seating area for the ladies and a blood-red blackjack table on which to wager a cool couple of million.

Rick's standing by the bar with four men I don't recognize. Tall, lean, dark haired, and vulturine… Someone once described him to me as a bird of prey who prefers to toy with his carcasses rather than pick at them. Put it this way: I wouldn't want to be his political opponent, in this life or the next.

"Aiden Knight." He peels away from the group to greet me with a handshake. You can tell a lot about a bad man from this gesture. Firm handshake. Firm trigger finger… And his nearly crushes my fingers.

"Senator Sanders. Congratulations on your recent re-election."

"I understand congratulations go both ways… Is she here?" I watch him nod at Frankie, who enters the room a couple of paces behind me.

"You'll meet her soon enough." I bend down to kiss his elegant wife who has appeared next to him. "This is an unexpected pleasure, Nina. What have you done with the kids? Checked them in at the door with your fur stole?"

"They're sleeping in their beds, I hope." She laughs, a pleasing bell of a sound. If Rick's a wide boy, then she's as soft and willowy as they come. She doesn't suffer fools, though. I've heard the stories.

"How are the paintings?"

Nina owns a successful private gallery in New York.

"Sales are excellent," she says with a contented sigh. "Rick's nefarious friends have a constant supply of cash to splash."

"*Clean cash*, I might add," drawls Rick, sliding his arm around his wife's waist in a classic mark of possession. "No doubt filtered, at some point or another, through this glorious casino. Am I right, Aiden?"

"I have no idea what you're referring to," I deadpan. "I run a legitimate business, Senator Sanders. As do you."

"Oh, fuck off," he says good-naturedly. "And get me another bourbon while you're at it."

I make eye contact with Adele, our hostess for the night, who sets to work on our drinks as I'm introduced to his group. They're mostly politicians and rich businessmen with port-wine faces who are just as bent as he is.

"Are you joining us tonight?" Rick takes his place at the table as the dealer waits for all the other players to follow suit.

I open my mouth to decline. Then I remember that a couple of hours ago I was decapitating the first of my father's killers, and yesterday I married a woman who despises the very ground I walk on. You could say that shit is upside down for me right now.

"It's your funeral, Sanders." I slip into the free chair next to him. "The house never wins in this casino... *I* do."

"Care to put your money where your balls are?"

"What can I say? My balls are feeling lucky." I nod in Frankie's direction, who returns it with a mild eyebrow quirk. He knows I never work the tables here. Nonetheless, a minute later he's delivering a million-euro gold case of chips to the table.

"I hope you enjoy life as a eunuch," taunts Rick. "I was taught to play by a Colombian who shot the fingers off those who didn't try hard enough." With that, he slams his hand down on the table, palms to the felt, to show me that all five of his fingers are still attached. "It's safe to say, I paid attention."

"Is there any reason why your other hand is still fixed to your wife's waist and out of sight?" I drawl back, signing the receipt for the chips and handing it back to Frankie. "Are you poker-facing me already, Sanders?"

"Do you think she'd look half as satisfied if I was missing any digits?"

I tip my head back and laugh as Frankie stacks the gold and black-flecked plastic into three neat piles in front of me, smallest denomination on the top. It's the sort of line I would have relished delivering myself.

"Rick," hisses Nina, her cheeks flushing the same color that Ielena's do. "Stop being an ass."

"Just telling it how it is, sweetheart."

She pushes him away with a small smile and goes to wait by the bar, curling onto a stool with her long legs crossed to the side.

Forty minutes later, Rick's not looking so smug. He's two hundred down and I'm running the show. The cards are rich for me, and I'm getting richer.

The first play in the next round is dealt. Turning up the corner of the card, I find it's another ace.

"Place your bets, please, gentlemen."

I'm sliding fifty grand's worth of chips into the betting box when I hear the door to the private room open behind me.

"Your balls really *are* lucky," murmurs Rick, glancing over.

"I told you I always win in my casino."

"Not the game, you British asshole. The woman."

Frowning, I follow his gaze and my world stops turning.

Ielena's standing just inside the doorway, blinking and unsure, but with her small chin jutted sky-high in an attempt to front it out. Tall and regal, with curves in all the right places, her bright red lipstick is a beacon for a mouth that I know, from sweet experience, tastes like ripe dark cherries on a summer's day. Her slinky satin cocktail dress and matching heels are the same color, the former being slashed to the waist to expose one of those slender pale legs that I keep envisioning wrapped around my body. The high neckline emphasizes the flawless arcs of her breasts and her slenderness, and there's no frigid, old woman chignon for her today—just a long curtain of glossy dark hair that reaches well past her ribcage.

She looks every bit of her twenty-two years and defiant as hell.

Not pretty.., Not beautiful... She's something even better.

A beat later, an unfamiliar emotion is blazing through me.

"Ielena." I rise to my feet, and she meets me halfway, which is a fucking leveler in itself. "I hear you've been playing captain with my ship." I press my cheek to hers and feel her body tremble. She doesn't lean away from me though, and I feel a buzz of admiration.

"I had to keep myself amused somehow, Aiden. The boring get bored, too."

She's mad at me, and I'm turned on as hell about it.

"There's nothing boring about that dress." I cast my gaze downward, drinking it all in. There's a grace about her that sets her apart from other women. "Your taste is improving day by day."

"What if I used the whore's gift you left on my bed to buy it? Would that make it a scarlet dress for a scarlet woman?"

My jaw clenches. "If it offended you so much, pay me back."

"Oh, I intend to. For everything." She shoots me a look that has me scrambling to decode it. "I wasn't expecting to see you here."

"That goes both ways."

"You must be the new Mrs. Knight." Rick's angling for a cut-in and I consider breaking his face for the intrusion.

"Rick, this is Ielena," I grit out. "Ielena, Senator Sanders."

"Please, call me Issa," she says graciously, shaking his hand like a true lady.

Fuck, that's hot. I imagine her asking me to tongue her pussy with the same refinement.

"Is it Issa or Ielena?" Rick looks confused.

"Issa."

She says it at the same time I growl, "Ielena."

There's a pause. "Friends and people I respect call me Issa," she says with a small laugh, managing to shrug it off and publicly kick me in the nuts at the same time.

Rick shoots me an amused look. "Issa, it is."

"Would you like a drink, *Ielena*?" I'm gritting my jaw so damn hard the fucking thing's about to crack.

"I'd love a glass of red... Do you have any Saint-Émilion?" She bats her eyelashes at me, as innocent as a baby fawn.

"I've heard the 2015 vintage is full of shit," I say coldly, ramming her with a 4x4 of a retort, imagining flailing limbs and bleating pleas as I do. Instead, she scrambles back up again with a sweet smile that hits me dead center of my dick.

"I've kept you from your game long enough." She turns to Rick. "It was lovely to meet you, Senator Sanders. I wish you every good fortune for tonight."

She drifts away to introduce herself to Nina while Rick and I resume our seats at the table. He doesn't say a word, but I know what he's thinking. For four years I've presided over the French Riviera with total authority. I staked my claim the minute I arrived. I crossed every line to gain respect because that's what needed to happen. The foundation of this whole damn casino is lined with dead bodies—men who tried to curb the meteoric rise of my star. I spread fear like a pandemic, but in four seconds flat some defiant teenager has waltzed in here and cut me down to size in front of one of the most powerful men in the world.

A cold, hard knot settles in the pit of my stomach and no amount of Glenfiddich is shifting it. My game disintegrates. I'm too distracted by the sound of my wife's laughter—she and Nina have clearly hit it off. I slide the felt when I need to stand, and stand when I need a hit. Over the next twenty minutes I manage to lose close to half a million.

"Fuck it, I'm done." Throwing down another piss-poor twenty-two, I slide the rest of my chips into my pants pocket and kick my chair back.

"Present company not satisfying enough for you, Knight?" inquires Rick slyly.

"On the contrary. It's high time I gave my new wife a tour of my casino. I'll be back for a late-night game. Save a cigar for me."

Striding up to Ielena, I take her by the waist, grinding our hips together and smiling coldly as she flinches away. "Time to go, *sweetheart*." She's about to learn that I'm not a man to play games with.

"So soon?" Nina's face falls in disappointment. "It was lovely to meet you, Issa," she gushes, seemingly oblivious of her transformation into a human rod of tension. "Keep up the drawing. I'd love to see some pieces. Make sure you send them to me. Aiden will give you the details of my gallery in New York."

"That's if Aiden ever decides to," I say in an undertone as I march Ielena toward the door. "What drawings is she referring to?"

"It doesn't matter," she says breathlessly. "You wouldn't be interested."

"Try me." But she's right. I'm not. I'm too busy thinking about how soft and supple she feels beneath my fingertips, and how much I'd like to pound my hardness and punishment into her like the callous bastard that I am.

"If you don't slow down, I'm going to trip in my heels," she warns.

"Is that an order?" My fingers tighten around her waist and I don't slow my pace for a second. "Where's all the belligerence gone, sweetheart? A few minutes ago you were drooling with it."

"Aiden—"

"I'll tell you what happened to it. It disappeared off to the same damn place as my half a mil." I guide her out into the glass atrium, her slender body still locked to mine. "And I was so looking forward to more of that verbal foreplay."

"You just lost half a million?" She looks stunned.

"The ownership of that is up for debate. Personally, I'm blaming you and that dress for the distraction. What the hell are you doing here?"

"I was bored! I said it already."

"Bullshit."

"You treat me like I'm non-existent."

"You have my attention now."

"I was angry—"

"*Angry*?" We reach the white and gold lobby and I spin her around to face me. "You know what, Ielena? That shit's transferable, because right now I'm fucking furious." I take a step closer, and she refuses to take a step back *again*, and my God, if that isn't the sexiest fucking thing ever. "Careful, princess," I murmur, fighting the urge to smash my mouth down onto hers again. "You're inching more and more into my frame, and that's never a safe place to be."

Chapter Twelve

ISSA

A bad decision is like a bad meal. The premise is good, the recommendations are excellent, but when the plate arrives half cold and you're forced to swallow it, you end up with a bad case of nausea and regret.

Picking a fight with my new husband is one of those bad decisions.

He's a criminal, a crook and, I strongly suspect, a cold-blooded killer. Basically, he's the worst kind of man to have a passive-aggressive showdown with and embarrass in front of a leading US senator.

I came here to learn about him, to try to understand him, to figure out why I've been forced to marry him… Now, I'll be lucky if I make it through the night.

So, what do I do?

I take all that nausea and regret and I choose to go down in flames with them.

"Good. I'm glad you're angry." Twisting out of his grip, I force a couple of feet between us, pushing my dark hair away from my face. "Maybe it shows we have more in common than we think. When people don't treat us with respect, we get mad."

I wish I didn't notice how handsome he looks in the light of a dozen crystal chandeliers. He's dressed in black again to color coordinate with his heart, and his rich tan is making his ceruleans flash like raging tempests.

"I disagree," he says coldly. "I've passed the 'mad' stage, and now I need to get the hell out of here before I start killing people." My body turns to ice as he beckons to the doorman. "I need my car right away."

"*Oui*, Monsieur Knight."

The guy scuttles off to call down to the parking lot as we pause our argument for a halftime break of seething resentment. There's another man standing just inside the lobby doors with us. He's rolling an unlit cigar between his fingers and watching us intently. He looks like the British playboy type—floppy hair, ruddy complexion, Daddy's disapproval threaded into the seams of his Savile Row suit...

His huge ego coughs up a smirk when he catches me staring back. *It wasn't a compliment, monsieur.* I look away, but I can still feel his eyes crawling up and under my dress like scarab beetles.

"Are you eye-fucking my wife, Landon?" Aiden's possessive growl echoes around the lobby, sounding like a transmission break in hell. Chatter ceases, the rest of the doormen evaporate, and Playboy's smirk drops faster than a gear change on his Ferrari. "Perhaps you'd like me to flip her dress up so you can see what a million-euro pussy looks like for yourself?"

"I had no idea she was your wife, Knight. I thought she was

a…" The word dies on Landon's lips when he realizes he just made his situation a thousand times worse.

"A what? A whore?" finishes Aiden casually.

I open my mouth to diffuse the tension, but he silences me with *that look*. It's too late. He's a lightbulb fizzing and spitting, and he's about to blow.

"Why don't you give your admirer a twirl, Ielena," he purrs, grabbing my hand and coercing me into a haphazard spin. "He hasn't even checked out the glorious back view yet."

I stumble on the downturn, but he catches me easily and brings me in close, crushing my ass against his front. *Oh my God.* Despite the dragging pain across my chest, it's my senses that are spinning like crazy now. He's hot and hard. An invitation and a warning. I've never been held by a man like this before, but when he palms my stomach to stop me from escaping, I push back on him out of some weird primitive reflex, absorbing the threat of his erection with a vicious thrill.

A low growl in my ear tells me he knows exactly what I'm doing.

"Will you be joining me in my cabin later?" he murmurs. "There's a sublime skill to hate fucking that I mastered a long time ago."

My insides turn to liquid fire. My pussy is a throbbing mess and I have to part my legs to ease the ache. Meanwhile, Playboy is inching closer and closer to the glass doors. Even Daddy's money isn't going to buy him out of this one.

"Isn't she beautiful, Landon?" Aiden lets go of me with a not-so-gentle push, leaving my body awash with neglect and confusion. Playboy's eyes dart to my face, and then back to Aiden's. "I said, *isn't she beautiful?*" Aiden roars suddenly, making all the chandeliers rattle.

"Yes, yes, very beautiful." Landon's not even looking at me as he says it. He's not even daring himself to. I'm the Gorgon—Medusa herself—but my savage husband is the one who will be turning him to stone.

A sleek, black Maserati has appeared out front.

"Would you like to taste her?" Aiden's voice slows to a thoughtful drawl, but it's just as terrifying as his roar. "Black cherries, Landon, all glazed with innocence…"

"N-no, thank you."

"Are you saying my own wife is less desirable than the girl you tried to rape in my hotel last night?"

Wait, *what?*

"Mr. Knight, I—"

"Shut the fuck up," he snarls. "Your speaking rights just got revoked. Indefinitely. You don't get to touch her. You don't get to speak to her. You don't even get to *think* about her, you piece of shit. Understood?" He swings back to me with more of that bubbling violence in his calm. "Ielena, sweetheart, I'm taking back what I said when we first met. When the revolution comes and the guillotines starts swinging, you won't be the first in line after all."

"Please don't do this," I whisper.

"I would have dealt with it before, but I've been a little…" His gaze flicks to the front of my dress. "*Preoccupied.* Frankie, get her out of here," he orders as footsteps approach. "Landon and I need to have ourselves a chat."

There's a shriek and a scuffle as Landon tries to make a run for it, but black-clad security guards have materialized at every exit.

"Come on, baby." Frankie takes my arm and gently tugs me toward the doors. "You don't need to see this."

I don't remember walking to the car. I don't remember Frankie opening the door for me, but suddenly I'm here, swathed in expensive cream leather and trying to digest the rotten swamp of the last ten minutes.

Hunkering down in the passenger seat, shivering for a million reasons other than the cold, I turn my back on the casino as muffled thuds and high-pitched male screams flood the balmy night. Aiden's oceans have volcanoes, and when they erupt, they're savage and bloody.

Five minutes pass.

Ten minutes.

It's coming up on twenty when the driver's door finally swings open. Aiden throws himself behind the wheel, reeking of sweat, triumph, and a raw, potent masculinity that, despite everything, settles like hateful, hot smoke between my thighs.

He doesn't say a word as he tears down the floodlit driveway and out onto the moonlight-drenched streets of Monte Carlo, breaking every speed limit. As for me, I have no desire to resurrect our disagreement in his present mood, not when the passing streetlights keep throwing up smears of blood on his knuckles. There's a strain in the air, which tells me that whatever violence spilled out of him is still molten and seeping.

He skids the Maserati to a halt by the quayside and one of his deck crew emerges from the shadows to take the keys. We make our way onto *The Cristo* still trapped behind our walls of silence, but when I try to peel away, he grabs my arm to stop me.

"Oh, no, you don't. I'm not done with you yet."

Depositing me on a couch in the main saloon, he stalks over to the bar and starts packing a white cloth with ice.

"What did you do to that man?" I ask softly.

"I gave him an etiquette lesson. Drink?"

"No, thank you."

"Tough. You're having one anyway."

Sighing in defeat, I slip off my heels and work the knots out of my toes. When I glance up again, he's watching me, with a whiskey in one hand and the ice pack wrapped round the other. He seems calmer now, as if the ice is chilling the worst of his temper, as well as his swollen hand.

"Why did you come to my casino tonight?" he asks again, handing me the glass.

I take the drink, even though I hate whiskey. "I wanted to see the place." I take a sip and try not to gag as the alcohol sets fire to my throat. "I've never set foot in a casino before. I was intrigued."

"*Intrigued*?" He laughs. "If you wanted an insight into my business, princess, you just had yourself one hell of a demonstration."

It appears that this devil celebrates his deeds with a stiff drink and sarcasm.

"You tell me next to nothing about yourself. I was filling in the blanks."

"Were you feeling inquisitive, *half-measure*?" He takes off his black jacket and throws it over the back of the couch.

"Please don't call me that. It's insulting."

"Don't kid yourself. You went to my casino to make trouble."

"No, I—"

"Enough." He saunters back to the bar. "I underestimated you, Ielena. In hindsight, calling you insipid was my first mistake."

"And the second?" I watch him pour himself a whiskey, honing in on his thick fingers and wondering how they'd feel inside me…fucking me… *Stop, Issa, stop.*

"Kidding myself that I wouldn't want to fuck you." I let out a gasp as our thought processes align seamlessly. "Fooling myself that you were unattractive. Laughing off your virginity as an inconvenience." He knocks his drink back, and then pours himself another, stripping me bare with his gaze.

"Where did you go last night, Aiden?" *I need to know. I don't want to know.*

He smirks again. "First lover was at eight p.m. Second one was at ten. I thought a third might be pushing it on my wedding night." More whiskey tips down his throat.

"I don't have to listen to this." Flying from the couch, I make it as far as the open-top Steinway before he's crowding me against the ivory keys, my ass landing on the bass notes and creating a sinister version of Beethoven's *Concerto No. 2.*

"Truth is, there is no other woman, *half-measure,*" he declares, crashing his hands down on either side of me. "And there won't be until I get the damn taste of black cherries off my tongue."

My weight shifts backward at his admission, and more notes are played in the tune of bewilderment. "Let me go, Aiden."

"Now why would I do a thing like that? You're just getting interesting." I turn my head to the side as he leans in even closer, getting me high on his whiskey breath as he nudges a knee between my thighs. I flinch when he brushes my décolleté with the back of his hand. "Do you still hate me, Ielena, or is it mixing up with something else now? I felt you pushing back on me in my casino. Your V-card is up for sale sooner than I thought."

"Don't you dare touch me!" But my words aren't matching up with my body's response.

"One last time… Why did you really come to my casino?"

He's leaning into me, scratching my skin with his words. I'm remembering the feel of his lips during our wedding ceremony. The darkness. The possession…

"I'm not some ornament you can stash away."

"I agree. You're definitely not a wallflower." He smirks, making me feel like I've stumbled into a private joke. "Turns out, you're far more intriguing than my Warhol will ever be."

"I'm a settled score, nothing more, remember? Rich bitches are last in the queue."

"That was before you went and red-dressed me," he says huskily, sending shivers up and down my spine. "Every man in my casino wanted you tonight… I didn't like it, Ielena." His fingers trail downward in between my breasts and I let out a cry of pain.

"What is it?" His hand retracts immediately

"Nothing," I whimper, but I'm not fooling anyone.

His knee drops from between my legs. "I've inflicted enough pain in my lifetime to know when the reaction's genuine. Frankie's right, what are you hiding?" Before I can stop him, he's sliding his fingers underneath the neckline of my dress and tugging down sharply.

The skinny straps disintegrate. I rush to catch the material, but not before the top half of my chest is exposed.

"Son of a bitch," he breathes, looking shocked. "Who did this to you?"

You wouldn't believe me if I said.

He takes a step back and an escape route opens up for me. I bolt for the door, clutching at scraps of silky red material to keep the rest of my dress from slipping to the floor.

"Ielena, wait!"

Never.

I run from his heavy footsteps all the way back to my cabin, and then into the en suite, ramming the bolt across as his fist starts pounding on the door.

Bang. Bang.

"Ielena, let me in."

"Go away!" I slide to my knees, burning up with shame and confusion.

"Tell me who the fuck did that to you!" He sounds ready to rip my cabin apart for an answer.

The tears start spilling down my cheeks. I thought I was stronger than this. I sat in that bar in Cannes, *his bar*, and swore to myself that they'd never break me. But his pity is the dam buster I never saw coming.

He waits.

I fall apart.

He waits some more.

I see the shadows of his feet under the door as he's forced to listen to my pain instead of seeing it stamped into my skin.

Why am I breaking now? I never showed them the same courtesy when they branded and beat me. *Why won't he leave me alone?* Aiden doesn't give a damn about me.

The shadows of his feet become something larger and more substantial as he sinks to the floor to join me. The hinges groan as he rests his back against the other side of the door.

Still mute.

Still waiting.

I feel a sudden compulsion to do the same. This betraying night is full of impulses and contradictions.

Crawling over, I press my shoulders into the wood, fooling myself that I can almost feel his body heat. We're connoisseurs of the strained silence, but this feels different somehow. It's not weighted with all the stuff we can't think of to say... This one's for all the words we can't bring ourselves to speak.

He shifts position to the soft scrape of an old-style lighter lid. "Are you done crying?"

"It depends," I croak, swiping wet palms across my cheeks. "When I open up, are you going to beat me, too?"

"Who do you think I am? Luca fucking Zaccaria? I earn my monster stripes in other ways, princess."

"You were acting like a crazy man tonight."

There's more movement and more clinking. "I'm not apologizing for kicking the shit out of that punk, Landon, if that's what you're asking for."

"Are you planning on beating up every man who looks at me?"

"I'm pleading the fifth on that."

"You can't plead the fifth. You're not American."

"Ielena?" he says patiently. "I can do whatever the fuck I want."

"Except divorce me."

This brings on another broody, moody silence until I can't bear it any longer.

"Don't you need to get back to the casino? Senator Sanders—"

"Can win the contents of my safe for all I care. I want answers first, and I'm prepared to wait for them. I'm a surprisingly patient man."

"What if I can't give them to you?"

"You will."

A delicious warmth filters down through my body.

"Did you kill him? The man in the lobby?"

"That's an ace of a question, sweetheart, with a fair amount of topspin."

"And?"

There's a beat. "I wanted to… He roughed up one of my… one of the women who work for me," he corrects swiftly.

"Have you killed before?"

"You wearing a wire?"

My heart shudders on a missed beat. "No. Just the remnants of a red dress and my ugly scars." *Some of which you've seen. Some of which you haven't.*

"I'm going to find out who did that to you eventually, Ielena." The threat in his voice is a new explosion of crimson in our lives.

I know you will.

"Do you still want me to hate you?"

"Not anymore… But I think it's an inevitability."

"Nothing's inevitable. Everything is built on shifting sands."

"Have you always been this smart?"

"Have you always been this fatalistic?"

"Occupational hazard." He laughs suddenly, and the vibrations feel like victory through the door. "Where the fuck did you come from, Ielena? You meet me in the middle every single time."

I find my lips curving into a reluctant smile. Our lightness has returned. It's a sweet, exotic oil that rises to the top no matter how much dark he pours on top of us.

"We *half-measures* find ourselves in the strangest equations."

There's a pause. "How come you know so much about red wine?"

"You really want to know?" I can feel my shoulders relaxing into the wood. "It's a silly, childish story."

"I skipped the whole childhood thing so feel free to fill in the blanks through a locked door."

"That's the first thing you've ever told me about yourself."

"Bullshit. I told you I had a casino. The childhood thing just now was an escaped firefly." *But I've caught it and stored it in a jar in my mind anyway.* "Red wine. Uptight wife. Go."

"When I was eleven, my father held a big party at our estate in Paris."

"Yawn. I'm bored already."

"You're so rude!"

More chuckling. "I like this bolder version of you. It's the two point oh improved model."

I like you more, even though you're a choice I'm finding harder and harder to make.

He's so charming when he wants to be—when you strip away the sneers and veneers, the death and decay.

"I was a shy child so I hid under the tables for most of it," I say, plowing on regardless. "I watched beautiful women dance and laugh and clutch at their wine glasses all night long. I convinced myself it was some kind of magic elixir." I shake my head at the absurdity of it all. "A couple of years later, I overheard Maxim telling my father he'd bought a couple of vineyards in Bordeaux."

"Elitist fuck," I hear him mutter.

"I begged him to teach me about wine. I thought knowing about the best vintages would be an easy pass to becoming one of those graceful women, instead of feeling so lost all the time." I smile again at the memory, of a man with half a face whom everyone feared patiently extolling the virtues of a merlot grape to me.

"You don't need the wine, you're in a class of your own," Aiden says suddenly, making my stomach flip. "Fucking irresponsible of Maxim, though. Turning a kid into an alcoholic."

"Were you born this hypocritical, or is it a condition you acquired?"

"What's the deal between you and him?"

"He looks out for me." *And Karina.* "You might think that everyone's out to...um, have sex with me, Aiden, but you're wrong. Maxim has never been anything other than a father figure."

"Papa Dubov didn't cut it?" He blows out a breath. "You're not lost either, Ielena."

"I'm still not found enough for you to call me Issa."

"Who gave that name to you?"

"The only person who ever cared about me. Why do people call you The Raven?"

"It's a nickname from my non-existent childhood that grew up, sprouted wings, and took on a whole different meaning."

Somewhere in my cabin, I hear a clock tick, and a strange compulsion overcomes me.

"They hurt me because I wouldn't tell them where my sister was."

"Who did?"

"I-I can't say."

"Is she worth it?"

I nod at the empty room. "I'll die before I tell them where she is, Aiden. I know Zaccaria will hurt her, maybe even kill her for humiliating his son."

Another question hangs between us, but instead of asking it outright, his shadow disappears from under the door. "I need a drink after all this adult conversation, and you can't spend the night on the floor of my en suite, no matter how expensive that marble was."

I don't want him to go, but I'm afraid of what will happen if he stays.

"Aiden?"

"What?"

"Thank you."

The door shuts and I scramble to my feet. Letting my dress fall to the floor, I slip into the white silk dressing gown that's hanging over the towel rail and unlock the door. He's switched the lights off on his way out, and the room is a welcoming swell of darkness.

I climb into bed to the sound of the waves lapping against the hull. I replay the events of tonight over and over until the film reel in my head warps and splits. Just as my exhausted body is drifting off to sleep, the cabin door opens again. He's a swaying silhouette in the light—tall and solid, with a half-empty bottle swinging between his fingers

"You asleep?" he slurs, propping himself up against the doorframe.

I sit up, pushing the clouds of dark hair from my face. "Not anymore."

"Good." He staggers toward the bed, and I wriggle to the far side. This man is unpredictable on a good day. Splash him with alcohol and he's liable to ignite like dry tinder.

The mattress dips and ripples as he collapses next to me with a groan. By some miracle, he manages to place the whiskey bottle on the nightstand without spilling it everywhere, and then he's taking all the spare pillows and lining them down the middle of the bed like the Hadrian's Wall of anti-seduction.

"What are you doing?"

"Safeguarding your virtue. I won't be held responsible for my actions if I see those legs in the state I'm in. They're rule breakers, pure and simple."

"Rule breakers?" For the first time in what feels like forever, I start giggling. "What about your self-control?"

"What about it?"

"You have six other cabins on your superyacht for you and your ego, Aiden Knight. You're richer than Croesus."

"Who the hell is he?" he rumbles. "Not another bastard I need to kick the shit out of, surely?"

"He's a dead king with lots of money."

"Hope he enjoyed it while it lasted." He yawns. "Now lie down like a good girl and go to sleep."

He's left the cabin door wide open, flooding light into all of our dark corners.

"Why are you being so nice to me?" I say, peeking over the pillows at him. He looks so *big* sprawled out on the bed next to me, with his black hair ruffled and his stubble more a meadow than a graze.

He yawns again and slots his elbow behind his head to look at me. "Because I'm drunk."

"You were drunk before."

"I was functional drunk. Now I'm fucked drunk."

"Why didn't you have a childhood?"

He blows out another breath. "I'd have to be both drunk *and* high to answer that. I'm sleeping now." He turns his head away and I drift back down to the mattress, listening as his breathing levels out. "You're a dangerous woman, Ielena," I hear him mutter.

"*Me?*" I lift my head above the pillow wall again. I'm shocked he would call me something that he exhales like air.

"Feel." He feeds the word into the space between us like a morsel of truth. "You're making me *feel*, princess. And that's the most dangerous thing of all."

Chapter Thirteen

AIDEN

"He branded her."

"He *what*?" Frankie grinds his cigarette into the ashtray and rips off his sunglasses, sizing me up for a lie and finding only certainty. "Jesus Christ."

Leaning back in my chair, I throw the casino's cost reports down next to my uneaten breakfast bagel. I'm not in the mood for figures. Not those ones anyway. I prefer them slender and toned… *Oh, for fuck's sake.*

The early morning sunshine is tanning the upper deck, but it's doing nothing to burn away the edges of my anger. "They got to her before they sent her up the aisle. She won't say who, but I guessed from her reaction." I take my father's old lighter out of my pocket and toss it next to the reports. "Dubov had the shit kicked out of his own daughter, and then he branded her like cattle—like he does to his whores in Paris—right across her heart. My guess is he did it the same day he found out she was marrying me instead of Zaccaria."

The more I think about it, the more I fantasize about adding another decapitation to this week's revenge roster. She was *mine* when he did this to her. He hurt something that was *mine*. I may be a vindictive piece of shit, but I always look after my property.

Frankie goes quiet for a moment. Quiet for him means thoughtful. Thoughtful means he's figuring out the best way to torture the living crap out of someone. He reaches across the table and takes Dad's lighter, flicking hard for a dead flame. Grinding metal for a spark that will never come. It's the same thing I did for most of last night, sat on the floor with my back to a woman who is sparking something inside me that can't seem to catch, either.

I don't want it. I don't need it. She's an Enigma code to crack, nothing more.

"You saw it?" he asks eventually.

"I saw the wing tips of the eagle. It's the *Semion* Bratva insignia."

"Poor kid."

"They did a bad job. It's red and infected. I have a doctor on his way from Marseille who specializes in third degree burns."

He lifts his eyebrows ever so slightly in my direction. It's still only eight a.m., and I've already tracked down this guy, paid him off, and sent my chopper down to Marseille to collect him. That's a lot to do for someone who I've said, repeatedly, I don't give a damn about.

"Where is she now?"

"Still sleeping." I trace the mouth of my highball with my finger, hearing our father's voice in my head again. *"To catch a hangover, you need to set a trap with vodka, son. Then you slam the key home with cold orange."*

The double shot is a requirement. After last night, my pretty little distraction is bordering on a temptation. I passed out in a drunken haze and came around to a sleeping angel. I punched a hole through the wall of pillows just to see the way her hair bled dark silk all over the white bedsheets. I left before I made the mistake of a lifetime.

I know it wasn't pity that drove me to back to her cabin at two a.m. Sometime in the last couple of days, my hate has turned to tolerance and sprouted wings of respect.

They beat her: *She didn't crack.*

They scarred her: *She took it all and more.*

My mind flits to the man I murdered in Siena yesterday, and how he'd begged and pleaded and pissed himself for forgiveness. He would have given up his sister's name while he was still lobbing oranges and lemons at me. He gave up Rossi's name easily enough.

"Was Maxim involved?" asks Frankie.

I shake my head. "They were acting too cutesy at the wedding. You don't smile at someone who just took a heated iron to your skin. How the hell is he still Dubov's *Brigadier* anyway? He's been banished to Cannes these past four years."

"You only have to look at his face to know he's wearing the answer."

I drum my fingers lightly on the wooden patio table. "I want you to find out, and do it quick. Are drinks with Dubov still scheduled for Wednesday?"

Frankie nods and picks up my uneaten bagel. "He's planning on coming to the casino in late evening," he says, taking a bite.

"I doubt my new father-in-law wants to apologize in person for missing his daughter's wedding."

"You want eyes on it?"

"Damn right I do. In every corner… I'm considering calling him out on his lax parenting skills."

"You sure that's wise?" says Frankie, chewing thoughtfully. "If you stir up shit with Dubov, you're in danger of killing the Riviera deal with Zaccaria. If that happens, he won't be so inclined to deliver on that second name. We could end up chasing our tails, not the truth, for another fourteen…" He shuts up suddenly as Ielena steps out of the saloon doors.

She's dressed in the same high-neck, white shift dress she was wearing the first day we met, but it doesn't look half as dull and uninteresting on her now.

I slide my gaze back to Frankie. His steady grays are already feeling me out for decisions so I give him the briefest of nods, even though it aches to do it. I can't divert a fourteen-year road trip because of a white rabbit in the road. I'll mitigate as much of the fallout as I can when it comes, but on this occasion my pain takes precedence.

"Nothing's changed," I tell him in an undertone. "We finish the job and then go after Rossi." Turning back to Ielena, I clear my throat and gesture to her outfit. "You regressing on me, sweetheart?"

She blushes. *Fuck, I love that blush. It's a streak-free window into her emotions.* "I start at Eloise's shop in an hour. I'll change into something else when I get there."

I'd forgotten about the job. The doctor's not due on board for another thirty minutes. She'll just have to be late.

I watch her give Frankie a shy smile and my chest feels like a belt got winched up a notch. As she folds into the chair next to me, we both catch the hiss of pain. When her blush starts to fade, she's as pale as a ghost underneath her light make-up.

Damn. The infection is setting in already.

"Up," I order, rising to my feet as Felix glides into the background with a tray of fresh juice. I send him away again with a look.

"I'd like some breakfast first." Her defiance is weaker today, but it's still there.

"You're sick. You can have it in bed."

"I am not sick, and I don't want to go back to bed." Her brow creases in confusion, and then a dawning outrage. "No, Aiden," she cries. "You said I could have this job for a week. You promised me!"

"Our wants are polar opposites when you're sick and you look like shit."

"Back to the insults so soon?" she says angrily. "I knew last night was too good to be true."

"Last night was a mistake."

Her head jerks up. "But nothing happ—"

"Frankie, leave us," I snarl, cutting her off.

"Temper, temper." Shooting me an amused look, he picks up my highball, drains it in one, and then crashes the glass back down on the table in his own personal "fuck you." I watch him take his sulky arse indoors before dealing with a pair of dark eyes that are glittering with betrayal. *She doesn't even know the half of it yet.*

She breaks first, dropping her gaze to her lap. "You weren't in bed when I woke up this morning."

"You make it sound like an accusation."

"I thought—"

"You thought what?" I shake my head at her, showering her in condescension. "I got drunk, I passed out, and I woke at five a.m. with a hangover from hell. Let's not romanticize it, princess," I say, shoving her back into a box named "irritant" again. Even so, I can't seem to shut the lid.

"That's not what I... Oh, forget it." With a roll of her eyes she neatly places me back in another named "fickle bastard." "I'm starting that job today, Aiden. I'm going to get my things together now." But as she stands, she starts to sway like the black and white tassels on the parasols.

"Jesus. Sit down before you fall down."

"No, I—"

I move like lightning, and for the second time in two days I catch her in my arms.

I'm staring up at that ring of gold again.

I blink and it becomes three.

I'm not in my cabin. I'm in the main saloon, stretched out on one of the soft blue couches with a gray check blanket thrown over me. Someone's undressed me. I'm wearing a man's black shirt that smells strongly of sandalwood and musk—*Aiden*—and nothing else except my underwear.

I try to sit up and feel a strange tugging sensation across my chest. Glancing down, I see the white corner of a hospital-grade gauze bandage peeking out from underneath the neckline of the shirt.

"It was infected. You've been out for two days."

My head jerks up. Aiden is sitting on the couch opposite, with a stack of papers on his lap and that ubiquitous whiskey in his hand. He takes a long swig before continuing. "The doctor cleaned it and dressed it, and gave you a shot of antibiotics and pain killers. We caught the worst of it just in time."

My stomach drops. "You saw it?"

"Yes, I saw it… I saw all of them." His eyes gleam, hard and blue. "We counted eleven bruises in total. That's eleven punches I'll be returning the favor on. I may even add a couple more for the inconvenience." He takes another vicious swig of his whiskey, his gaze never leaving my face. "If there's anything important you'd like to say to your father, I'd do it quickly if I were you. I'll be severing the family ties for good sometime in the next forty-eight hours."

"What makes you think it was—"

"Don't." His anger reverberates off the walls, shocking me into silence again. "I know what the *Semion* insignia is, Ielena, and I know why he did it."

"I-I don't understand."

"He wants me to reject you. That way he keeps the deal and gets one over on the Italians," he adds grimly. "I was the consolation prize, the retaliation for your sister's bad deed… I'm not even a made man, sweetheart. I'm a fixer. I'm an associate to opportunity. I get tipsy on the potential, and then high on the challenge. I'm the bastard who's prepared to do what it takes, the man who puts down his roots in the hardest of soils, and the one who gets what he wants by any means necessary… I was chosen because it shames your family to be married to me instead of one of Zaccaria's bastards. Your daddy got pissed about it and bought himself a branding iron. He ruined you to send his own message back to *La Famiglia*."

"You think I'm ruined?" I say quietly.

"No. I think you're free."

Free? The air comes whooshing out at my mouth. *I'm stuck on a yacht. I'm trapped in a marriage. I'm bound to a lie. And he thinks I'm* free?

"Free of your father," he corrects tersely, seeing my expression. "It was all about keeping the deal alive between the *Semion* and the *Cosa Nostra* while not losing face. That's the only thing he cares about. Are you stinging from the truth yet?"

God, he's relentless. He's goading and pushing us across county lines into a place that neither of us wants to be.

"I don't understand why you're telling me all this."

"You showed me one of your secrets. I'm repaying you with one of my own."

My hand drifts toward my bandage again. "You stole my secret from me while I was unconscious."

"So I'm offering mine freely in return," he counters with a crooked grin. "Take it. Exploit it. It's rarer than you know."

"I don't care about the reasons why we're married." I glance down to find I'm twirling the ends of the cashmere throw around my fingers and making pits in the yarn with my thumb. "I don't care if you're not a Zaccaria. We can't divorce otherwise the deal falls through and you don't get your world." My gaze finds the empty deck outside. "Whatever happens, I'm never going back to Paris."

"Good, because I lost the fucking receipt on you the moment you grew a pair."

Don't you do it, Aiden Knight. Don't you undo my resolve with your throwaway respect.

"Did they hurt your sister, too?" he asks.

I shake my head. "Karina ran long before they had a chance to…" I trail off as my wound starts to ache.

"Do you know where she is?"

I think of a beach. I think of waves crashing against a wooden breaker that's green with algae and age.

"No."

The lie comes easily enough. After everything I've done to protect it so far, it has an unbreakable wax seal.

He nods slowly, accepting this.

I smooth the throw over my bare legs. "My father ordered his men to do this to me, and my mother is a drunk." I fix him with a challenging look. "Go ahead, Aiden. Call me a poor little rich girl. I know you're dying to."

He finishes up his drink and loses the glass to the coffee table in front of him. "Poor little rich girls whine about the color of their ponies. You've been concealing third-degree burns from me for the last few days."

"Dapple gray… I always wanted a bay."

It's me who's clawing for our unexpected lightness now. His revelations don't lessen my burden—the path back to Karina is still overgrown with thorns—but I'm craving some of his sweet relief.

"Don't go reinforcing those stereotypes, Ielena," he says mildly. "You know I'll give you hell for it."

"You know I'll give you hell back."

His slow grin turns into a laugh. It's one of his looser sounds, letting all of the tension drain away from us. "Your father's coming into my casino tomorrow night." He cocks his head to gauge my reaction. "If I didn't know any better, I'd say he's come to gloat."

"Do you have business with him?"

"I did, but after the last twenty-four hours it's under serious review."

"I don't want you to start a war."

"I'm at the epicenter of so many damn wars, they're thinking of naming an atomic bomb after me." He comes over and sits down on the couch. So close. Too close. "I called the weird cat-dress lady earlier. You can start tomorrow, but *only* if you're feeling up to it."

"You called Eloise?" I'm shocked.

"There are five hundred people working for me on the Riviera. I know how employer/employee relations work. I figured you'd want her to know about your double-day absence. You owe her money, after all." He props his elbow on the top of the couch and rests the side of his head on the heel of his hand. It's one of those casually masculine gestures of his that does wild things to my core.

"Did you tell her why?"

"She didn't ask questions. I presume she saw the evidence when she was warning you all about me in that dressing room for half an hour."

"You heard that?" I whisper.

He laughs. "I hear everything."

"Please don't hurt her."

"I will if she does it again," he counters silkily.

"I told her I fell from a horse."

"And got trampled by eagle-shaped hooves?"

I search my mind frantically for a change of subject.

"I liked Senator Sanders…"

His smirk vanishes. "You shouldn't. That man's a savage."

"All the best women seem to be married to one."

He cocks his eyebrow at me, but doesn't comment. "If you fancy a nightmare sometime, I'll share his life story. Does it hurt?" He gestures to my chest.

"It's…better," I say, feeling shy suddenly. "The pain is more of a dull, throbbing ache." I catch my hand drifting toward the burn again.

"Why didn't you tell me?"

"I didn't want to be mocked for it," I say, slapping him with the truth. "You would have used it. Abused it. Admit it, Aiden… One person's wound is just another thing for you to jab your thumb into."

"I have zero interest in being in this marriage," he states, slapping me back with a force even harder than mine. "I make no secret about it. But I was offered something I've wanted for a very long time, and you happened to be the deal. It doesn't mean I want to see you beaten or branded because of it."

The times when he doesn't know he's being cruel are so much worse than the times he does.

"What did Zaccaria offer you?" I say, keeping my voice even.

"The greatest thing on earth." He reaches into his pants pocket and pulls out an old Zippo lighter. Scuffed black on one side. Stainless steel on the other. When he scratches the flint, I recognize the sound from last night.

"What's that?"

"Reasons."

"The greatest thing on earth is 'reasons'?"

"No, the lighter is."

I wonder if he cultivates his air of mystery on purpose, or if he's just one big unsolvable riddle. I suspect the latter. His truth is as twisted up for him as is it for me.

"Thanks for calling the doctor…" I trail off when I catch sight of the Steinway piano over his shoulder.

Heat.

Sin.

Wanted.

Reaching out, I run my finger over the lid of the Zippo. He

doesn't move away, even when our fingers connect. I can see the tattoo of a black raven on the inside of his wrist. "You're like a two-speed dryer, Aiden," I say jokily. "You only blow hot and cold—"

"As far as I'm aware, no one's blowing anyone around here."

"You treat me with contempt, and then you act like the husband I'd hoped you'd be. Maybe one of these wars you speak of is a war with yourself."

"Enough." He moves fast then, curling a large hand around my neck and pitching me forward until our foreheads are pressed up tight against each other. I can feel his whiskey breath on my face. Everywhere I look is glorious, dangerous *him.* "Godammit, Ielena. You are *not* what I expected. You are so much worse and so much better. You are a universe gone haywire."

"You want to fuck me," I state, stumbling over the word and despising my innocence.

"I want to fuck you," he confirms.

"Do I really taste like black cherries?"

He groans, as if in pain. "Dark black cherries in the summertime. In the park with the broken swing on the council estate back home. You taste of possibilities and a future," he adds huskily, strained even, as if he's forcing the words from his mouth.

"You taste of color, Aiden Knight."

Clashing color.

He's a bad man, but there's a deep reservoir of melancholy inside him. I stood on the banks last night and caught the silver ripples of the tide in the moonlight.

The hand around my neck tightens. It's a blunt reminder that he could kill me anytime he wanted. He opens his mouth to say something else, but his cell phone does all the talking for him.

"Shit." The spell breaks. He lets go of me abruptly. By the time I've recovered he's halfway across the room. "Yes?" I hear him say. "When? Good. I'm on my way." Hanging up, he returns to the couch to collect his jacket, avoid my scrutiny, and resurrect a distance between us that's far more than the present three feet. "Business," he announces, as if the last ten minutes never happened.

"What sort of business?"

"My sort," he says, striding toward the door. "Get some rest. Felix will bring you anything you need. I'll be back later."

It's impossible to fall asleep once he's gone. For every *tick-tock* of the clock above the bar, there's another splinter of our conversation to digest. He's just gone and given me the one thing I never expected from this marriage: honesty.

In the end, I kick the quilt off my legs and head back to my cabin for my sketchbook and pencil. For the first time in a week, I can move without razorblades slitting open my chest. Whatever the doctor gave me, I'm hoping he left Aiden a repeat script.

The cabin is quiet and empty. It's exactly how I left it two days ago. The closet door is still ajar and bright sunshine is bouncing off the make-up lids I left scattered across the dresser. My red and pink dress still drapes limply over an ivory stool.

I go to pick up my sketchbook from my nightstand when I notice a strange cell phone resting right on top of it. It's an older model than my iPhone, the kind that my father and his men use. *The illegal burner kind.*

It starts ringing while I'm still staring at it.

No Caller ID.

"Hello?" I say hesitantly.

"Don't say a word," orders Maxim. "The whole place is bugged, but I've had the closet cleaned and sound-proofed. Hang up and go straight there. In the top drawer on the left you'll find another cell. Shut the door, lock it, and then wait for me to call you. Tell me I'm a wrong number. Quickly, Issa!"

"Sorry, wrong number," I say mechanically to a dead dial tone, before placing the cell back down on the nightstand and rushing into the closet as instructed.

The new cell starts ringing as I'm still pulling out the drawer.

"Maxim—?"

"Has he hurt you?" he demands "I heard the doctor was called on board two days ago."

"No, it's not like that."

"Tell me, *zvezda moya*," he urges. "Tell me you're okay."

"Paris. Last week," I whisper, closing my eyes, choking down the nausea as I force myself to relive the memory. "He wanted to know where Karina was. When I wouldn't say he-he…" The lie gets stuck in my throat.

"What did he do to you, Issa?"

"I can't…"

"Tell me!"

When I don't answer, he demands it again and again, until I'm drawing in a ragged breath and leaving raw clues in my reticence.

"No." His voice is a rasp of shock. He knows what my father excels at. "*Mudak*! I'll kill him. Issa—"

"There's no way you could have stopped it. You were five hundred miles away in Cannes. Besides, I wouldn't have let you.

You can't blow your cover, Maxim, any more than I can."

A stream of guilt and apologies filter down the line.

"Stop," I beg. "If you think for one moment that your love for my sister drove me into this, you're wrong. I would have made the same sacrifice, with or without you."

When the Riviera deal was first mooted four weeks ago, we knew we had to get Karina out of Paris as soon as possible. Her illness was a secret we couldn't hide any longer, and there was no guarantee Luca Zaccaria would have provided her with the treatment she needed. I knew he was a bastard with a bad reputation even before Aiden confirmed my suspicions. He would have let her die in agony.

In the end, Maxim cut a deal against his nature, in exchange for information that only someone close to the *La Famiglia* could get.

"They called an hour ago." His words are gruff, distracted... He's still struggling to get a handle on his anger. "They've confirmed that the donor at the hospital is a match."

I suck in a sharp breath. "Have they given her a date for the operation?"

"Tomorrow, all being well. They still need to run some final tests." There's a pause. "She's going to get through this, Issa. She's strong, like you. As soon as she's well enough..."

"I know." I say it calmly and slowly in an attempt to reassure us both.

"How are things there? Is he treating you well?"

"Why is my cabin bugged?" I interrupt suddenly, a bitter chill washing over me. "You don't think—?"

"Knight is a naturally suspicious man, *zvezda moya*. He doesn't let anyone in. He's watching your every move to ascertain if he can trust you. Earn that trust, Issa. It'll lead us back to Karina."

But at what price?

"Have you heard him mention someone called Mattia Rossi?"

"Not Rossi…" I drag my mind back to last night. "I was introduced to a man called Rick Sanders…"

"No, not the senator. He's affiliated with the Santiago Cartel in Colombia. Mattia Rossi is the head of a New York mafia outfit. They think he's a key player in *La Società Villefort*."

"What do they need me to do? Ask Aiden about him?"

"No. They want you in on this deal meeting with Zaccaria, Knight, and your father at the end of the week. They need you to wear a wire. It's the only opportunity we'll have to slip a tracking device on Zaccaria as well. They can't touch him in Sicily. His protection is too great. It's one of the reasons he rarely leaves Italy."

My heart sinks as the impossible drops a couple of levels. "How, Maxim?" I say helplessly.

"They'll inform us nearer the time. Meanwhile, your father has a drink planned with Knight tomorrow."

"I know. Aiden told me."

"We may need an in on that, as well. I'm awaiting confirmation."

The thought of seeing my father again brings tears to my eyes. The narrow closet starts to feel like a tomb. "I can't," I whisper.

"You must. Think of Karina. Think of our new life." He sighs heavily, as if the Judgement of Paris is bearing down upon him, too. "How do I stop myself from ripping your father apart after what he did to you?"

"Fake it," I urge. "Fake it like I'm faking it. For my sake…

For Karina's…"

But even as I say it, I know I'm a liar. Whatever this thing is with Aiden, it transformed into something dangerously real last night. I push that thought from my mind.

"How did you get the burner cells into my cabin?"

"There's an undercover agent working in Knight's crew. He's keeping an eye on you, Issa. He won't let Knight get too rough."

"Aiden won't get rough," I clarify quickly.

"You don't know him like I do. If things go south, he'll take you down with him. There's more blood on his hands than your father's." He stops and sighs again. "As much as it hurts me to say this, I need you to continue what you're doing. It's working. You've caught his attention. You're the best chance we have."

I can feel the weight of expectation crushing my shoulders. *Please don't hang all of our hopes on me.*

"I'm meeting with our handler again today. Do you have a message for Karina?"

"Tell her that I love her." My voice cracks. "Tell her to be strong. Tell her that one day I'll be sitting with her on that veranda, painting her portrait instead of a silly fantasy in my head."

It's only after I hang up that I allow myself to disintegrate.

Chapter Fifteen

ISSA

I can't relax in my cabin after learning about Aiden's surveillance. Is it audio? Visual? I keep seeing imaginary *camera live* red dots in dark corners. In the end I rip out all the pages of quaint English cottages from my sketchbook and stuff them into the wastepaper basket before taking my paranoia outside.

Karina's operation is weighing heavily on my mind. I know how much of a big deal it is—her whole life is hanging in the balance—so I do what I always do when the walls of my life are closing in on me: I sketch memories from the past to create a cocoon of comfort.

My first picture is of two young teenage sisters racing their ponies bareback in the heat of the Paris sun. Once done, I flip the page over to capture a bid for adventure that same summer, and how it led us to the old lake on the edge of our father's estate. I draw the flecks of sunshine that pierced the water and dappled the ground beneath the trees. I add the sad branches of a weeping willow hovering just above the surface. My toes start to tingle when I remember how the cold water felt on my skin as we kicked and splashed and laughed while our ponies stood patiently in the shade of an old oak, whisking flies away with their tails. My nose is filled with the phantom scents of damp river earth, ponies, and the exotic spice of the nearby meadow.

I draw pages and pages of happiness as the sun tumbles into the Mediterranean, detonating on impact with rose-gold debris. The sunsets are spectacular on the Riviera and I'm momentarily distracted before I start to draw what I know will be the last thing Karina thinks about when the anesthetic is administered. Running my finger lightly over the finished picture, I whisper promises to the wind to keep her safe from harm. I'm learning to be brave from her, as only the sick and dying can teach.

When I look down a couple of minutes later, I'm shocked to see that I'm standing on the bow of the yacht, with the sea breeze molding Aiden's black shirt to my body, my fingers curled tightly around the stainless-steel handrail, and my loose hair fanning out behind me. The sunset must be weaving her dark spells because the water doesn't seem to be scaring me right now. I'm having one of those rare "anything is possible" moments, with my lungs so full of salty sea air that I feel like I'm choking on life itself.

"If you jump, you're drowning alone," clips a voice. "I'm not wrecking this Tom Ford for some stupid Di Caprio stunt move."

Aiden is standing in the doorway of the saloon in his usual devastating attire of black shirt and black suit, looking like the tall drink of Devil and God that I'm craving more than anything right now. The sunset's hellfire is lighting up his dark hair. His eyes are the darkest shades of blue.

He moves toward me, cat-like, as I silently will him closer. I'm frightened. I'm lost. He's wrong. He's right. Two days ago, I believed that a dress would make me feel alive. Now, I need something else…something more tangible. Something only he can offer.

I'm thinking things I shouldn't be.

The worst kinds of things…

The best.

"Kiss me," I blurt out, not recognizing the neediness in my voice. Ignoring everything he is and everything I am. Pushing it so far from my mind, it's lost to the ocean. "Kiss me like you did on our wedding day, Aiden. Without asking questions or drenching me in scorn." *Make me feel desired, even if it's the stupidest decision I'll ever make.*

He stops dead and eyes me suspiciously. "Are you drunk?"

I bite my lip and shake my head.

"Good, because I don't kiss, suck, or fuck compromised women."

A beat later, his palms are gripping the sides of my jaw and his fingers are digging into my hair. I see a flash of hunger, the smirk of a conquering predator, and then his warm lips are crashing into mine. My arms tangle around his neck as a forceful tongue drives between my lips and lays waste to my mouth in slow, dominant sweeps. "Mine." He groans it into the kiss, and I swallow down every drop of his possession like it's my favorite poison.

Madness… Harmony… I must be drunk on his whiskey breath again. His hands drop to my ass, encouraging me to wrap my legs around his waist, and then I'm being laid down on the cream couch by the Jacuzzi, the leather chilling the backs of my thighs as the warmth of his body hovers over me, but never close enough to touch my scars.

This is escalating fast.

I could tell myself a thousand lies about why I'm under him right now, but the truth is baser:

I want him.

I want this beautiful, complicated, vicious bastard of a man.

I want his corruption and I want his sin, and I want him to grind it all into me, making me forget that I'm just as bad as he is.

"I should be home late more often," he murmurs as his mouth moves to the hollow of my neck.

I moan when I feel him next on my jawline, another stab of desire coursing through me and pooling in the place I want him to defile the most. Unhooking my legs from his waist, he kneels on the deck between them and pushes my thighs apart.

"Wait." My hands shoot out to cover myself.

"No." He catches them, and pins them roughly above my head. "You coming to me like this, you wanting this, *you consenting to this*, is the only fucking decision you get to make around here. If I want you spread, Ielena, you arch your back for me and you show me *everything*. Do you understand?" He lets go, and a second later there's a sharp tug across my pelvis as my white lace underwear is ripped away. "Keep your hands where they are or I'll flip you over and take your ass first."

"I don't... I've never..." I trail off breathlessly.

"Relax," he croons, switching tack. "I'm warming you up tonight. I'm not giving you my cock until you're ready for it." Our gazes catch as he removes his jacket and loosens his top button. Our eyes are still holding as he dips his head between my legs, spreading my lips wide and blowing on my clit.

"Oh my *God*."

"Like that, do you?"

He does it again and the sweetest ache has me whimpering out his name.

"Ielena, I'm going to break you in so easy, you'll be begging me to fill you up."

The lust in his voice has me throbbing and squirming. This is so much more than just being alive. It's emotions and connections, screaming nerve endings and wild impulses. My cheeks explode with heat as his drives a hard lick straight through my center, before wrapping those wicked lips around my clit as his finger starts to massage my entrance.

The end of my innocence is wild and frantic. He circles and nips, his teeth dragging me closer and closer to the edge as his stubble grazes the most sensitive parts of me. I start to thrust, demanding more and more friction from his finger.

"Did you ever make yourself come late at night, princess?" he croons. "All alone in your empty Parisian palace?"

"Once." I shut my eyes as the intensity of the feeling steals my breath away.

"Was it good?"

I moan in response.

"Did you lift your hips to ride the waves over some college boy who wears a tweed hunting jacket on the weekend?"

"No," I croak.

"No?" He lifts his head to glare at me, his mouth glistening with my arousal, his ceruleans cool and demanding.

"I thought of you," I gasp out. "That day we first met."

Demanding switches to pure satisfaction. "Tell me more."

"Naked," I moan as he fucks me with his tongue, tipping my head back and shutting my eyes again. "On all fours. On my bed."

He growls his approval. "Did you come all over your fingers for me, Ielena?

"Yes!"

"Did you scream my name into the pillow?

"Yes!"

"Was it nice?"

The best.

"Spoiler alert," he snarls suddenly. "The real thing isn't nice. I'm about to cause a fucking tsunami in your pussy." With that, he drives his fingers so deep inside that even the roar of the waves can't muffle my cries. There's no pain though, just more of that thrilling, rapacious need. "Shit," I hear him hiss. "So fucking pure and tight…" He plugs his next words by rearing up and stealing a kiss from my lips, his finger still moving inside me.

"More," I beg, lifting my hips so he slides in even deeper.

In response, he slams his palm across my mouth. "What did I tell you about giving me orders? Now I'm really going to make you scream."

With one elbow by my head and a knee wedged between my legs, he leans over me like the severest shadow as he pumps mercilessly in and out of my body. The wet sound of his finger-fucking is spicing up the early evening stillness. The inside of my thighs… The leather beneath my ass… It's all dripping with the results of his expert manipulation.

He forces a second finger in and the world goes white. It's not a tsunami. It's an earthquake. It's me, gasping and clutching at a wrist that doesn't let up until I'm crashing back down to earth.

"Fuck," I hear him mutter, withdrawing his fingers slowly as I race to catch my breath. He trails them up to my lower stomach. There, he spells out that same word he growled into my mouth earlier, but this time with my wetness—with the sea breeze icing it into my skin.

Mine.

Afterward, he sinks back down to his knees, his blue eyes glittering with triumph as he pulls down the tails of my borrowed shirt to cover up my immodesty. "I need a cold shower." He drops another kiss on my lips. "Better still, I need a swim."

I watch through heavy-lidded eyes as he stands to strip, kicking off his shoes and socks and tearing at the buttons of his own shirt to reveal a scene-stealing torso that dips and grooves with muscle in all the right places. Sometime in the last half an hour, soft circular lights around the edges of the deck and the Jacuzzi have sparked to life. The glow is deepening his golden skin to a dark amber hue.

Tossing his shirt at his feet, I catch a glimpse of a jagged trail of dark chest hair as he turns toward the ocean, his fingers reaching for his belt buckle. Striding over to a gap in the handrail, he drops his black pants and black boxers, and then dives headfirst into the water in a perfect arc of machismo.

"Aiden!" I cry, rushing over to see his body disappearing into the water. These are the last moments of the sunset, and the choppy waves are like the dying licks of flames.

Seconds drag and I start to panic. I'm looking around for a life preserver or ring when a dark head bursts through the surface again. Slicing through the waves in great, powerful strokes, he reaches the swim platform at the back of his yacht in seconds, where a member of his deck crew is already waiting for him with a white towel. Wrapping it around his lower body, he climbs the steps to the main deck to rejoin me, slaking water droplets from his dark hair as he goes.

I can't tear my eyes away. There are no two, three, or even a dozen colors I could mix together to replicate the golden lines of his skin, or the same savage blue in his gaze. He's his very own masterpiece, and he knows it, too.

"Enjoying the show?" He shoots me a crooked grin as he makes his way toward the saloon, smelling of salty water and thigh-clenching musk. "Dinner's in half an hour. I picked up a few things for you in town earlier." His voice follows him inside, sounding like a threat and a caress, and a lo-fi beacon flashing in the darkness. "I left them in your cabin.

"Aiden."

"Get dressed."

"Where should I meet you? I don't really know this yacht yet."

"The same place you always meet me, Ielena," he says, re-appearing in the doorway with a whiskey and a grin. "Middle deck. Sky lounge. Between your cabin and mine." He takes a long swig and undresses me with his gaze. "In other words, you'll meet me halfway, as usual."

Chapter Sixteen

AIDEN

I don't believe in karma.

If I did, there'd be some serious recompense on my part. Point me in the direction of a confessional and I wouldn't be out of that wooden box for a week. Maybe that's why I hated living in Italy for all those years. The Catholics are so full of guilt they built a church on every block. It's tougher to dodge salvation when it's offered up like a whore's mouth.

I started doubting my views when my wife came so damn hard I felt her muscles clenching. I figured I must have been paying some kind of due for not allowing myself to climb inside her virgin pussy when it was offered up so sweetly.

The ocean swim isn't enough. My cock is still a misguided missile. Stepping into the shower in my en suite, I'm barely under the punishing jets of water before I'm taking the matter into my own hand. I pump hard and fast, tasting black cherries, imagining her soft body trembling beneath me, remembering the way her lips parted as she lost control of that good girl poise.

Before long, I'm groaning in relief as pleasure shoots up and down my spine and thick ropes of cum are hitting the white and gray marble tiles in front of me.

"Shit," I breathe, slamming my palms down on either side of it, feeling a rush like no other, needing to go again because I'm not even partway satisfied yet. *This woman is going to be the death of me.*

My cell phone is ringing when I step back into the cabin.

"What is it, Frankie?" Moving over to the desk, I flick up the lid of my laptop and check the security feed on Ielena's room. It's a ritual I seem to be doing a million times a day. I watch her fall upon the three dresses I left for her on the bed, and I can tell by the wide smile on her face that she recognizes the designs. She won't take my money, but she'll take a loan on Eloise Dubois' threads. She'll have to work another couple of weeks to pay them off, but something tells me she'll be okay with that.

"Rossi got your message."

I pause. "How so?" I watch Ielena drop my shirt to the floor and do a long, slow swirl around her cabin—giving me the floorshow to end all floorshows. She's naked, except for the fading patchwork of bruises across her chest and the white bandage, and if I didn't know any better, I'd say she knew I was watching her.

Dubov might have stamped his Bratva insignia across her heart, but it's no more than an inch squared. The bandage doesn't cover up her small breasts or her slender waist. It sure as hell doesn't cover up her long, coltish legs and the tempting strip of dark hair between them…

And just like that, I'm hard as stone again.

"I'm looking at his offshore banks accounts," I hear Frankie say. "The ones in the Cayman Islands are looking fruity. He even bought himself a brand-new superyacht to keep up with the Knights. He's looking like a man ready to run."

"What the fuck?" I bang the laptop lid down again. "Regardless of the fact that he's meant to be under this top secret, untouchable *La Società Villefort* protection, why would the boss of a prominent New York crime syndicate get spooked by the decapitated head of a long-forgotten *soldato*? He must have done worse in his sleep. Tell Zaccaria I want to speak to him. Any news on Maxim and the case of his disappearing face?"

"Still working on it. Any progress with your wife?"

"Still working it," I counter grimly. "But the night is young and the wine is expensive."

He laughs. "Are you living dangerously with a Saint-Émilion?"

"I figured a rich, full-bodied Chianti would be more in keeping with what I had in mind. Is Rick Sanders returning to the casino tonight?"

"No, he had to fly back to the States. He mentioned something about throwing a surprise birthday party for a certain Colombian friend of his."

"Tell him he can have my casino for free if Dante Santiago considers us for future business opportunities."

"Raven, are you serious?" splutters Frankie, shaken out of his usual cool. "That's dancing with a whole other devil."

"Maybe I'm in the mood for a partner swap. Speaking of which, I want an extra fifty in the building for this thing with Dubov."

Hanging up, I opt for black jeans and a thin, black V-neck sweater.

Stepping into the sky lounge five minutes later, I discover

Ielena's beaten me to it. She's curled up on a stool at the bar in a short, blue and gold color explosion of a dress, and she's making small talk with Felix as he fixes her a cocktail. She looks up as I enter with that smile still etched into her delicate features.

I have a theory about facial expressions as well as handshakes. You can always fake the motion, but you can't fake it forever. I'm betting my entire fortune that Ielena has worn that smile from her cabin all the way here. That smile, my friends, is the real deal.

A strange feeling steals across my chest. It's as if one of those three fists that grabbed a hold of my heart at sixteen is loosening its grip. But at the same time, I can feel my father's lighter weighing down my back pocket. *I gave that smile to her, and I'll be the bastard who takes it away again.*

"You found yourself to halfway." I drop a kiss on the top of her head as I direct Felix to the Glenfiddich bottle.

"It was easier than I thought… The dress is beautiful, by the way," she adds, blushing slightly. Not as much as she usually does, though. Her loss of innocence is leaching away my ability to read her emotions. *When I finally fuck her, will it be gone for good?* "It's Eloise's design, isn't it?"

"When I called her to let you know you weren't working, I requested a few pieces for my driver to collect."

"Do you like them?"

"I prefer women's dresses on my bedroom floor."

She rolls her eyes, forgetting herself for a moment, but I ease up on the chastisement. I want her undone. I want her comfortable around me.

"How do you know her?" I ask.

"I spent a summer in Cannes when I was thirteen. One day, I was sat in a café just behind *La Croisette* and she was sat at the next table. She was wearing the most beautiful jade dress and I couldn't take my eyes off it. I told her how much I liked it and she invited me to sit with her. For the next three weeks, we met every day in the same café. She knew I was interested in art and design, so she taught me all about different fabrics and colors and textures…"

I can't stop staring at her mouth. She's talking about something that doesn't interest me in the slightest, but she's making it sound like the greatest money deal I never heard about.

"Sorry, I'm boring you," she says shyly, dropping her gaze to her margarita.

"What did you warn me about the first day I met you?"

"That I'd never be boring."

And she's not. Because she's got me hanging onto her every word, and it's not to catch the secrets that could come tumbling out at any moment. Suddenly, I want to find out every detail about her.

"Did I ruin your suit the other day?"

"Among other things…"

"Do I have to work to pay it off as well?"

"Mrs. Knight, are you flirting with me?"

I can do mock-scandal as well as the next horny-as-fuck man.

"Would it be so terrible if I were?"

"It's a slippery slope, princess… One minute you're flirting, the next you're—"

"Sir, the captain's asked me to let you know we've arrived," interrupts Felix, handing me my drink.

"Thanks. Shall we?" I say, taking her hand and tugging her off her stool.

I lead her out onto the middle deck and over to the stainless-steel handrails. The moon and stars above us are as bright as the yacht's underwater LED lights.

"What were you just about to say in there?" she asks.

"Something so filthy poor Felix would be in therapy for a month."

She laughs, gazing out at the inky horizon. "Where are we?"

"Bay of Marseilles." I move to stand behind her, smirking into her hair when I feel her body tremble. She lifts her hand to calm her billowing hair and I catch sight of her engagement ring. I dropped two hundred thousand on a diamond to suit the woman I thought she was. Now, all I see is an insult. That ring is a disservice to everything sweet, gutsy, and true about her.

"Hey!" She flinches away as I grab her finger and wrench it off. "What are you doing?"

"Redressing a situation." With a flick of my wrist I chuck the ring into the ocean. "Some local fisherman will be making the catch of his life tomorrow."

"Why did you do that?" She looks sideways at me as if I'm insane. Which I probably am… Even I can't explain the rightness of what I just did.

"Doesn't suit the dress," I say mildly. "You can't expect to be a psychedelic sixties clone with a rock like that on your finger. Now hush. I brought you here for a reason. Look over there."

She follows my outstretched arm. "Is that an island?"

"*Chateau d'If.* Technically, it's an islet, which means it's smaller, but we don't go in for small things around here." She laughs again, and my dick pays attention. The cherry thing must be contagious because her whole body smells of it tonight. "Can you see the fortress? The battlements are illuminated in orange."

"Yes, I see them. What is this place?"

"The French built it in 1524 to protect Marseilles from

invaders. Eventually, they turned it into a state prison."

She lets out a soft cry of recognition. "Oh, I've read about *Chateau d'If*. It's the prison from *The Count of Monte Cristo*."

Well, at least Papa Bratva gave her an education along with the bruises.

"You know your dumb arse."

"It's Alexandre *Dumas*," she says with a groan at my crass attempt at humor. "I had a lack of love, but an expensive education... Fourteen years," she declares suddenly, and I nearly drop my whiskey into the ocean. "I remember the story now. That's the length of time Edmond Dantès was locked up for a crime he didn't commit."

Or for a crime he planned to.

"Can you imagine the rage he must have felt?" she muses. "Chained to a place he was never meant to be in for fourteen years. No wonder his vengeance was so cold."

"Vengeance is a form of redemption."

"But it will never be as powerful as forgiveness."

"Jesus. You're hurting my ears."

"Dantès was an antihero—"

"As all the great men are."

"He believed he was some kind of God handing down his judgements."

"I bet he didn't make his wife come as hard as I did, though."

She spins around to face me, her softness brushing against my erection and making me grunt at the lightest of touches. "Is that what you and Zaccaria do? Play God and hand down judgements to people who have wronged you?"

"No, Ielena. We make a shit load of money together, the bad guy way."

"When did you meet?"

"Fourteen years ago," I say, trying not to smirk.

She mulls this around her pretty head for a beat or two. "You could almost identify with Edmond Dantès, then."

"I doubt it. I've never seen the inside of a prison cell…yet. Unless, of course, you're counting this marriage."

Her smile vanishes, like I knew it would. I'm the fucking smile-catcher when I want to be. It's her fault. She flicked the switch, and now this conversation is too charged for my liking. My truth is a burning pyre. Anyone who dances too close gets burned.

"What did Zaccaria really promise you for my hand?" she asks curiously. "And don't give me 'the world' or any of your other asinine non-answers."

I lean down to graze her cheek with my next words. "Why do you want to know so badly?" At the same time, I move in closer, grinding my erection against the conclave of her stomach. She presses back even harder, like I knew she would. "Bad girl… Still, sexual intimidation is so much more fun when it's reciprocated."

"I'm not your *half-measure* anymore, Aiden." She tips her head back, aligning her perfect rosebud of a mouth with mine.

"Is your pussy still wet for me?"

She nods, holding my gaze. "As hard as your cock is for me."

"Spoken like a true non-virgin. I don't think you blinked once. Shall we continue your education here on this deck?"

I watch her chew gently on her lower lip. "Teach me how to make you come like that."

A slow grin creeps across my face. "I don't come like that, Ielena. Not like the whole sky just crashed down on me. I learned self-discipline a long time ago."

"Along with hate fucking, if I remember rightly. Does sex bore you?"

"I've never found anyone to keep me interested in it."

And that's changing right here, right now.

"Mouth or fingers?" she gasps out. "What are you going to teach me first?"

I've had enough of this. She's fire dancing again.

I wrap my hand around the back of her neck and bring her in so close our lips are almost touching. "Are you my lover or my whore?" I ask nonchalantly, fighting my natural urge to force her to her knees and take what I want from her body.

"I'm your wife," she rasps, but I see the flash of fear in her eyes.

"Then fucking act like it." I let go of her neck and point to the sky lounge. "Get inside, and wait for me there."

I listen as the *click* of her heels grows progressively quicker as her poise starts to slip. I'm a bastard for treating her like this, but for a second there she made me forget I was the predator, not the prey.

"Wait," I say irritably, losing a war with my conscience.

She freezes to the spot, dressed in blue and gold and confusion.

"Ielena—"

"Do you have a lover?" Her voice is hesitant… *Fearful.* I remember her accusing me of this on our wedding night. "Is this marriage a conflict for you?"

"Not presently," I lie, striding up to her. "But if my apology gets accepted, I might get lucky by the end of the night."

"I thought all mafia men had a million girlfriends," she says, smiling weakly.

"I'm not 'all mafia,' *halfway.* I'm an associate to anyone

who makes me money. I'm a veritable criminal mongrel."

"I asked too many questions. That's why you got angry with me."

"Ask me no questions and I'll tell you no lies."

"Karina used to say that to me all the time." She glances back toward the ocean. "She was always stealing my clothes and evading my cross-examinations with clever phrases like that."

"And now she's stolen your life."

A gasp catches in her throat. "If Luca Zaccaria is as awful as you say he is, I'm happy with the trade-off."

"Go back to your cabin and polish your halo," I mock, heading over to the bar. "There's no room for your martyrdom on this deck."

"Haven't you ever loved someone, Aiden?" she asks, following in my footsteps. "I don't mean a woman," she adds quickly, seeing my expression.

"Not for fourteen years, as it happens." I reach for the scotch. *Put the fireguard up, Ielena, or those flames are going to bite you again.* "Except for Frankie, but he's more like a big dog with teeth." *And knives. And guns. And shovels.*

"I like Frankie."

"There you go again. Saying you like men who you really shouldn't." I down my double and pour another. "So tell me something. If this deal never existed, if you'd never been forced to marry me, if your sister wasn't on the run from the Italians, would you guys have left Paris together?"

"That was the plan. Maybe after working for a year or two first… Before all this, I had a job placement at *The Louvre* lined up."

"What would you have done? Bum around Europe on the Interrail with the rest of the Z generation? Or move to a quiet little island and be all self-sufficient and worthy?"

Caught up in the unexpected amiability of the conversation, she opens her mouth to answer me, *she fucking opens her mouth*, and then she shuts it again.

I watch her turn away quickly to compose herself, and in that moment I know that my pretty little Russian Doll knows *exactly* where her sister is.

Pain won't break her, so it's time to dial up the pleasure.

Chapter Seventeen

ISSA

We eat dinner on the top deck with the flickering lights of the Riviera serving as our background entertainment. Aiden's instructed that his yacht return to berth at *Port Hercule* in Monte Carlo, but the travel motion isn't distracting me from my appetite. It's been days since I last had a proper meal, and I'm falling on the salmon mousseline like a starved animal.

"The doctor will be back tomorrow morning to change the dressing." I glance up to find him watching me with an irritated expression on his face. "Christ. Didn't Felix feed you while I was gone?"

"I wasn't hungry before."

"Then today is a day for new appetites."

I swing the knife and fork together with a contented sigh. "That was delicious. My compliments to the chef."

"No dessert. We're going out." He seems impatient. He's up on his feet already.

"Where are we going?" I ask, placing my napkin down on

the table.

"I'm combining business and pleasure for the rest of the evening." His eyes gleam with untold sin and my stomach dips in nervous apprehension. "And you, princess, are very much the latter."

His black Maserati is waiting for us at the quayside. He sees me into the passenger seat, and then we're weaving our way through the back streets of the town in the direction of his casino.

"Did you take your meds tonight?"

"I did."

"How does the wound feel?"

"Better, thank you."

He seems pleased with the answer, in much the same way a hunter would be if his prized prey had shaken off an injury. He doesn't have to treat me like glass anymore. I'm fair game.

When he places a warm palm on my leg, the fire between us flickers back to life. He pushes the pedal to the floor as his fingers start to trail upward, the snarl of the powerful engine disguising the thundering of my heart. By the time his fingers have reached their destination, the car is pushing fifty kilometers per hour.

"Aiden, stop," I tell him with a groan, but at the same time I'm parting my legs to give him access.

"Never." With his trademark smirk, he hits sixty as he starts to massage my clit through my damp panties. A delicious burning sensation is spreading out across my pelvis. I throw my arm up around the headrest as his touch grows even more insistent. The vibrations of the car are making it hard to get any kind of traction on my self-control.

"Are you going to come for me, Ielena?"

"Yes," I rasp.

"Maybe later if you behave yourself." His fingers disappear.

The car slows. "Pull your dress down. We're arriving at my casino, and I'd prefer not to have to beat the shit out of any more of your admirers. It's not good for business."

It's agony to be that close to the edge and be denied. He wants me desperate. Helpless. And I'm playing into his hands like a dream.

"Ielena?" he says with an edge. "*Dress*."

"Sorry." I scramble to comply, even though my mind is in the gutter and my panties are soaked through.

He takes one look at the state of me, and he's still chuckling as he exits the car and hands the keys to the valet. When he opens my door, he pulls me into his arms and plants a rough kiss on my lips before I've had a chance to fix my hair. I'm wearing it loose again tonight, and writhing against a car seat as my sadistic new husband toys with my body has left it in a revealingly untidy state.

"What sweet, exotic torture I'm inflicting on you," he croons, skimming the outside curve of my left breast with the backs of his fingers "And this is only the beginning… Hold tight, your education is about to take an *unpredictable* turn."

How can one word turn the light pulse between my legs into a solid, painful beat? I'm practically panting as he takes my arm and leads me through the gold and marble-lined casino lobby and out onto the main gaming floor, under its striking domed ceilings and arched windows. In another time, when my body's impulses weren't dictating my every move, I would have stopped and admired all the artwork on the walls, but Aiden is a man on a mission and I'm too eager to follow him into the unknown.

The smell of money is everywhere. It's woody and fresh with each new shout of success, while an acrid tang accompanies the groans and losses. It's wall-to-wall beauty, from the throngs gathered around each table to all the supermodels and A-listers drifting through to their private gaming rooms.

The jeers, the chimes... I'm consumed by it all, but not as much as I am by the man next to me whose body heat is blasting into my skin, and whose raw masculinity is the most potent scent of all. A couple of days ago, in a bar in Cannes, I barely had his attention. Tonight, people are hailing him from all sides, but he's ignoring them all in favor of me.

I could pretend to be cool about it. I could remind myself of my imminent betrayal. I could even tell myself that I'm nothing but a passing vogue for a man who has used and discarded half of the Riviera. The truth of the matter is he's making me feel wanted for the first in my life, and that's his most wicked seduction of all.

"Where are you taking me?" I ask breathlessly as he leads me through another set of gilt-framed double doors.

"My office."

I feel another vicious thrill.

Out through the great glass atrium and up another red-carpeted staircase, then he pauses by a large black door. Smashing a security code into a silver-gray box, he stands aside to let me enter first, a dangerously still expression on his face.

Oh God.

Can I do this?

In true Aiden form, he doesn't give me a chance to debate it.

Before I've a chance to register the huge circular office, he's pushing me up against a floor-to-ceiling window running the expanse of one wall and overlooking the gaming floor below. My hands are held above my head. My dress is dragged above my hips... Aiden's touch is hovering on the edge of violence, and it's forcing me to confront things I never knew about myself:

like the fact that his total domination is silencing my duplicity, and when he treats me this way I can feel my juices dripping down the inside of my thighs. *I need his corruption more than I need air.*

"I could go easy on you, Ielena," I hear him purr. "I could steal your virginity in a soft bed with soft kisses, but that's not the kind of man I am. I'm a sadistic bastard, and you're about to get a taste of how much."

"Show me," I croak, as his hand wraps around my throat. The chill of the glass against my back is making my burning skin rash up.

"Still up for meeting me halfway?"

His mocking tone has me gritting out my answer. "Every time."

"We'll see." With this, his spins me around. "It's tinted glass, Ielena," he reassures as I expose myself to the entire casino. "No one gets to see this glorious sight but me." The next thing I know, my panties are hitting the floor and he's kicking my legs apart. "Time to finish what we started." I can feel the imprint of his erection against my naked ass. "How much do you want me?"

"So much," I say with a groan. It's taking all of my willpower not to relieve the throbbing pulse between my legs myself.

"How much are you willing to sacrifice?"

"Everything."

"Tongue or fingers?"

"Cock," I whisper, grinding my forehead into the glass.

"Cock?" He sounds amused. "Why, you have to earn that first." He spins me back around and I'm mesmerized by the blazing lust on his face.

He's a liar. He's a goddamn liar. He's swaying on the edge of his self-control, just as much as I am.

"Get down on your knees. Second lesson starts now."

For a second, I falter. "Here?"

I watch him snap open his belt. "I can drag you downstairs and we can do it on top of blackjack table if you like, but I'd have a hell of a lot of murder on my hands afterward."

He's not joking.

I glance at the shut door. "What if someone comes in?"

"Then I'd shoot them in the head, too." As if to prove the point, he takes out a gun from his waistband and slams it down on the dark mahogany table next to us. "Now, do as I ask, I'm losing patience."

I sink to my knees and run my fingers over the huge bulge in his trousers. I've fallen a long, long way from untouchable Bratva princess to this: a compromising position in a master criminal's lair and so blindsided by desire it's holding all my senses hostage. But when he reaches to undo his zipper, my fingers are already there.

"Eager, sweetheart?" he says as I tug his pants and boxers down and his cock springs free. Warm and smooth, I run my hand up and down his shaft a few times before lapping at his head and slit, hearing him curse my name as he braces his hands on the glass above me. "Shit, baby, you're a natural."

Feeling bolder, I wrap my lips around him, and guide him into my mouth. Flat palms become clenched fists.

"Fuck…"

"Is this okay?"

"No, it's shit," he gasps out. "But keep going anyway."

"I don't believe you, Aiden Knight."

"I don't believe me, either."

I move faster, sucking harder. It's me who is on a mission

now. I bob my head in time with his harsh curses, feeling him so deep at the back of my throat that I'm forced to breathe through my nose before his hand is crashing down on the back of my head and he's driving in even deeper. "You want it? Then fucking take it."

Seconds later, he's pressing my face into his crotch and holding it there, groaning out my name as a liquid heat starts pumping down my throat. Salty. Generous. His cum is a never-ending spurt.

Our eyes meet as he slides out of my mouth. His expression is glazed and there's a slight sheen of sweat on his forehead. "You have some serious explaining to do," he says roughly, tucking himself back inside his pants and winching the belt together again. "That was fucking incredible."

I swipe the back of my hand across my wet chin. "I said I was a virgin, but I never said of what."

He pauses. "What the fuck did you just say?"

"Joke," I say, backtracking quickly. This man is proprietorial, uncompromising... Alpha is at the heart of his DNA. He doesn't like to share. He doesn't even like to consider it.

"It better be." He hauls me up and folds me into his arms, my dress still tucked up around my waist. "I'm taking all your firsts, your lasts, your sexual everything..." He carries me over to a large black desk and with one hand sweeps a pile of papers onto the floor.

"I thought people only did that in movies." He drops me on top, and then drags me to the edge by my ankles.

"Lie back and close your eyes, Ielena," he orders as he pushes my legs apart. "I'm about to shine your fucking star."

I didn't realize he was being gentle before. What he does next to my body is total devastation.

Pretty soon he's devouring my pussy with his tongue—sucking, fucking—plunging two fingers inside me before I can brace myself for the intrusion. In a bid to anchor myself to the chaos, I swing my arms above my head and grasp the lip of the desk for all I'm worth.

"Aiden!" I scream as he slides a third finger inside me, driving me so far into heaven thoughts scatter and nothing else exists.

"I'm bigger than this," I hear him say huskily. "So you better get used to it."

"Please!"

"Please, what?"

I don't even know what I'm begging for anymore. I'm all fireworks and broken lullabies.

"Maybe your sister made the wrong choice. Rumors are Luca Zaccaria fucks just as hard as I do."

"She never had a choice! She never had a choice!"

His mouth and fingers disappear and I hear the clink of his belt buckle again.

"Where did she go, Ielena?" he whispers, sliding his cock up and down my pussy—soaking himself, and teasing me to distraction. When I don't answer, he slides his cock an inch or so into me.

I arch my back into the delicious burn, but he withdraws again to wrap my legs around his waist.

"I've been wanting you to do that since the day we met."

"More," I pant.

"So fucking greedy for it, aren't you?" His accent has slipped into a London dialect I don't recognize. All our bare bones are being exposed. "My perfect, soon-to-not-be-so-innocent wife... Do you really want to lose it like a whore, on my desk?"

"Better a whore than a virgin. I'm done with my innocence."

"Debatable." With that, he thrusts back inside me, driving even deeper as I cry out in pain and relief. "You're so fucking tight," he grunts. "A whore can never come close to this." He pushes in even further. *How can heaven and hell be this perfect a combination?* "Is she in trouble, baby?" His soft words are like a caress.

"Yes." *But not as much trouble as I'm in right now.* I'm losing my mind.

"Tell me."

"Harder."

He drives all the way in, silencing my next scream with a brutal kiss as I let go of the desk to dig my fingers into his silky, black hair. He pauses once he's buried up to the hilt and we're bathing in each other's ragged breaths. "Mine," he growls, seeking out my mouth again. "Too much has been taken from me, but not you. No one else will ever feel this, fuck this, taste this... Do you understand?" He's almost feral in his possession. "Answer me, Ielena. Who does this body belong to?"

"You," I croak as he finally starts to move—thrusting deep and slow, touching and tainting.

"Say it again," he demands, increasing his pace, grinding so deep he's stealing the air from my lungs. "I'm taking your innocence and painting it black."

"You!"

I'm right on the edge of that pleasure void again—falling, falling—and he's the only one who can catch me. His fingers slide into my mouth and I can taste my own arousal on his skin.

"Bite down, baby," he orders. "This is where it gets rough."

He takes me like the animal that he is—slamming harder and harder—as lost in this moment as I am. As for me, I'm biting, moaning, and tearing at his hair as my orgasm detonates inside me. He follows me down with a labored curse. I can feel his cock jerking as my inner muscles squeeze every last drop of cum from his body.

Exhausted, my fingers slide for his hair and my legs tumble from around his waist.

"Tell me, Ielena," he murmurs, resting his weight on his elbows. "Tell me where she is."

"Dying," I whisper.

Chapter Eighteen

AIDEN

Dying?

My head jerks up for confirmation, but she's already drifting in and out of consciousness.

What the ever-loving hell?

Even in my freshly fucked haze I can feel the shock of the word echoing through me. I wanted to pound the truth out of her. I wanted her sweet lips to bring me ever closer to my vengeance... I never considered that it would tug at something Tommaso Zaccaria had beaten out of me fourteen years ago.

She winces as my cock slides from her body. I've hurt her in the best ways possible, but I shouldn't have lost control like that. *I never lose control.*

Fixing my pants and belt, I walk over to my en suite for a clean hand towel. Running it under the hot tap for a minute, I return to the desk. She's still lying where I left her, but she's drawn her knees together and rocked them to one side. She looks vulnerable. *Used.*

"Okay, baby, this'll make it feel better." I part her legs and she whimpers in protest, but she doesn't stop me. I press the warm towel to her and she flinches as I set about wiping the inside of her thighs clean.

"I can't believe I did that," she whispers, lifting her head to watch me.

Is she referring to the slip-up over her sister or the out-of-this-world fuck?

As I suspected, there's no blush on her cheeks anymore, just the remnants of exertion and sin. I've killed the last of Ielena Dubova over my desk tonight. She's a fallen Knight now.

"I've broken you in, sweetheart. This is where the fun starts."

Who am I fooling? It doesn't get much better than that.

Removing the towel, I can still see the residue of my cum glistening at the apex of her thighs. I fight a primal urge to push it back inside her. I want a part of me corrupting her at all times, because she's so fucking corruptible.

Instead, I toss the towel on the floor and help her up to a seated position. Her hand flies to her hair again, but no amount of frantic patting is going to disguise what just went down in here.

"You look fine." I reach down and smooth it away from her face. *She looks beautiful.*

"Is it always like that?" she says, gazing up at me. "My mind went blank. I feel like I've just lost thirty minutes of my life."

Good job, too, sweetheart. Your secret is very unsafe *with me.* Even so, I'm having that feeling again, that guilt-type feeling, which can fuck right off.

"Let me fill you in." I take her delicate jaw between my fingers. "You told me I was a god, you professed your undying sexual love to me, you swore my body was a temple, and then you screamed out that my dick was the eighth wonder of the world... Sound about right?"

She grins slowly, that rosebud unfolding just for me. "I have no recollection of any of that."

"You also switched between four different languages, so it's a good thing I'm multilingual. 'Fuck me harder' sounds so much sexier in Russian."

"You're a wicked man, Aiden Knight."

"And you're his wicked wife."

Dying.

Karina Dubova is dying.

I let go of her with a frown. "Okay, so I may have paraphrased." We're interrupted by a knock at the door. "Go away!" I snarl.

"Aiden. Let me in."

It's Frankie's serious we-have-a-huge-fucking-problem voice.

"Hang on a minute." Blowing out a breath, I walk over to the sideboard where I left my gun and slide it back into my waistband. "Stay here," I tell Ielena. "Help yourself to a drink." I jab my finger at the well-stocked bar in the corner, and then to the door next to it. "En suite is over there."

Frankie is leaning against the far wall with a scowl a mile wide. "New aftershave, Raven?"

The smell of sex is clinging to my skin like a hippie's incense stick.

"Hanging out by the keyhole, were we?" I shoot back. "I never figured you as the voyeur type."

"Hard not to listen either when she's drowning out the slot machines. There's a man downstairs who's calling himself

Rocco Rossi. Says he's here to deliver a message from his father. I'll give you two guesses who that is."

"A hand-delivered message in return for a decapitated-head one," I muse. "We need to get ourselves a couple of email accounts. Hey, Louis!" I shout.

One of my men emerges from the room next door. "Yes, Monsieur Knight?"

"Stand here, and don't let my wife out of my office under any circumstances. Do you hear me?"

He nods as I turn back to Frankie, who's already checking the clip in his Glock. "Let's go and see what the bastard wants…"

I lead the way, with Frankie and two more of our men dropping in behind us.

"I take it this isn't going to be a friendly message?"

"All he offered was a shit-eating grin and a business card." Frankie hands it over as we take the stairs together. The card is unfussy, white and elegant: three words, with a symbol of a key stamped in blood-red ink above the writing.

La Società Villefort

"Looks like we've hit a nerve with someone," I say, resisting the urge to crush it in my fist. "Has Zaccaria got back to you yet? Maybe he can shed some light."

"Not yet."

"Order security to close the front gates. No one comes in or out until Mr. Rossi says what he needs to say."

Frankie pulls out his cell and issues the instruction.

"One more thing." I jerk him to a stop as we reach the bottom stair. "Karina Dubov is sick," I say, lowering my voice. "Get a detailed description, and then send it wide to every major hospital in Europe. I want all our contacts working on this as well."

Frankie doesn't respond, but there's a hell of a lot going on in his silence.

"No need to bother with the US or Canada. I doubt she would have been able to travel further afield."

His stone-gray gaze is demanding more information, but I'm already walking away. "Whatever you find out, keep the information between us."

Rocco Rossi is standing by the lobby doors. He has his back to me—which is pretty audacious if he knows of my reputation—staring out at the floodlit fountain beyond the forecourt.

He turns when he hears our footsteps approaching. Dressed in black tails, with his bowtie undone, he's a '60s Frank Sinatra clone who took a deeper dip on the Italian side. He's younger than me by a couple of years, but his smirk is at least a foot wider.

"Mr. Knight." He holds his hand out to me. "Thank you for your time."

"Signor Rossi." I take it briefly. *Firm as fuck.* "What brings you to Black Skies Riviera?"

"Black Skies?" He quirks an eyebrow at the nickname

"This is my home. My territory. If I don't like what people are selling, I turn their lives a shade of that color."

My threat is in my delivery, not my words, and, as expected, his smirk slips.

"I travel when needs must, Mr. Knight."

"An interesting turn of phrase... Shall we take this somewhere a little more private?"

Behind us, a square-jawed A-lister is arriving at the casino, and he's making a meal of his entrance with his twenty-person strong entourage.

"No, this won't take long. My flight back to New York

departs in an hour." He gestures to a car out front. The back door is open and the engine is idling. I know a getaway car when I see it.

"I take it Rossi got my postcard from Siena?" I say mildly.

Rocco chuckles and runs his hand across his jaw. "Yes, we received it. Although the writing got smeared in transit."

"How did you know it was me?"

"We followed a trail. With Gambino's links to our organization and so much bad blood between my father and Tommaso Zaccaria, we assumed it would be one of his." He sweeps his gaze over my face and I see a begrudging respect in his eyes. "And we were right. One of his former favorites, too."

"I'm not one of his anything," I respond coldly. "I work for everybody, and everybody works for me."

"No, Mr. Knight," he responds dryly. "Your entire empire is built on one thing, and one thing only. Black Skies... The Raven... All these nicknames and really, they're just the color of your vengeance."

This guy is starting to irritate me.

"Who the hell do you think you are, coming into my casino and talking this shit to me?"

"If you don't finish what you started, Mr. Knight," he says, not even flinching, "I fear your empire may crumble."

"Not me, I'm indestructible. Gambino, on the other hand—"

"Was last seen on a security camera in London fourteen years ago, near the same council estate where your parents lived," he interrupts tersely. "A day later he vanished into thin air."

"What footage?" I'm working hard to keep my expression in neutral.

"Footage that has only very recently come to light. Until

a few weeks ago, those police reports were lost in a vault somewhere underneath Brixton police station. A suspicious mind might assume that they'd been buried on purpose… From those, it was simply a matter of figuring out a motive."

"Why the fuck are you telling me this?"

"It's a peace offering. My father wishes to know what your intentions are toward him."

"Oh, I think he's guessed already, don't you?" I flash him a chilling smile. "Care to explain this?" I hold up the business card and I watch his tan skin pale.

"It was placed in the *pizzicheria* window next to Gambino's head," he explains quickly. "We have friends in the Siena *Carabinieri* who were anxious to share their findings with us. Did you leave it there?"

"No. Is your father a full paid-up member of *La Società Villefort*?"

He shakes his head. "He was denied membership a long time ago."

I glance sideways at Frankie. This is unexpected. Back in Siena, Gambino had confessed that Mattia Rossi was up to his eyes with the secret society shit.

"Next, you'll be denying Gambino was one of yours."

Rocco exhales slowly. "He *was* one of ours until he disappeared from New York fourteen years ago."

"Straight to Italy via a short stay in London, as ordered by *your father*." My trigger finger is starting to itch again.

Rocco shakes his head again. "He never gave that order to kill your family."

"Bullshit," I scoff, getting right up in his face. To his credit, he doesn't back away.

"A man pleading for his life will say anything to divert

the bullet, Mr. Knight. Wouldn't you agree? When Gambino joined the hit crew on your father, he was already on the run after stealing fifty grand from one of our close associates. The only reason we hadn't located him yet was because he was under protection from *La Società*. At the risk of repeating myself, that same protection was revoked a few weeks ago for reasons unknown."

"What the hell are you saying?"

"Whoever ordered the hit on your parents has nothing to do with the Rossi *Famiglia*, Mr. Knight. My father has sent me here in person to reassure you of that fact."

"And I'm supposed to believe what some old *Capo* has word-vomited over his wild boar ragù?"

His face tightens. "It's the truth, and I'd ask you refrain from the insults."

Enraged, I flick the business card at his chest and it drops to the ground between us like a dead bullet shell. "Seems we have ourselves a mystery, Rocco. If the *'Ndrangheta* didn't leave this, and I didn't leave this, then who the hell did?"

"I suggest you ask Zaccaria." He eases up the distance between us and glances at his car, acting all edgy suddenly at the mention of his name. "I'm assuming he's the one who told you about Gambino in the first place."

I shrug, my hand straying to the loaded weapon tucked into my back waistband. "What makes you say that?"

"Because Zaccaria will always be the man holding the smoking gun at the end, but I don't need to tell *you* that. You've worked for him for nearly half your life."

"Tell me about the war between him and Rossi," I demand, ignoring his veiled provocation. "Who cried first over their spilt *Aperol*?"

Rocco grimaces and slides his hands back into his pockets. "That's another question for your *Capo Dei Capi*." He switches his gaze to Frankie. "I hope you're taking notes."

Frankie's resultant growl has me slapping my hand across his chest. "Careful, Rocco," I murmur. "I have a trained Rottweiler and I'm not afraid to use him."

"Then I apologize," he says swiftly. "I am not here to make waves. I am here to smooth oceans."

"Oceans calm enough to sail into the sunset? I know your father's about to run, Rocco." I watch him recoil in surprise. "Don't try to deny it. We've seen the offshore bank accounts."

"My family's intentions have no bearing on you and your vengeance," he bites back, his composure slipping.

"Is he scared of Zaccaria?"

"Everyone is scared of Zaccaria. And you should be, too." He tidies his expression with difficulty and re-extends his hand. "I have a plane to catch, Mr. Knight. I wish you every fortune in finding your parents' killers."

"I want those London police files," I say, gripping his hand so tight he winces.

"You'll have them in the next hour. However, I should warn you there's nothing in them to identify who Gambino's co-conspirator was that night. The man is still under the protection of *La Società Villefort*."

No pre-empting Zaccaria, then… Karina Dubova is still a caveat in our agreement, albeit a dying one. *We need to find her, and fast.*

I follow him to the doors to see him out.

"Don't trust him," he says, stopping suddenly.

"Who?"

"Zaccaria."

"Why?"

"This Riviera deal with the Russians he has going on out here. Ask yourself why a man like that would want to share the wealth."

"When I want an opinion, Rossi, I'll pay a whore to keep the silence."

"Then it's your funeral," he mutters, resuming his walk to the car, but once he reaches it, he's turning and frowning in my direction again, looking like a man on the cusp of enlightenment.

He opens his mouth to say something, then the scream of an engine fills the night. I see the glint of the gun through the open window before Rocco does.

"Get down!" I roar, reaching for my own gun, but it's too late. The black sedan is already level with us, and five well-placed bullets are ripping the Italian's body apart.

He hits the ground as I fire my first shot into the fleeing car, taking out the back windshield. It's not enough to break the pace. My second and third just put scratches in the paintwork. Frankie takes over, but by then the sedan is nearly at the end of the driveway.

"Why the fuck aren't the gates shut?" I bellow at him, but he's already sprinting after it.

By the time I reach Rocco Rossi's side he's dead.

Chapter Nineteen

ISSA

I'm busy ransacking Aiden's desk drawer when the first shots ring out.

Slamming it shut again, I kick off my heels and rush to the window. The gaming floor below is a spectacle of well-heeled hysteria. White-shirted casino employees are frantically waving their arms around and urging everyone toward the back exit and away from the front lobby.

Aiden.

Where the hell is Aiden?

Yanking the door open, I go careering into a tall wall of unfriendly muscle.

"Let me past!" I gasp at the security guard.

"Sorry, can't do that." Strong arms wrap around me and usher me backward into the office. "I have my orders, Madame Knight." He delivers his words with a grim smile, a shaky French accent, and an extra firm push.

"Please, I need to…" I trail off when I see Aiden vaulting up the stairs behind him with a gun in his hand and a dark expression on his face.

The relief I feel is overwhelming. The more he slithers into my heart like this, the sharper the parting glass will be.

I glance down at his hands. They're covered in crimson paint.

Not paint.

"Let me through," he orders, and his man steps sideways.

"Aiden? What's happened?"

"Fun time's over. We're leaving." He grabs my hand and drags me out into the hallway with him. He's clearly not in a reassuring state of mind. "Get the hell out of here too, Louis," he adds over his shoulder. "The cops will be crawling all over this place in less than five minutes."

"My shoes," I cry, realizing I'm still barefoot.

"Leave them." He picks up the pace, and I break into a jog to keep up.

"Aiden, you're scaring me."

At this, he stops dead—dragging me into his arms and slamming a furious kiss down on my lips. "Thank God you stayed in my office and didn't defy me," he mutters. "I want you in *my* way, not harm's way. You got that, *halfway*?"

Halfway?

With that bombshell of a declaration, he's ushering me down the stairs.

"I need to get you out of here."

"Whose blood is that? Is that Frankie's?"

"No. It was a warning, a pretty effective one at that. We're getting too close to the truth."

It's like he's speaking the words to himself, not me.

"What truth?"

"My truth."

Panic floods my body. *What secrets are you hiding, Aiden? Are they even worse than mine?*

We've reached the lobby and it's swarming with his men. There's an arc of bullet holes sullying the casino's glass facade, and the usual shoot-out debris of broken glass and discarded belongings is scattered all over the white marble floor. Outside, there's a car with blown-out windows and a man's body lying face down in a pool of blood. Frankie's on his cell nearby, pacing up and down, not looking his usual stoic, laid-back self.

"Is he dead?" I say quietly.

"Permanently sleeping." He throws a heavy arm around my shoulders and leads me out the front entrance, tucking me to his side to shield my view of the corpse. My head only comes up to his shoulders, making me feel like a whisper of an afterthought, but the darkest of plans lurk in the smallest of places. "Can you drive a stick shift?" he demands suddenly.

"Yes." I bury my face into his powerful scent. Musk. Sweat. *Him.*

"More's the pity." He leads me over to his Maserati. "Frankie," he hollers out. "Keys." A flash of silver comes sailing through the air at us and he catches them easily. Opening the driver's door, he presses them into my hand, and then tugs me into his arms again. "Keep to the speed limits," he orders, imprinting more warmth and scent onto me. "Don't crash it. I'll meet you back at *The Cristo*."

"*The Cristo*?" I say, frowning up at him.

"It's the name of my yacht. The route is already programmed into the GPS. Now go." In the distance I can hear the wailing of police cars. He guides me into the driver's seat, before leaning over to switch the ignition on. "Clutch down, baby."

"Did you kill that man?" I say, grabbing hold of the front of his sweater.

"No," he says calmly, prizing off my fingers, one by one. "But I'll consider killing you if you're not pressing that accelerator pedal in the next five seconds."

"If you stay, will you be arrested?"

He chucks my chin, his eyes glinting with amusement. "The cops can't touch me, but I need to stick around and clean up the mess. I want you gone in case the shooter comes back for round two." With that, he rears back and slams the door. "Go!"

Men like him don't pay for their sins. They use them as currency. I jam my foot down and fly down the driveway. I've barely traveled a hundred meters on the main road when a cavalry of red and blue comes screaming past me in the opposite direction.

Unsure of the route to *Port Hercule*, I pull over into an empty gas station and bring up the GPS like he told me to. My fingers are shaking so badly I can't press the home button. A couple of attempts later, I'm tapping into the saved destinations and I'm ready to go.

Dropping my hand to the hand break, I notice a bright light flashing up in the coin pocket underneath the screen. Intrigued, I lean in closer. It's Aiden's cell. He must have left it here earlier. Neither of us was in a fit state to remember our senses, let alone our personal effects. He wanted me just as much as I wanted him.

Still want him.

Still feel him.

Still smell him.

The screen keeps lighting up as new messages appear. I

glance at the top one before the screen starts to fade. It's written in part English, part Italian, but I'm fluent in both.

O: Has The Raven consumed his little bird yet?

The passing traffic fades to white noise as I scramble to make meanings from the words. The Raven is Aiden, but that would mean—

O: Two days, and counting.

What happens in two days? Is the little bird *me*? Who is O?

"We're getting closer to the truth."

"My truth."

This night is an emotional gauntlet, and it's not even nine p.m. yet.

Pointing the car at the gas station's exit, I make my way through the pretty streets of Monte Carlo toward *Port Hercule*. Strips of orange streetlight keep flashing across my face like the bars of a prison cell, trapping me inside my head with my thoughts. I'm going over and over the messages in my mind— picking apart, fretting, interpreting…

Felix and another of Aiden's deck crew are waiting for me on the quayside. He steps forward to open my door. "Mrs. Knight," he says silkily, looking as composed as always. "Follow me. Philipe will take care of the car."

A blue pashmina is tucked around my shoulders as I'm led up onto the yacht. I glance up at the portside bow as I cross the gangplank.

That name.

So black. So bold.

How did I not notice it before? It's a sixty-foot Easter egg for the man I married a couple of days ago.

Aiden was trying to share something with me earlier. It's

something drowning in his lake of melancholy that he wants to dive down and rescue. I rack my brains to remember the ebb and flow of our conversation, but there's nothing except the feel of his arms and the taste of his lips...

"This way, *madame*," I hear Felix say as we enter my cabin. "You're shivering. Let's pick you out something warmer to wear."

He ushers me toward the walk-in closet and stands aside to let me enter. I don't register his overfamiliarity until he's slamming the closet door and advancing on me with his cool expression curled up into a vicious snarl.

"What the fuck happened in the casino tonight?"

"Wh-what?" I stagger backward in shock, my shoulder colliding with a rail of dresses.

"Don't lie to me, Ielena." *Why is he using my first name?* He grabs my arm and twists it, the pain registering as sharp and threatening. "I've been working this case for two years... Two fucking years as an undercover agent for Interpol, nailing Knight for money laundering, and then you appear on the scene like some wrecking-ball ninja. You're about to side-kick everything we've worked for out of this yacht's port holes."

Interpol? The International Criminal Police Organization?

"I don't know what you're talking about." I wrench my arm away with a wince.

"Don't play dumb with me." His usual meek and compliant act has gone. He looks like a man on the edge. "You know exactly what the deal is between Zaccaria and Dubov. You were sold like meat off the back of it. Now, tell me about tonight!"

"Some guy was shot dead outside the casino," I gasp out. "I don't know any details. I think it was a drive-by."

"Did Knight order the hit?"

"He swore he didn't." The fog of shock starts to clear. "You're the guy Maxim told me about. You planted the cell phones in my room. You soundproofed this closet." I glance around the small space and realize he's blocking the only exit.

"Maxim Lebedev should learn to keep his big mouth shut." He grabs my arm again and gives me a brutal shake, my exhausted body reacting with a silent scream like an Edvard Munch painting. "I was doing MI6 a favor planting those cells, but I'm not liking what I'm getting in return. I've risked everything to bring Knight down. My life, my job, my family... That Riviera deal between the *Scmion* and the *Cosa Nostra* needs to be signed off in two days' time, and you're going to make sure it happens."

"Get the hell off me!" I wrench my arm away from him for a second time. "I have no intention of sabotaging that deal. If you know who I am, then you'll know why I'm here. You know what I have to do, and my reasons for doing it."

"You're wrecking it anyway, whether you realize it or not. Daddy left his Bratva claw marks behind on your precious skin and Knight doesn't like it when people play rough with his toys." His upper lip curls in disgust. "You should have seen him when the doctor was here the other day. Mouthing off like he actually gave a shit about you. He's more likely to put a bullet in your father's head than let him sit down with Zaccaria now."

"It wasn't my fault!"

"But it's both of our problems now, thanks to you and your golden snatch." His scornful gaze drips hot wax on my body. "Knight was all about the money and power before you came along. He never even screwed the same woman twice."

"Stop," I whisper. "I'm just trying to get close to Zaccaria and his secrets. I'm working undercover, too—"

"Don't you dare compare yourself to trained agents like

me. You're nothing but a spoiled mafia princess who's had to interrupt her spray tan schedule to spread her legs for the greater cause."

"Don't presume you know anything about me, Felix, or whatever the hell your name is," I rasp, jabbing back with a weak punch of my own. "I'm living my own lie here. I'm drowning in it so deep, the path up to the surface is a trail of dissolving air bubbles."

"Spare me the pity party," he snarls. "Go tell it to your diary." I open my mouth to argue again, but he shuts me down with his next words: "I don't give a damn what British Intelligence offered you and Lebedev... I have no interest in blowing apart some top-secret, lick-arse society that Zaccaria claims to be a member of. That's their gig. Their problem. My target is Knight. My target has always been Knight. Two billion has passed through his casino and come out squeaky clean, and that's a big deal for me and the people I work for."

My mind starts reeling.

I think of Aiden's reaction when I asked if he might be arrested earlier. I think of the ravens at the Tower of London— the ones with clipped wings to stop them flying away. They were denied their freedom. They never had a choice but to stay.

The Cristo.

Fourteen years.

Aiden's been stuck working for Zaccaria for fourteen years.

Why?

Felix starts pacing the small space, so I back myself into the far wall. The smell of his sweat and frustration is permeating the air and making my stomach turn.

"My objective is linking Knight to your father and Zaccaria, which means it's imperative to have them all in the same room together. Nothing can deviate us from that."

"There's no way you can bring down those three men all by yourself," I blurt out. "I can't speak for my father, but you know who and what protects Zaccaria."

"Then you better work harder, *princess*," he sneers. "My success is dependent on yours, so I want to see blisters on those knees, and a goddamn spring in Knight's step for the next day or so. If it all goes to plan, he'll be facing life imprisonment by the end of the week. With a bit of luck, *La Società Villefort* will be crumbling from the inside out as well."

Is it possible to hate anything more than I do this twisted fate?

"Tell me what else I need to do," I say dully.

"Make Knight believe that you've forgiven your father for what he did to you. Keep him sweet. Keep them both sweet. They're having a drink together tomorrow night at Dubov's request, and I don't want any nasty surprises. If you speak to Lebedev, tell him I want him working just as hard from his end to keep the peace."

Do I tell him about Aiden's cell phone in the car? He could tap into the data and bug it in no time, but he's stripped me of my dignity along with my good will with this horrible ambush, so I'm thinking he can go straight to hell.

"Focus, Ielena. On Thursday I want to be lighting up the Monaco skies with more red and blue than a French laser show."

"Fine," I mutter, staring straight past his shoulders at the door. "Can I go now?"

"Just so long as you realize what's at stake…" As I draw level, he jabs his finger into the wound on my chest and I cry out in pain. "Don't fail me, bitch," he hisses, lording his threat over my doubled-up body. "I have a special hotline to British

Intelligence, too. One call and the nurses in your sister's hospital ward might accidently be attaching the wrong drip at two a.m. in the morning."

"No!" I gasp out.

"You can build up a lot of animosity for a person in two years, and that's all I feel for that bastard husband of yours. His past is murky. His sins are an ever-growing list. Did you know he used to fix for Zaccaria for ten years before he arrived here to terrorize the *Cote d'Azur*? He made all of his boss's little problems go away. He's not a businessman, he's a thug and a killer, and you're just an extension of him now."

I force my body to unfurl. This man doesn't deserve to see my pain.

"Disappointed men aren't known for their rationality, Mrs. Knight," he continues.

"Neither are disappointed women." I summon all the energy I have left to shove him away. "Why don't you slither back undercover and fetch me another juice like a good employee?"

His pale face turns magenta. He raises his fist to strike me and I hate myself for cringing away. "I'm warning you—"

"Fuck you!" I'm getting used to saying those words. They slip so much easier from my mouth that they used to. "I could take you down, too, Felix. If my sister dies before the authorities catch up with Aiden, I'll make sure you're finished. I'll blow your cover and your whole operation. And don't bother intimidating me with more retaliation. Without my sister, I'd be dead inside anyway."

It's not true. My heart beats for more than just Karina these days, but I'm learning to play this game by all its twisted rules.

He glares at me—weighing options, making judgements— and then he's dropping his hand to his pocket. "Say hi to the

British for me." He slams a new burner cell down on the top of the bureau. "Eight o'clock tomorrow morning. I suggest you answer it... They're not as tolerant as I am."

I quickly shove it in a nearby drawer, despising him not so much for his insults and threats as for his acid truths about Aiden.

"Try not to choke on all that conflict inside you, Felix," I say, glaring at him.

"Likewise," he replies with a bitter laugh. "I'm betting you choke first, though."

I spend the rest of the evening looking for a soft place to fall, but all I find are sharp edges and empty staterooms. My lungs are like lead again, my footsteps slow and deliberate. It's not easy drawing breath when your soul is this battered and compromised.

I'm craving Maxim's solid reassurance. I need him to tell me that everything's going to be okay, but he's a million miles away wrestling with his own demons—namely my father, a man whom I know he despises even more than Felix does Aiden. I shut my eyes and I see a white hospital room with blue disposable curtains. I see a team of blond- and black-haired surgeons. I see a bright red box, packed with ice, and the burgundy-colored organ that's going to save her life.

After tomorrow, that life is going to be peaceful and unpolluted, and far, far away from my father and his cruel decisions. Aleksandr Dubov is the bad guy from every fairytale. He thrives on misery and he despises happily ever afters, most of all his own daughters'.

Preoccupied, I wander past my cabin, past the sky lounge,

past the saloon into a different part of *The Cristo*. Somewhere along the way, I lose my bearings. I frown at strange doors. I double-back down unfamiliar passages. I'm as lost and found on Aiden's yacht as I am in Aiden's arms.

The next door I try greets me with a familiar scent so strong I have no choice but to slip inside. It's another cabin, twice the size of mine, with a huge king size and a long black desk with a silver laptop that's dead when I open it up.

In the en suite, I run my fingers over the uncapped shampoos and cologne bottles on the counter, picturing him washing and grooming. He always looks so perfect with his carefully tousled black bed hair. It's an appearance that I know belies the storm inside.

Returning to the cabin, I climb into his king size and wrap myself up in his granite-gray sheets.

Has The Raven consumed his little bird yet?

If the message is referring to me, the answer is unequivocal. The ache between my legs is just the physical evidence. More substantial proof lies in my current state of restlessness. It's like he's awoken a part of me that will never sleep again.

I glance at the digital clock on his nightstand. Ten p.m. *Is that all?* Some nights pass in the flutter of soft kisses and sweet dreams. Others march on and on in lonely, wide-eyed solitude.

This is one of those.

Awake.

Alone.

Lying discarded next to the clock is the old lighter he was toying with yesterday. I reach out and turn it over in my hand. There are two faded letters stamped into the scuffed brushed steel that I didn't notice before:

J. K.

On the flip side is the faint outline of a bird. *Is that a raven?* I looked up the reference on my iPhone yesterday. It's from an old Edgar Allen Poe poem. If what Eloise alluded about him is correct, he's holding onto something from his past so tightly it's staining every aspect of his present.

Next, I think about what Felix said—about all the awful things he's supposed to have done in the name of Tommaso Zaccaria. Am I supposed to be repulsed by it? Horrified? The world isn't as cut and dry to me as it was six months ago. People do bad things for a variety of reasons. Desperate reasons. Look at me. Look at Maxim.

I can't condemn him until I learn his true motives.

Not everyone with dark feathers and black hearts deserve their freedom, but I can sense there's more to him than a dangerous smirk and a killer reputation.

I can't let Interpol take him down, but I can't let my sister die, either.

At some point I must have fallen asleep. The next thing I know, it's pitch-black outside and the mattress is dipping with heat beside me. Insistent fingers start circling my hipbone. Sweet and sour whiskey breath is lacing the nape of my neck. A beat later, I'm being yanked backward into his open-armed den of safety.

I don't care that it's weaved with loose lies and deception. I don't care much about anything when he's wrapped around me like this.

"You're home."

"Home," he murmurs, and we both take a moment to decipher a word that's complicated and unfamiliar to us. His hand seeks out the lighter, and he plucks it from my fingers. "Where did you find this?"

"Nightstand… J. K… Is that—?"

"My father," he answers gruffly, closing his fist around it.

There's a pause. "What happened to him?"

"Dead." He tosses it onto the bedsheet beside me and his fingers start wandering again, this time up to my breast to tease my nipple through the thin fabric of my dress until it's stiff and tender.

"Is that long dead or recent dead?" I wriggle my ass up against him, feeling his erection, needing him…

"Fourteen years dead."

I freeze. "Is this a Zaccaria-linked death or—?"

He hisses under his breath. "Stop fire dancing again, sweetheart. It's been a hell of a night."

Fire dancing? I refrain from arguing that it was him who started this breadcrumb trail in the first place.

"What are you doing in my cabin anyway?"

"I got lost." *Lost for you. The minute you sat down, uninvited, in a bar in Cannes and mocked your way into my life.*

"Do you need me to draw you a map?"

"Of your yacht or of your body?" I tease, striving for our lightness once more. "We could call it the next lesson."

He growls out a laugh. "You shouldn't say such inflammatory things." His fingers trail downward again. "It's been a long time since I let a woman stay over in my cabin, if ever… Are you a bed invader as well, Issa?"

My pulse rate spikes. Issa. *He called me Issa.*

The first time he said my nickname it was drenched in contempt. Tonight, it's bathed in deference.

He's bending, learning…

Conceding.

"As well as what?" I rasp back, pressing into his warmth

again, but I never get my answer with words.

Instead, for the next two hours, he lets his lust do all the talking for him.

Chapter Twenty

ISSA

I wake to brilliant sunshine streaming in through the cabin's windows and gently warming my face. My mother used to say that a circadian rhythm is best broken at sunrise, but how she knew that is a mystery to me. For as long as I can remember, she only left her bed for her pre-lunch aperitifs.

My limbs are heavy with sleep as I yawn and stretch, and familiarize myself with my surroundings. It feels too natural to be waking up in his bed. It's that soft place to fall I was searching for all of last night. Whatever happens between us, there's a part of me that will always yearn to be back in the comfort of this moment.

A rustle of sheets has my stomach dipping in anticipation. I turn and find myself face-to-face with my newest life conundrum: how a napping Aiden is equally as desirable to me as a wide-awake one, albeit less liable to quip, ridicule, or fuck me to avoid the questions one might…

His sin isn't so full frontal this morning. There's a softness in his expression, even though his graze of dark stubble is hinting at a less than perfect soul. With his eyes closed, those wicked blues aren't glinting at me like treasure at the bottom of the ocean, but he's all about the colors in other ways: golden skin. Gray sheets. Black hair. *Faded pink stains on his forearms…*

The events of last night come rushing back. There's a phone call to take in a couple of hours from MI6. There are lives to save, and lives to ruin.

The weight of a traitor's responsibility entices me to shut my eyes and return to oblivion, but I force my legs out of bed regardless. That's when a strong arm hooks around my waist and pulls me back into his safety nook again.

"Where the hell do you think you're going?" he rumbles, his deep cadence thickened with sleep.

"I have a new job," I say, smiling into the pillow, filling my voice with that same emotion before I have a chance to conceal it. "And the doctor is returning first thing to change my dressing."

Yawning, he lets go of me and rolls onto his back. "Does it still hurt?"

I brush my hand across the white bandage. "It's much better, thank you."

"Such a polite little *halfway*, except when she's on her knees—"

"I think we get the picture," I interject hastily.

"But I had it in glorious Technicolor."

I watch him doze himself awake for a minute or two. The wound in my chest may be healing, but resentment is still bleeding from it. Every time I look in the mirror, every time I lay with him, that eagle insignia will be there to chase the light away.

"Give it a couple of months and you can tattoo over it," he says, as if reading my mind.

"With what? A skull and crossbones?" I wrap the sheet around my chest with a sigh.

"It's a blip, nothing more. The rest of your body is fucking perfect, so one minor flaw is acceptable."

I cluck at him reprovingly. "It's too early in the morning for you to be handing out compliments."

"You're right. Mornings are good for one thing, and one thing only." At this, he rolls onto his front to blast me with the glorious temptation of his thick web of back muscles.

"Which is…?" I run my fingers lightly up his spine. I can't seem to stop touching him.

"More sleep," comes the muffled reply.

"Are we going to talk about last night?"

"The fun part or the not-so-fun part?"

"The dead man in front of your casino part."

"It's business." He turns his head to glare me into submission, but I'm not so easily dissuaded.

"You always say that when you don't want to talk about it."

"Maybe you should take the hint."

"Maybe you should stop being so dismissive, and then I might."

"Fuck, I love it when you talk dirty." He strikes like a snake, flipping me onto my back and pinning my hips with his weight. "Next you'll be telling me you'd miss me." He swallows up my shocked gasp with a kiss.

"Can a marriage get annulled in the first year or is it still a divorce?" I say, ripping my mouth away.

"Oh, baby, you couldn't get rid of me if you tried." He nuzzles into my hair, making my head spin from his heavy blanket of maleness. Our banter is turning him on, judging from the twitching hardness against my thigh. It's our foreplay. Our very own back and forth. He dishes it out, and I'm learning to take it and return it. "Get up." He removes his leg and kicks the remainder of the gray sheet away. "You're having a shower with me."

Right away, panic clouds up my insides. "I don't want to have a shower with you."

"Tough. It's non-negotiable. I want to scrub us clean before I go and sully my reputation with *my business* again."

I watch him rise from the bed like a golden Adonis. "Seriously, Aiden, I don't want one. Not here. I'll go back to my own cabin."

But he sees right through my paper-thin excuse. "Is this about the water thing?" he says irritably.

"I don't want to talk about it."

"What happened? Did Papa Bratva drop you in the swimming pool as a kid?"

"Please leave it." I scrabble off the bed, refusing to give him any more reasons to hate my father.

He grabs hold of my hand, but I flinch away. "I want to know, Issa. I have my suspicions, but I want to hear the words from your mouth."

"If you know, then you don't need me to confirm it."

"Maybe I like to corroborate my sources." He drags me closer to him, locking me into the force field of his body. We're both naked and breathing hard with resentment. "Tell me."

"I can't!"

"He waterboarded you, didn't he? The same night he beat you and branded you. Am I right?"

My mouth is like a roulette wheel. All the right words are spinning away from me.

"Why does he want to find your sister so badly? This is more than just honor, sweetheart. This is about something bigger."

"I don't know what you're talking about." I try to shove past him, but he just pushes me back onto the bed.

"Don't lie to me."

"Fine! He did it to send a warning!" I dig my nails into the mattress, feeling fragile and exposed—bruises, scars, and all.

"To whom?" Driving one knee between my legs, he covers me on all fours, caging me in with his arms.

"Stop, Aiden."

"I said I was a patient man, but my God you're really testing me."

There's a secret burning a hole in the pocket of my resolve. I need to tell him something, *anything*, to shine that spotlight away from this spiraling intensity.

"Maxim," I whisper. "He did it as a warning to Maxim."

He rears back in surprise. "*Maxim*?" I watch the flash of shock turn to fury as he jumps to the wrong conclusion again. "I fucking knew it... That slimy bastard was all over you on our wedding day."

"It's not like that—"

"Do I have a defective model? Was my pretty little Russian doll ruined before I had a chance to break her in?"

"No!" I cry out in fear as he drags me to the edge of the bed and catches my jaw between his fingers. "No," I repeat, this time as a whisper. "My father is jealous of our closeness. Maxim is more of a parent to me than he'll ever be. That's why my father banished him to Cannes."

"Did he fuck you good, Ielena?" *Not Issa.* The cold look he's giving me is like a bomb exploding inside my chest. "Did he make your tight pussy cream as much as I do? Do the scars on his back from your nails match the ones on his face?"

"Why won't you listen to me?"

"Because I'm not particularly liking what you have to say. Did you suck his dick, too? Maybe you let him finger fuck you in your pretty pink palace bedroom. Was he a sweet sixteen present to yourself?"

"He's not in love with me!"

"Sex ain't love, princess," he grits out, that strange British dialect of his making an unwelcome return. "It's a far more enjoyable experience than that. And here I was thinking that your father had hurt you to get back at Zaccaria and me. Christ, I even felt guilty about it for all of three seconds, and I never feel guilty about anything."

"He's in love with my sister!" I scream, unable to take his look of disgust anymore, the one that's searing my skin far deeper than my father's branding iron.

He lets go of my face immediately. "*What*?"

"He's been in love with my sister since she was nineteen years old." And just like that my tears are threatening to make the second unwelcome appearance of the morning. Still, I refuse to look away from him. "I've never kissed a man, touched a man, *lain* with a man before you."

"Convince me."

I gape at him in shock. "Wasn't it obvious last night?"

"Not that," he clips. "Convince me that they're in love."

"Are you going to tell Zaccaria?" It comes out sounding like a dare, but it couldn't be further than the truth. Inside, I'm begging and pleading for him not to. If the Italians decide to torture Maxim, I know he'd rather die than give away Karina's location, but it's still a dangerous risk to take.

"I'll consider it, but only on one condition."

I stare up at him—wanting to believe him. I need so badly

for him to be on our side.

"Ielena," he says sharply. "Did you hear what I said?"

"Yes."

"I need you to tell me everything."

That's non-negotiable. But I can give you a breadcrumb trail of your own.

"Maxim hates my father."

"Tell him to join the queue… It's not generally in the job description of a *Pakhan's Brigadier*, though." He reaches for a pair of black jeans hanging over a nearby chair. At the same time, I flip the gray sheet back over my nakedness. I barely feel the brushed cotton against my skin. I'm too numbed by our conversation and its potential consequences. I'm putting all of our lives in the hands of a man I don't entirely trust yet. "Are you saying he's screwing your sister to get back at Daddy?"

"No." I shake my head. "That's not… Shit, it's coming out all wrong."

"Then start from the beginning." He takes a step back and eases up on his tone, but all I see is red.

"Is this how you torture people?" My swell of anger catches us both by surprise. "Sprinkle in the sweetness when the sour gets too salty?"

"I don't have the tolerance to torture people, Ielena," he snaps back. "If they don't give me what I want in the first five minutes, my bullets tend to direct the conversation."

"Are you going to shoot me, too?"

"No, *halfway*," he says, killing the distance between us instead. "I have a much better idea that that." He rips off the sheet and grabs my ankle. As he flips me over onto my front, I slam my elbows down to stop my scars and bruises from hitting the mattress.

"Get off me!"

"Never going to happen." He crashes his own elbows down next to mine, grinding his fury against my ass.

"Wh-what are you doing?"

"Incentivizing." He scuffs my shoulder with his stubble, driving heat between my legs. "Demanding…" He moves to nip my ear and throat with his teeth, and I let out a soft moan. "*Apologizing…*" My eyes flutter open again as his mouth moves to the nape of my neck. "I shouldn't have doubted you. I shouldn't have spoken to you like that. But the thought of you…" He trails off with a groan. "Damn, woman, I'm losing all fucking sense and reason around you."

I know how that feels.

"You're still a bastard," I hiss.

"Yes, but I'm *your* bastard." He moves onto his side and runs his hand up the back of my thigh. I try to wriggle away, but he only yanks me back again. "Don't tempt me, Issa." *Back to Issa again.* "I like a good hate fuck as much as the next man."

"What do you want from me?"

"I want some embellishment on what you just revealed. As much as I dislike talking about Maxim when you're naked like this in my bed, on this occasion, needs must. What does he have against your father?"

"I can't tell you… I've already said too much."

"Zaccaria," he growls threateningly

One name. One threat. One conclusion.

"He doesn't agree with the way my father treats Karina and me," I blurt out. *Hating him. Hating me.* I've backed myself so far into a corner over this I'm tasting paint. "We grew up as toys to be paraded about when he felt like it, but most of the time we were packed away and forgotten about. I didn't even know he was a *Pakhan* until six months ago. I was led to believe he was a successful businessman from Russia who'd made a name for himself after relocating to Paris. Then, one night, a man came to dinner. He and my father had words. I sneaked out for a late-night walk and I watched from the shadows as Maxim beat him, over and over, until my father pulled out a gun. That was my introduction to the Bratva world."

"Cute story," he says mildly. "Did it come with Pepsi and popcorn?"

I drop my head between my shoulders, too exhausted to smile, too exhausted to fight. "It was like someone shook up a Paris snow globe souvenir of my life. When the glitter settled, I finally started paying attention. I worked out the key players in his organization—"

"And the two Russian lovebirds?"

I can feel my nails digging deep into the mattress again. I'm a double, *triple* traitor for sharing their intimacy with him.

"I caught their secret smiles across rooms. I stumbled across notes." *I watched their love bud, blossom, and bloom.* I omit that part though, knowing it would make a man like Aiden gag. "Last year, I confronted her and she told me everything: That they'd been in love for four years. That it had started the day she turned nineteen. That whenever she could, she'd sneak down here to the Riviera to be with him." I blow out a breath. "And then she got sick."

"Sick?"

I shoot him a look, but he doesn't flicker. In turn, I feel a spark of uneasiness. I know exactly what I let slip to him by accident last night, so why is he pretending otherwise?

"What's wrong with her?"

"She needs a kidney transplant."

"Ah."

So now *he looks shocked?*

"A couple of months ago she started getting confused. She'd sleep all day and be in constant agony all night… With our mother in her perpetual cocktail hour state of mind and my father spending most of his time in his *6th Arrondissement* apartment with Marie, it was easy to hide it. When Maxim found out, he—"

"Why the hell would you hide something like that? Papa Bratva can buy her the best doctors in the world."

"Our *father* has a strong contempt for weakness." I collapse down to the bed, too exhausted to hold myself up any longer. "It's another reason he's so eager to find her. He doesn't take too kindly to humiliation, same as Zaccaria. Although who'd inflict her with the most pain if they ever tracked her down…" I leave that question to the unpartisan stillness of the room. Both men are as cruel and malicious as each other.

We're interrupted by the harsh beep of a cell phone.

Aiden reaches out across the bed and steals it from the nightstand. "What is it?" There's a pause. "Tell him I'm not interested… I don't give a damn, Frankie. Just do it." He hangs up and tosses the device back to where it came from.

"What was that about?" I ask. *And how did you get a new cell phone that fast?*

"A persistent problem, but it'll all be sorted soon enough." He flips a lock of my hair away from my shoulder blade and runs the pad of his thumb along my lips. I shudder at the tender gesture, still hating him for earlier. "Where's your sister now?"

"Maxim found a top medical team in Europe and she became a priority candidate for a donor. They planned to leave together last month, and then her health deteriorated even more. The next day, Zaccaria approached my father about the Riviera deal. It was as if the hangman was coming to claim his prize. We needed to move fast, so Maxim fixed it to look like Karina had ran away. He managed to charter a medical helicopter across the channel, while he and I stayed behind to add texture to the lie."

"As simple as that?"

"As simple as that," I say, leaving out the biggest part of all. The digital clock is blinking seven a.m. at me. *Sixty minutes.*

"Does your father know about Karina and Maxim?"

"Do you think Maxim would still be alive if he did?"

"True." He rolls me onto my back again and nudges his leg between my thighs. "He's a dickhead, but he's a smart dickhead."

"Will you do something for me, Aiden?" I say, reaching up to cup his jaw, thinking fast.

"Only if it's illegal." He gives me a flash of that wolfish grin that I'm starting to crave like a fine wine. I wouldn't like it half as much if his apology hadn't been half as genuine.

"I need you to play nice with my father." His grin slips. "I don't want the Monaco Police Force to find him washed up on a Riviera beach. He needs to sit down with Zaccaria on Thursday. Whatever happens, that deal needs to be made so they can choke on their arrogance and their future billions, and forget all about my sister."

"You ask too much." He pushes my hand away with a frown. "I'm not letting him get away with what he did to you."

"But don't you see? You're not rejecting me because of it, which means he's already lost the battle. Or are you…?" There's a trace of vulnerability in my voice.

"What the hell do *you* think?" He moves in closer and plants a soft kiss to my lips. It's a painter's kiss, or rather an abstract impressionist's kiss—as subtle as a Rothko, with the heart-stopping punch of a Picasso.

"Can I trust you, Aiden?" I see a flicker of something moving behind his eyes that both scares and thrills me in equal measure. We're comets locked on a collision course—me, him, Karina, and Maxim—and we're entering the final descent.

"Give up your most precious secret to me, and I'll show you how much."

Now it's my turn to kiss him, to daub his lips with a surrealist's dreamscape that has him moaning into my mouth. "Do what I ask of you tonight," I say, breaking away, "and I'll give you everything."

Chapter Twenty-One

AIDEN

She slips from my cabin thirty minutes later like the ghost she was when she first arrived last night. I watched the security feed. I saw her check out my laptop, the same way I saw her rifle through the top drawer in my office before Rocco Rossi decorated the front of my casino in his very own shade of crimson.

She closes the door behind her with a shy smile, tossed at me like a winner's salute over her shoulder. It has me reflecting on that word "honesty," and how open it is to interpretation. Issa and I seem to have very different construals in that respect. As touching as her story is, I know when someone's holding back.

She lied to me. I lied to her.

It's the yin and yang of dysfunctional marriages up and down the Riviera. In truth, torturing a person is a fucking high for me. I enjoy breaking the body, but not half as much as I do breaking the mind. In that respect, I played along. I told her what she wanted to hear. I paid attention when she slipped up…

Rising from the bed, I tap a number into my cell as I'm

walking toward the en suite. Frankie answers on the first ring.

"What did she say?"

"I haven't broached the subject yet." I run my hands through the black hair of the fraud who's reflecting back at me above the sink. "I know where her sister is, though."

There's a pause. "Where?"

"The UK."

"He managed to charter a helicopter across the channel."

There's only one channel she could possibly be referring to, and I've crossed it a fair few times myself.

"Frankie, make a list of all the major hospitals with transplant units."

"I'll redirect the teams immediately. We'll start in London—"

"Start with Cambridge. Call it a hunch."

"Jesus, Raven," he exclaims with a laugh. "Is this the part where I'm meant to be impressed? You're one kinky motherfucker… It only took you five days to get her to talk. Is Zaccaria offering bonuses?"

"My dick can't take the credit for this one, and I want nothing from Zaccaria when this is all over. I have the money to pay back his loan and to buy the casino outright. He can keep the bars and clubs."

It's a muted celebration. My vengeance isn't lighting up the same fires as it used to. I want that last name on the list, but the cost is rising with every minute I spend in her company.

"Shades of gray?" he says, reading between the lines.

"Shade of gray," I confirm reluctantly. "But we still have a job to do, so let's keep our eyes on the prize."

"Eyes on the prize," he echoes. "Why Cambridge?"

I reach under the mattress and slide out a drawing of a

white cottage with blue shutters, and the taste of black cherries explodes on my tongue. *Did she draw them from memory or from her imagination?* "Maxim has a beach house listed on his private property portfolio about eighty miles from there. It's under the name Victor Morrel, and it's the only one he owns in the UK. Find her, Frankie," I growl. "Zaccaria was the one who raised the stakes, not me. If he wants to play hardball again, this time I'm planning on leverage."

Chapter Twenty-Two

ISSA

We reach *La Croisette* at around nine a.m. The palm trees that greet us are like a gently swaying audience, while the white hotels set back from the road are in the cheap seats. The ocean on my left is glinting the same hard, cerulean-blue that is fast becoming my favorite color.

Aiden insisted on keeping his yacht in Monte Carlo and driving me the hour or so to Eloise's store in Cannes. He hasn't said much on the journey, and our silence is far from easy. There's something weighing heavily on his mind. There's something weighing heavily on mine. Our tension is darkening the shades of his cream leather interior. It's causing my stomach to fizz and dip like I'm on a rollercoaster with broken brakes.

The problem with deceit is that it comes with many coats of paranoia, like an ageing supermodel with her spoils of war. I took the call from MI6 earlier. I listened closely to their plans for tomorrow night. I accepted Felix's new "gift" in my walk-in closet drawer, and now the micro listening device is nestled deep at the bottom of my purse.

Aiden pulls over when we reach an empty side street close to *Rue Meynadier*. The black Escalade that's been tailgating us all the way from Monaco pulls over, too. He switches off the engine and we listen to the whirr of the cooling system for a moment.

"Louis is coming with you today. No arguments."

"Is that really necessary?" In the side mirror I watch the beast of the man who held me hostage for all of five seconds last night exit the vehicle. He lights up a cigarette and blows smoke rings at the crystal-blue sky.

"I said no arguments. Don't worry; he'll stay outside the store. I wouldn't want one of my best men losing his fucking mind in the realm of malachite and shocking pink. Why the hell do you like her stuff so much anyway?"

He says it like an accusation, so I reward him with another truth.

"Color breaks up the darkness."

"It's not like you need the money."

"It was never about the money."

"Don't kid yourself, sweetheart. We're all paying a price for something, even if we can't see the debt."

"Aiden…"

"Louis stays. Deal with it. You're a Knight now and that means you're target practice for all the petty chancers and criminals on the Riviera. You saw what happened at the casino yesterday."

"Do you think someone's trying to kill me?" I whisper.

"If there's a chance it could hurt me, then yes."

If?

I study his profile, noting the frown lines and the set jaw.

He's like a card from a deck, with one side always ready for the game while the other stays a blank expression. I'm definitely getting the latter today.

Dammit, Aiden.

I want our flashes of lightness back. I want a taste of what we could have been before it's gone forever.

"Fine, I won't fight you anymore." I drop my iPhone into my purse. "I accept your complete and utter overprotectiveness, but only because you're a control freak and I make allowances for it...and because it's hot."

"Hot?"

"Yes, hot." Leaning over, I go to seal the deal with a kiss to his cheek, but he turns at the last second and captures my mouth with his own.

"How hot are we talking here, exactly?" he growls, switching tack, trapping me in place with a firm hand wrapped around the base of my neck. It's sending out ripples of hot lust that are congregating between my legs. "Second base over the tits hot, or sliding my middle finger into your pussy right up to the knuckle hot?"

I let out a moan of lust, glazing his face with it. This man has a hotline to all my turn-ons. He holds the key to the cage of my inhibitions. When he took my virginity last night, he set me free, and now I have years of sexual ingenuity to catch up on.

"How about riding you so hard your eyes roll back in their sockets hot?"

"Okay, so now I'm interested." A beat later, I'm straddling his lap and his hands are in my hair—tugging, wanting, claiming. He drives his tongue between my teeth and I accept everything—tugging, wanting, *claiming* him right back—rocking my hips over his huge erection as a rush of need floods my senses.

My dress gets yanked up to my waist again as his hand slides between my legs.

"Yesterday, you told me off for talking like that, Aiden… Oh *God*." His fingers brush against my clit, zinging my swollen nerve endings and making me squirm.

"Turns out I like my wife's mouth as filthy as mine." A couple of early-rise shoppers are wandering past the car as he tugs my damp panties to the side. "Good thing these windows are tinted. We'd get arrested for what I'm about to do to you."

"Thought you didn't get arrested?"

"Turn of phrase, Issa." He groans as his fingers glide effortlessly toward their destination in a sea of slickness. "You're the only one who can lay their hands on me."

My heart gives a vicious flutter. "Then what are you waiting for?" I tell him, breathless and frantic as I reach for his belt. "I gave you my permission at least thirty seconds ago."

"Good girl gone bad. One day a virgin, and the next a nymphomaniac… I'm liking the progression." He chuckles darkly into my mouth. "It's my progression only, though. You're—"

"I'm yours," I whisper, dropping his zipper and pressing a hand to his mouth. We're bound by lies, by depravity, by injustice. But we're also bound by two souls that fit together perfectly in the heat of these moments, when all the other bad stuff falls away. He felt it first, and now I'm catching up and overtaking him.

Rising up on my knees, I invite him to banish the conflict, to take what he wants because I know he'll be giving me so much more in return. I don't want to think about anything else except us—not Karina's operation or tomorrow's deception— just glorious, incomparable us.

"You're a goddamn tease, Mrs. Knight," he says, shaking my hand off his mouth. "Be careful what you wish for." With that, he gives good on his promise, thrusting two thick fingers inside me with just the right amount of savagery.

I curse in French and Russian as I feel my inner muscles clamp greedily around his digits, and then he's pressing his thumb against my clit and moving it in slow circles. I'm still sore from last night, but my red-hot arousal is mixing everything up into a sensory paroxysm.

"Ride it," he orders through gritted teeth. "You're not leaving this fucking car until your juices are all over the front of my pants, do you hear? When we're through, I better be as soaked as you are."

"Yes!" The desire to drive him deeper into my body is all I can focus on. Gripping the headrest, I tilt my pelvis as he curls his fingers inside me to hit a spot that has me groaning again. "Aiden!" I shudder to a halt. The waves are lapping harder and faster. I'm too consumed to do anything but surf the incoming storm.

"That's right, baby. It's my name on those rosebuds, no one else's."

I quiver and shake as the tipping point looms.

"Self-control, Issa," he chides. "We went through this the other day."

"I'm falling…"

"Then let's fall together." With his other hand, he grips my hair so tightly my eyes start to sting. At the same time, he starts pumping his fingers in and out of me with a breath-taking violence that pushes me over the edge and beyond.

Wrung out and spiraling, I collapse against his body as the thunder of his heartbeat forces its way past the scars and bruises and into my own chest.

"I hope you brought a change of underwear," he muses, sliding his fingers out of me.

"I hope you brought a change of pants," I mumble into his shirt.

"No chance. I'm wearing you with pride for the rest of the day. When I meet your father later, I'm planning to rub his fucking nose in it like a dog who did wrong."

I pull back to look at him, pushing my damp hair out of my eyes. "You promised, Aiden…"

The corners of his mouth twitch. "I said I'd keep my bullets at bay, I never said I'd play fair." We stare at each other for a moment. "Get your soaking-wet pussy to work. I'll pick you up at six."

"Thank you," I whisper, teasing kisses along his jawline.

"For the orgasm or for the lift?"

For being you, I want to say. *Demanding, compromised, insecure, broken, sexy-as-hell you…*

But instead, like always, I hide that truth in a smile.

———————

His eyes are burning me up as I cross the street in front of his car. I'm amazed I can put one foot in front of the other. My good girl tendencies have been shaken to their roots, and the rest of me is stuck in the violent aftershocks. I've never been more aware of the creases in the dress I'm wearing—mid-length, amber and white striped silk—or the tell-tale flush in my cheeks.

He parked a good fifteen-minute walk from Eloise's store, so that's fifteen minutes to loosen the scent of sweat and sex from my skin with the help of the ocean breezes. Just before

Louis and I reach *Rue Meynadier*, I come across a small perfume stall, but all they sell is old school Calvin Klein, so now I smell like Kate Moss heroin chic as well.

I can still feel the sting of his fingers inside me—thieving and conquering—as I pass under the russet entrance sign with Louis trailing five paces behind. Every time we touch, we're crossing lines and smashing barriers. It's becoming rougher, dirtier… I sense the monster. We feel each other's fraud. There are parts of us that want to lay all our secrets bare, and the only method we trust is by fucking them into the open.

Leaving Louis loitering like a pit bull next to the racks of holiday postcards and cheap sunglasses of the store next door, I push the door open and step inside. Right away, I'm greeted with overjoyed smiles and open arms by an elegant vision in full-length burgundy with white cap sleeves.

"Issa! Oh my goodness. How are you feeling, *ma chérie*?"

"I'm better, thank you." Once again, I accept her embrace like it's a rescue remedy, breathing in the scent of lavender and coconut oil from her soft, iron-gray hair which has been coiled into a neat bun on the top of her head. "I missed you. I wish I could have been here two days ago… Aiden said he called?"

To her credit, she keeps her smile bright and unwavering at the mention of his name. "Yes, he called. He sounded *concerned*." She pauses to give me a chance to fill in the blanks. Instead, a clock ticks and the chatter from the street filters into the store, but she soon takes the hint. "So…colors!" She spins away and claps her hands briskly at the shelves and rails as if her dresses are her children and it's time for the day to begin.

"It was my father," I say quietly, and she spins back again, her Chanel red lipstick frozen into a perfect O. "The marks you saw on my chest? He gave them to me last week, or rather, his men did."

Eloise looks stunned. "No, no, no, Issa, there must be some mistake. The Aleksandr Dubov I knew would never have been so cruel to his daughter."

"The Aleksandr Dubov *I* know would never have been so kind," I say, hurt by her reaction. *Half-measure…halfway…half-truths.* The story behind my scars is far more complicated than I'm letting on, but my father deserves vitriol, not compassion, for everything else he's done to me in the past.

"Distant, maybe." She takes a couple of hesitant steps toward me as a form on contrition. "Perhaps more absent than he should have been, but it was only to protect you from his work."

"His *work*?" I splutter. "You mean all the murder, extortion, and fun stuff that a *Bratva Pakhan* excels in?"

She glances nervously at the door. "When I knew your parents—"

"How exactly *did* you know my parents?" I say, frowning. At the age of thirteen, I'd never once stopped to question such things. I'd been too swept up in the notion of not being ignored for once. My café visits had been allowed to continue, and that was enough for me.

"We met that summer." She seems hesitant to elaborate. "It started when your mother sent for me. She'd heard all about your little art and textiles meeting with the lady in jade."

"I never told my mother anything about you. I spoke to her even less than I spoke to my father."

She waves the mystery away as if it's nothing more than a fly. "That afternoon I found myself in the summer room on your father's estate in *La Californie*. Your mother was such a beauty, Issa," she gushes. "You remind me so much of her. She was a muse for all ages."

"Except when she's drunk." My newly acquired acid tongue is creeping into Aiden Knight territory now. "Then she's only a muse for Gordon's and Tanqueray."

Eloise lifts a reproving eyebrow. "I can still picture her, you know—reclining on a crushed velvet antique Louis XV, with the sunlight streaming through the open window and setting fire to her hair."

"With a cocktail in one hand and her responsibilities in the other," I say, pouring even more burning oil on the memory. "Shall we take a guess at which one she dropped first?"

I'm done listening to romantic notions when it comes to either one of my parents. My mother lives her days like she's an eighteenth-century courtesan. When the shit hit the fan four weeks ago, she made sure it was her daughters who faced the guillotine, not her.

"She's fragile. She can't comprehend—"

"She's cruel!"

"She was married too young to a man she didn't know," she argues gently. "He came with more baggage than she could handle."

"You're telling me you garnered all this from an afternoon in her company?" I walk over to the counter and drop my purse on top of it. All of a sudden, I don't care about the unexploded bomb inside it. Call it a fleeting fuck you to MI6 and the gun they're holding against my head.

"She was thrust into a world that frightened and ostracized her…"

"It's not a parallel with my own life, Eloise." I'm growing tired of her case for the defense. In my mind, my mother will always be tried and found guilty, the same as my father. "Life is what you make of it. We all face decisions that rip the fabric of our souls apart. That's when you need to stay true to the people you love."

Am I staying true to Aiden?

I pause, feeling like a con artist again. I don't love my husband. I *can't* love my husband. You can't throw that word at people you've only known for five days, even if they feel like holy water in your hands. Okay, wrong analogy for a man like him, but still.

I watch her pick invisible lint off the dress on the mannequin. "Sometimes there are decisions behind decisions… Like a wall of mirrors in a fairground attraction, the illusion never ends."

"I always hated fairground attractions." I sigh and tuck a loose strand of hair behind my ear. I only ever seem to wear it down these days. "I swore to myself that I'd never become like her, Eloise. I told myself I was stronger… Kinder. That if I ever had children, I would never be complicit in their pain, not like she was in mine. She had the choice to love Karina and me unconditionally, but she didn't. She chose to love her misery instead."

"Affairs of the family are as closely guarded as affairs of the heart," she says, reaching out to run her hands lightly up and down my arms as if she's trying to rub her point of view into me. "I cannot possibly try to understand the motives of your parents for treating you that way. I can only go on what I perceived for myself that summer all those years ago. I sat with her for three hours, *ma chérie*. Afterward, I was summoned to your father's study, where I sat with him for two more. I came away from his estate content in the knowledge that you had two parents who loved you deeply."

I shake my head in disbelief. "You're mistaken. So very mistaken. You're trying to touch up a portrait that was framed

260

and forgotten about a long time ago."

The bell above the door chimes, and a customer enters the store.

Concluding our conversation with a tight smile, Eloise steps forward to greet the newcomer.

We don't speak about it again for the rest of the day. Some topics aren't so easy to resurrect when they're driven by differences.

By midday, we're so busy, I don't even get the chance to panic about all the things I need to panic about. Eloise's designs are as popular as I remembered, and her small store is a thoroughfare. I find myself lost in someone else's moment, one that's full of fabric, small talk, and laughter as I fetch different sizes and offer opinions to everyone from passing tourists to wealthy regulars. I even manage to sketch a couple of new designs when I'm meant to be stocktaking, my pencil flying over the paper as a rush of inspiration takes hold.

It doesn't feel like I'm drawing memories today. It feels like I'm outlining a cautious future. *Is there a gentler fate awaiting me once all of this is over?* Something simple and safe with Karina and Maxim? We could own a store like this, or maybe even a café… No more guns. No more Bratva. No more danger and deceiving.

I don't have the chance to ask Eloise about Aiden until the afternoon heat is waning, our last customer is exiting, and Louis is acting less like a well-trained pit bull and more like a pacing tiger.

"Is he one of *Le Corbeau's*?"

I nod as I catch her glancing out the window. "Have you only just noticed him?" I ask, nudging the cash register shut.

"Oh, I noticed him. I just wasn't sure if you wanted to

talk about his employer or not." She comes over and starts rearranging a display of scarves on the counter that don't need the interference.

"Tell me about him, Eloise… Tell me everything you've heard."

She considers me thoughtfully for a moment. "Does he treat you well?"

"Not at first." I try to conceal my smile, but it bursts through anyway. "I guess men like him aren't supposed to. To them we're trophies. Playthings. Pretty ornaments to use and abuse… I tried to show him I was different."

"And he liked that?" She sounds surprised.

"No other Bratva or mafia man would have let his wife work here today. They'd see it as an insult, whereas he sees it as a turn-on." I flick her a grin and she swats my arm with a honeyed laugh. "He doesn't hide what he is, and I know he's never going to change. But he's smart in a way I never expected him to be, and the best parts of him shine through the dark clouds when you least expect it."

"If he's good to you, then things like pasts and bad reputations are nothing but sandstorms." She leans over and strokes my cheek affectionately. "Let them blow over you, Issa. Make yourselves a home in what's left behind."

A pang of regret hits me. *There will never be the chance for that.*

"The problem with sand is it lingers." I glance at my iPhone. Six p.m. Aiden will be here any minute. "It seeps into every crevice. It's immortalized in nicknames…" I think about his father's lighter with the raven insignia. Feeling weary suddenly, I lean over the counter, resting my elbows on the glass. "Sometimes he drops clues to a past he has no intention of sharing. Then he accuses me of fire dancing when I ask too many questions."

The bell chimes again and the man in question stalks in, filling the store with his powerful presence.

Urbane.

Savage.

Beautiful.

He's all the things I first thought about him and more... and he's *still* wearing the same black suit that he had on this morning. A shiver of longing zips up and down my spine. He wasn't kidding when he said he intended to wear our desire as a victory prize tonight.

"Are you done?" He nods at Eloise, who gives him a cautious wave.

"I am." I slide my purse onto my shoulder, and give her a quick kiss on the cheek. "Thanks for today, I loved every minute."

"Me too, Issa. *A bientôt.*"

"I'll see you tomorrow."

"How does it feel to be working class?" He leads me out onto the street with his hand clamped to the base of my spine. Louis and two other men fall in behind.

"Good. How does it feel to be criminal class?"

"Fucking awesome."

I burst out laughing and slip my arm around his waist. It's another stunning early evening in Cannes, rich in both heat and atmosphere. Many of the boutiques and stores are still open and a surfeit from the bars and cafés is spilling out into the streets. Aiden's casual arrogance makes every head turn. More than once, I see the mouths drop open on some very beautiful, rapacious faces.

They don't exist to him. He doesn't even glance their way, and it makes me wonder about all the women who have come before me. Did he bore easily? Is that the reason they never stayed the night? Am I the first to figure out that this complicated man needs complicated in return? There's a part of him that has never truly loved anything, and another part that has simply learned to never expect it.

"How much have you earned today?" His hand slips from my back to my waist to mirror mine.

"About a hundred euros, and a hundred pounds in weight. I didn't sit down all day."

"I'm proud of you, baby," he says, making my heart flutter again.

"Did you murder anyone today?" I enquire.

"Not yet…"

"Then I'm proud of you too, baby," I intone, and he laughs that wonderful loose tenor I love so much.

"*Halfway*," he accuses.

"*Overkill*," I return.

We walk the next couple of steps in a contented silence, so different from our car journey this morning. That *thing* I crave is back in spades, and I want to dig my three-inch heels into the present and never let it go.

"What did you want to be when you were a kid, Issa?" he asks.

"I didn't care so long as I could draw it." When he doesn't respond, I feel obligated to continue. "There's a small town called Collioure on the *Côte Vermeille* about five hours drive up the coast from here. Artists like Matisse, Rennie McIntosh, Picasso… They all lived there at one time or another, infecting it with their magic. My *adult* dream is to sit in a beachfront café there, sketching the waves in the shallow bay all day and drinking in the inspiration…"

"Thought you said you hated water?"

"I'm learning to appreciate it from afar. What about you?"

"I wanted to be a survivor."

"Congratulations. It looks like you made it."

He turns and catches my face between his hands, his thumbs tracing the arcs of my cheekbones "We should take *The Cristo* up the coast to Collioure. I want to see you sketch waves."

There's a yearning in his voice that takes my breath away.

"What would you do while I sketched?"

"Drink whiskey, dream up new ways to defile you, show the local gangsters who's boss."

"Buy up a load of property," I say with a grin. "Open a casino…"

"At least I'd be free of the smart retorts for a couple of hours. You know what they do to me." His eyes start gleaming with wicked intent again. "We won't be making our dinner reservation at this rate."

"That's a shame," I say lightly. "Do you have something better in mind?"

"Yes, you're wearing it. On second thought…" He drops his hands and plunges his face into the crook of my neck briefly, making my head spin. "Why on earth do you smell like a nineties rave?"

"Extra vintage Calvin Klein." I flash my wrists at him and he pretends to gag.

"What is it with you and bad perfume?"

"I'll tell you what, why don't you buy me something that's not going to make you do the scrunchy-up face thing?"

"What scrunchy-up face thing?"

"This scrunchy-up face thing," I say, reaching up to smooth the frown lines from his face, feeling him shudder beneath my touch.

"Challenge accepted."

Taking my hand, he leads me into the next street where there's a perfumery that's miles swankier than the one I found this morning. "Stay here," he says to his men as he guides me up the stone steps and into the empty shop.

Standing under the glare of the strip lighting, with rows and rows of choice swirling before my eyes, I try to eavesdrop as Aiden starts chatting to the man behind the counter.

"What sort of thing do you like?" he barks at me over his shoulder.

"I guess this isn't a great time to tell you I don't like perfume," I say sheepishly. "I find them too florid or too extravagant. They're like flowers at a wedding that wilt before the night is through."

"No such problem at ours. Chanel Allure," I hear him say, and I watch the man spray a white tester strip and hand it over to him.

"Is this what you give to all of your girlfriends to make them smell the same?"

"No, sweetheart," he drawls. "This is what I give to my wife."

I swear if my heart does this fluttering thing again, I'm going to be dead by the morning.

He hands me the stick and of course it's perfect. Fresh and sensuous, with a spice that is quintessentially *me*. It's scary how he's managed to soak up all my quirks so quickly. He's flaying me open with every unexpected gesture.

I give him a shy smile, and ten seconds later we're leaving

the store two hundred euros down.

"I'm paying you back."

"I wouldn't expect anything less." He hands the paper bag to me with a smirk. "I should warn you though, I charge interest."

I watch him pull his keys out of his jacket pocket, wanting to climb in there myself and never leave. "You have hidden talents, Aiden. You're a perfumer as well as a master criminal."

"Let's just say I'm good at covering stuff up. Started from a young age, and I graduated with honors." I wait for him to elaborate but, of course, he doesn't. "You still hungry?" he asks when we reach his Maserati.

"Not particularly."

"Right answer." Coming in close behind me, he leans over to open the passenger door, but it's just a pretense for him to slide his hand between my legs and cup my heat. I push back on him with a soft moan as his fingers press harder. "Naughty girl," he murmurs. "I can feel you throbbing for me already."

"Why is it the right answer?" I whisper as he shifts his body to screen his actions from his men.

"Because the only thing I want to eat tonight," he growls, "is you wearing fuck all but this perfume."

Chapter Twenty-Three

AIDEN

I left her sleeping in my cabin, sore yet sated.

In the space of twenty-four hours, I've unleashed sexual heaven and hell. Her reticence was unfounded. Her innocence was a sham. Underneath it all, my wife is an insatiable minx, and I want to dye her every shade of filthy. When I close the door behind me, I do it with scratch marks down my back, a bleeding lip from demanding teeth, and a deep satisfaction inside that's slaked my appetite until I can return to her arms again.

I make my way across the gangplank and onto the quayside where Frankie's waiting for me, an unlit cigarette clamped between his teeth. Instead of a greeting, I snatch it off him and flick it into the ocean.

"I needed that," he grumbles.

"I need you more, preferably not dead from a lung disease. Give me an update on the casino." We walk toward his parked black Escalade together, falling into an easy step.

"Business as usual, if not better. A good murder always

brings in the crowd. The new front window was fitted and approved, the front entrance is so clean you could eat your new wife's pussy off it." He shoots me a grin. "And the cops are sitting pretty with the story we're selling."

I slide into the passenger seat as Frankie takes the wheel. "Make contact with Rossi. He needs to know we had nothing to do with his son's death."

"Already done. As to whether he believes us…" He shrugs his massive shoulders. "No black hands in the mail yet, but they only repatriated the body this afternoon."

I check my watch. Nine fifty p.m. "And Dubov?"

"He arrived at the casino fifteen minutes ago with Maxim and a couple of others."

"How many others?"

"Ten. Right now, they're happy gamblers in a private room."

"What about the—?"

"Yeah, I sorted it." He clucks in disapproval and rakes his hand through his hair. "Are you a hundred percent sure about this? Zaccaria—"

"Fuck Zaccaria," I say. "This has nothing to do with him. It's a family matter, between my father-in-law and me. If he wants Karina Dubova's head so badly, he'll stay the hell out of it."

Promises are easy to make in my world. They're even easier to break. I warned Issa at the beginning that they were temporary structures which could crumble at any moment.

"Have we located her?"

Frankie hesitates. "Cambridge, like you said. She came out of surgery six hours ago."

"And?"

"Successful. Time will tell if her body rejects it." He drops the clutch and we ease through the center of town. "Are we going to discuss the clusterfuck of revelations that Rossi dropped on us last night?"

"I'm still deliberating on it."

"You're also bleeding on it. Your lip's a mess. Did you get into a fight with a whiskey bottle?"

I brush my jacket sleeve across my mouth. "My kitty cat has claws."

Frankie laughs. "I guess it's going to be even harder to rehome her tomorrow night, then."

"Step on it, would you?" I say irritably. "There's a Russian bastard waiting for a reckoning."

I don't want to think about Issa, let alone talk about her. Not in the same context of fucking her over, when all I want to do is the fucking part.

Frankie does as he's told and the Escalade surges forward. "If Rossi didn't order the hit fourteen years ago, who did?"

I chew on his words as I check my cell. "Someone yanked the strings and it wasn't the *'Ndrangheta*. Why would anyone want to kill Rossi's son anyway? Find out who Rossi's enemies…" I trail off and we catch each other's eye. "Son of a bitch," I mutter.

"There's something else." He pulls out his own iPhone from his inside pocket and hands it to me. "It's unrelated, but it's surprising."

"*Surprising*?" I pick on the word with a scowl. "Are you trying to kamikaze my evening?"

"Yeah, well, see what you think of it first. Scroll down to my emails. It's the last one from Gabriel. He was monitoring Eloise's store security like you requested. She had a visitor a couple of hours ago, and you'll never guess who."

"Cindy fucking Crawford?" I pull up the video clip and

start playing it. All of a sudden, my mind's not on supermodels anymore.

I watch Issa's friend rush forward to greet the new arrival. I watch her place a tender hand to his cheek in a gesture that pushes all the casual relationship rules to the limit.

"What the hell?" I breathe. "Is that—?"

"Yep."

"Do we have audio?"

"Not yet. Dubov carries a jamming device. Gabriel's working on it right now."

"Tell him I'll buy him a new pair of angel wings if he unscrambles it tonight."

We pull up to the casino with my mind working overtime. I leave Frankie to deal with the car and head straight up to my office to pour myself a double.

I drink it straight—no ice, no frills. I think of Issa lying naked in my bed as the first taste slithers heat across my tongue. When it slips down my throat, I consider all of the pain I'll never be able to share with her. When it burns acid-sweet in my stomach, I remember a note stuffed into my dead's father mouth that bought me a one-way ticket to this hell.

I was content making billions, corrupting the system, and killing in the name of anarchy and sin. I had a purpose. I had a goal...

Issa hints at better.

She hints at more.

But hints don't disperse the darkness, and forgiveness will never triumph over vengeance. Somewhere still trapped inside me is a kid of sixteen who's still kicking about the park with his mates and a four-pack of Stella, with a future like a child's twisting kaleidoscope. There isn't a clear focus yet, but there's a hell of a lot of color.

Issa has color.

Two men stole that life from me. A third gave the order. All will die before I allow myself to taste that kind of happiness again.

There's a knock at the door as I'm pouring out a second.

"Come in."

A Russian platoon comes marching into my office, with Maxim leading the charge. Frankie shoots me a look from the doorway and I give him a nod. A beat later, ten of my own are filing in after them and lining the back wall. It's a dick swinging display at its finest, and my guys have the edge.

The office is large enough to accommodate the bodies, but not the atmosphere. Tension is rising up like a convection current, and then dripping down on French, English, and Russian alike.

"Knight," says Maxim gruffly, stepping forward and holding out his hand.

"Lebedev."

The scars on the left side of his face look livid under this yellow lighting. Is he frowning? Scowling? *Smiling?* It's impossible to tell. The scars are a disguise—a liar's dance of an expression. His one good eye is giving him away, though. It's refusing to focus, darting about my face like a black hummingbird. He's stressed as fuck, and so he should be. The love of his life just had a kidney transplant...

That's when it hits me. Why is he still hanging around with Dubov when he could have disappeared into a hospital sunset four weeks ago?

"It's an honor to introduce you to my *Pakhan*." Could he sound any more insincere? He stands aside to let the man behind him into my limelight. "Aleksandr Dubov... Aiden Knight."

Dubov is taller than I expected, with thick pewter hair that matches the color of his three-piece. He and Zaccaria are the same age, but he's more maligned with the weight of his avarice than the Italian is. There's a slight stoop to his shoulders as he leans in to shake my hand, and his face is a patchwork of jagged, crisscrossing lines. I recognize his eyes, though. Dark, intelligent, soul stealing...

"Welcome to my casino," I say, slipping into Russian. "I trust you've been made to feel welcome in my absence? I apologize for the delay. I was unexpectedly detained."

"Nothing too taxing, I hope?" he says gruffly, sounding like a Moscow-vodka-bar-drinking-fifty-pack regular.

"Taxing in the best of ways." I toss him a smirk. "I was busy fucking my wife for the third time today. You know how demanding new brides can be."

The sly smile drops from his face. His hand follows suite.

Suck my dick, you bastard. I just set the tone for this meeting perfectly. My territory. My rules. My wife's perfect alabaster skin.

"Frankie? Drinks." I direct Dubov to the leather chair in front of my desk. "This is the reason you requested to see me, is it not?"

The Russian fixes me with a narrow gaze. There's a hell of a lot going on behind his set expression, but I don't scare easily. "Leave us," he snaps, waving at his men. "All except you, Maxim. I wish to speak to Mr. Knight alone."

This is unexpected. I'd anticipated a ten-men cull before the first toast at least.

No one speaks as they file out of my office one by one, like unpaired arc animals.

"Sit down, please, Mr. Knight," he says, sweeping his gaze back to me.

"That's my line." I lift my eyebrows, refusing to budge.

There's a tense standoff before he's conceding with a grunt and lowering himself into the chair. Circling my desk, I do the same, refraining from throwing my feet up on the desk to show him the diamonds.

"For a gambling man, you play your hand too early," he declares with a sneer.

"Just because I own a casino, don't go casting those aspersions." I throw him another smirk as Frankie places two whiskeys down on the desk between us. I don't bother asking how Dubov takes it. He hurt Issa.

He hurt Issa.

My mind is a raging inferno suddenly. I have to fight the urge to reach out across the desk, grab his tie, and smash his face into the expensive joinery until he's choking on the splinters.

"You're unhappy with me," he states, watching me carefully.

"What on earth would give you that idea?" I singsong back at him.

"Eleven bruises and the *Semion* eagle."

Before I know it, I'm on my feet and reaching for my gun.

"No!" he thunders, and it takes me a second to realize he's shouting his command at Maxim. His *Brigadier* has gone one further and is already aiming in our direction. "Put your weapon down, Lebedev. Mr. Knight is well within his rights to be angry with me for what I did to Ielena."

"Issa," I say automatically, earning a sharp look from Maxim. I shoot him one back, the duplicitous motherfucker. I open my mouth to spill his dirty secret, and then I notice he's aiming his gun more at his *Pakhan's* head, not mine.

Issa was right. Maxim fucking hates her father.

My expression turns quizzical, and he drops his arm first.

"It is just as I feared," sighs Dubov, crashing back down to his seat. "You have fallen in love with my daughter, and she with you."

This brings me up short.

Love?

I don't do love.

It's a tired, old emotion for the weak and directionless. I know exactly where my life is headed: murder, vengeance, and a massive alcohol problem.

"I'm not in love with her, Dubov," I respond coldly. "But I'm not rejecting her for what you did, either."

"You should. For her sake."

I've had enough of this.

"I particularly enjoyed the waterboarding touch, you piece of shit," I say, losing my cool. "It brings a whole new meaning to a father-daughter bonding session."

He frowns. "What waterboarding?"

"I wouldn't get too hung up on it, if I were you. It's the least of your crimes." His confusion is niggling at me, though. "Her extreme fear of water?" I prompt. "It doesn't take a genius to figure out—"

"Ielena has always had a fear of water," he interrupts tersely. "Ever since she was six years old."

"*What?*"

A slow tic appears in Dubov's cheek. "She watched her sister drown. She tried to save her, but she wasn't strong enough to fight the currents."

Bullshit.

"Would this be the same daughter who vanished into thin air

two decades later?" I slide my gaze to Maxim again, and watch the unblemished side of his face pale. I let him choke on the knowledge that I know about him and Karina before swinging it back to his *Pakhan.*

"No. Not Karina. I had a third daughter. Annika." There's pain skulking behind his blank expression now. It's strange, considering he doesn't give a damn about the daughters who did survive. "My wife has never recovered. She tries to forget it in her own way." *You mean the cocktail way.* "I wasn't there when it happened. I was in Russia on business. Because of this, my daughters blamed me." That tic in his cheek is working overtime now.

"What's with the sudden oversharing, Dubov? You don't seem the type."

"You were forced into this marriage too, Mr. Knight. You deserve to know the truth." He holds up his hand for me to let him finish. "Grief forged an unbreakable bond between Karina and Ielena. I am almost certain she knows where her sister is."

"So, you tortured her for it?"

"I never tortured her. She'd die before she ever gave up that secret to me. Wherever Karina is, I only pray that she's happy."

My head is starting to ache. "Are you saying that you're *not* looking for her?"

"Only insomuch as to check on her welfare."

Well, it's pretty fucked right about now. "She disgraced you. I thought Bratva was all 'honor amongst thieves'?"

"We bend the rules, as and when it's required." He motions with his glass for a top up for his whiskey.

"Did you help her escape?"

He shakes his head. "That would have meant a certain death sentence from Zaccaria. For me, and for every member of my family."

"What do you mean you didn't torture Issa?" says Frankie, moving closer.

"Next, you'll be telling me she asked for it," I say with a snarl.

"She did." He takes a painfully slow sip, reminding me of that age and refinement thing that Zaccaria preached about in a Trattoria in Sicily fourteen years ago. "The beatings, the branding... It was all her idea."

Fucking.

Bastard

Surprises.

Even Maxim looks like someone just swapped his Glock 21 for a water pistol.

"So let me get this straight," I say, leaning forward in my chair—heart pounding, fists clenching. "You're saying that your daughter, my wife, *asked* for you to scar her with your insignia?" I go to take a swig of my whiskey and find that my glass is already empty. "Why would she do that? Why would you consent to it?"

"She wanted the man she married to think of her as damaged goods."

I guessed that part right. Shame it didn't translate to my cock.

So, my halfway princess wanted to marry me even less than I wanted to marry her... *Does she still feel that way?*

He studies his own glass for a moment, holding it up to catch the overhead light. "It wasn't a decision I took lightly. She begged and she pleaded. She said I owed it to her after what happened to Annika." He grimaces. "I have loved my daughters from behind a glass wall for many years, Mr. Knight. It doesn't mean I don't share their suffering. It doesn't mean that I stayed in the room when my men carried out my orders. It doesn't mean that I didn't feel every blow, every agony. We both know that Luca Zaccaria would have done much worse to her than I did."

I feel like I'm back in the game with Rick Sanders from a few nights ago, but this time I'm losing a hundred million, not a half.

"Are you a weak man or just a stupid one?" I say, groping for some equilibrium in this shitshow of a conversation.

He bangs his glass down on the table. "I am a man who is trying to set my daughter free! *That* is the real reason why I am here tonight... Tomorrow, there will be a choice for you. I fear that you will choose poorly and destroy my daughter's heart, as I did to my own wife's heart when the same choice was mine."

"Dubov," I say patiently. "I'm turning up tomorrow to discuss terms for a Riviera deal between the *Cosa Nostra* and the *Semion* that I stand to benefit greatly from. My only choice will be between wearing a blue Tom Ford suit or a black Armani one."

"Do I need to beg?"

What the fuck?

"You'll be begging on behalf of a daughter who hates your guts. Jesus!" I exclaim. "Your family life is even more messed up than mine is."

"Oh, I doubt that very much." His dark eyes start glinting like a night of a thousand shit secrets.

"What's that supposed to mean?"

He shrugs. "That's a question for Zaccaria."

There are a lot of questions for fucking Zaccaria.

"I am not in love with your daughter, Dubov," I repeat, "but neither do I think of her as damaged goods. I fuck her out of duty. I fuck her to keep my end of the bargain."

I don't love liars.

I can't.

I'm including myself in that rhetoric.

"Then her plan has failed spectacularly, and so has mine, by all accounts. Please… Just think about what I have said." I watch his features rearrange themselves into something even colder. The introspective part of the evening is done, and now it's time for business. "There is another reason why I came here tonight," he says, clearing his throat. "I came to thank you for your services these past few years, and to let you know that they are no longer required. The *Semion* has found a suitable replacement in Marseille."

My blinding inferno starts raging again. I don't want his business, but he's gone and stolen my thunder.

"A fake for a wife and a loss of fifty million a year revenue in laundered money." My smirk is a shadow of its former itself. "This is a truly illuminating evening, Dubov. May I ask why you've taken this decision?"

"I believe it is for best."

"Did you come to it yourself, or did Eloise Dubois have any input? I understand she's not such a big fan of mine."

He goes very still.

"Why did you visit her two hours ago?" I say idly. "Store closing is at six p.m. You're a Bratva *Pakhan*, not a fire starter. There's no need to go about rekindling old flames on my Riviera."

"She has nothing to do with this." He rises to his feet and slams his fists down on my desk. "She is an old friend, nothing more."

"I believe this is the most animated you've been since you stepped into my office," I drawl. "Does your wife know, or is she still hedging her bets on Marie replacing her? Speaking of which, where is shark-bait this evening? I must thank her for her piss poor contribution to Ielena's wedding outfit."

Ielena, not Issa.

"Your parentage is the only thing that is stopping me from razing your casino to the ground, Knight."

"My *parentage*?" I let out a rough chuckle. "If I'm reliant on them, I'm screwed. They were murdered in a London council estate flat fourteen years ago. I have no lines. No origin. My family tree is as barren as the Virgin fucking Mary before God decided to switch up the game plan."

"Is that so?"

That dark glint is back, making me want to scoop out his eyeballs and crush the mysteries out of them.

Instead, I rise to my feet, my patience paper thin and flaking. "I think it's time for you to leave now, Dubov. But before you do, I have a parting gift." There's a dull thud as the butt of Frankie's gun connects with Maxim's temple.

By the time Dubov reaches for his own gun, mine is already kissing his forehead.

Chapter Twenty-Four

ISSA

I wake to suffocating stillness, with the sheets tangled around my legs and my hair slick with sweat. Even the lapping waves at the hull sound dull and distant somehow. The blinds are down, and the dark is a disorientating blur of shapes and angles.

Stretching my hand out, I caress air and emptiness.

Aiden.

My father.

I sit bolt upright as my iPhone starts beeping. Tracking the white glow across the room to his desk, I fish the device out of my purse. My stomach lurches when I see who's calling.

"Maxim?" I gasp out. "Why are you calling me on an unsecured line?"

"He knows," he slurs. "How the hell does he know, *Dorogaya moya*? How does Aiden Knight know about Karina and me?"

"Are you drunk? Have the British been in contact about her? Was her operation successful?"

"So far so good."

"Thank God." I tip my head back to stop the tears of relief. "Did you sell us out, Issa?"

"Never!" I'm horrified he would think that. "You two are my family, Maxim. I'd do anything for you. I'm *doing* everything for you." I grab a white towel from Aiden's en suite and wrap it around my naked body. "He was asking and asking. I had to tell him *something*. He doesn't know about... He promised me he wouldn't say anything to Zaccaria. Did he tell my father?"

"Not yet."

"This time tomorrow, Maxim." A sob swells up in my chest with an army of many. "This time tomorrow we'll be gone, and none of this will matter anymore."

But it will... I know this week is going to haunt me forever.

"Your *ublyudok* of a husband can do a lot of damage in twenty-four hours. You should see what he's done tonight in two." There's a loud crash in the background and a volley of angry Russian. "There's something else... Why didn't you tell me—?" This time there's a bang and the line goes loud and fuzzy, as if the device if being pressed tightly against fabric.

"Maxim?" I urge. "Are you there?"

"You need to get off his yacht, Issa." My body goes cold. "He's on his way back right now and he's not happy... I've got to go."

"Maxim!"

I stare at my dead cell, long after the lights have faded and I'm lost in the darkness again.

What does Aiden know?

Fear kickstarts my adrenaline. I throw on my dress and grab my shoes and purse. I sprint, barefoot, all the way down to my cabin, my thoughts dashing against the rocks in a turbulent storm.

Crashing through the door, I'm heading for the closet when a heavy hand clamps across my mouth and pushes me headfirst into the bed. The mattress muffles my screams before I'm flipped over onto my back and straddled by a dead weight across my hips and thighs.

"Can't breathe," I wheeze as my hands are wretched above my head and held there, and I'm left blinking frantically in this new darkness.

"That's the least of your problems, bitch," growls a cut-glass accent that chills my skin.

"Felix? What are you doing? Let me go."

"Nope, uh-uh. Not happening. Not until you explain why Knight went all judge and jury on your father tonight." *He did? But he—* "Did you know? Did you fucking know?"

"Know what?" I croak.

"It's tit for tat in the criminal world. Shit went down tonight, and now tomorrow's deal is looking mighty shaky."

"No, I—"

"You gave me your word, Issa, so it's punishment time for lying bitches."

There's a shadow of movement above me, and then a rocket is exploding across my left cheek—the *crack* of the brutal slap echoing around the cabin. It's pain on a double beat. Another explodes across my jaw, and the taste of metal erupts into my mouth.

I'm gasping and spluttering as he shifts his weight to aim another at my rib cage. My pitiful noises turn to groans. Terrified, I try to roll over and crawl away, but he yanks me back by my foot.

"Knight's lost his mind over you, so I'm intrigued to find

out what golden pussy tastes like." The next thing I know, my dress is being ripped from my body. "You tell anyone about this and he gets an anonymous phone call about his wife. You hear me?"

"No!" Kicking out frantically, my heel connects with his crotch.

"You fucking whore!" he hisses, letting go of me immediately.

My eyes are adjusting to the lack of light. I can see a large dark shadow bent over by the bed. Scrabbling backward on my elbows, I run out of mattress and end up as a crumpled heap on the floor. I'm half-crawling, half-stumbling toward the en suite, when I'm yanked backward by my hair and thrown onto the bed again.

"Someone help me!" I scream before his hand is smothering my mouth again and his full weight is pressing me down into the mattress.

He punches me in the side of the head, and then a blinding white light hits my streaming eyes. Cringing away, I feel his weight leave my body, followed by a dull thud as his hits the floor.

"You mixing up your fucking pay grade, Felix?" comes a familiar drawl. "Attempted rape of my wife isn't included in your benefits package."

Slick, savage sounds of fist on bone come next, interspersed with sickening crunches, whimpers of pain and grunts of exertion.

Wincing, I yank the remains of my dress down as Aiden pulls out his gun from his back waistband and calmly fires three bullets into the crumpled white and red heap on the floor.

After that, there are no more whimpers.

With his gun still outstretched toward the body, he lifts his gaze to meet mine, his heavy brows knitting together with a fresh fury as he takes in the state of my face.

"That motherfucker," he growls, firing another three rounds into the dead body as Frankie bursts into the cabin.

"What the hell is going on?"

I watch him glance between the corpse and me as Maxim's words filter into my brain, past all the hurt and the shock.

"You need to get the hell off his yacht, Issa. He knows."

"It's a goddamn mess, that's what's going on. Clean it up," orders Aiden, sliding his gun back into his waistband and turning his attention back to me. "You okay there, *halfway*?" He takes a step in my direction and I flinch away. His eyes are violent seas. His anger hasn't dissipated, and I'm next in the firing line.

"Well, look what we have here," exclaims Frankie as he checks the body, holding up a couple of blood-stained burner cell phones and a gun. "Interpol standard issue, if I'm not mistaken. They love their archaic shit."

Aiden's head snaps back to him. "That limey bastard. He's been working for me for two years…"

"He *is* Interpol," I rasp.

"How the hell do you know that?"

"Whoever he is, his contract's been officially terminated, both as a deckhand and an undercover agent." Frankie makes to stand, clucking in annoyance. "I'll get onto the clean-up crew right away. I'll see if I can track down his handler as well."

I swing my legs off the bed. There's a deep ache resonating in my body as I stagger toward the en suite. Ramming the bolt home, I stare at the wreck of me in the mirror above the sink. My top lip has split and my left cheek is swelling. I look like a manifestation of all the chaos going on inside me.

I'm exhausted.

Exhausted from the lies, the deceit... From pretending I don't care about this man, *this killer*, when every fiber of my being is screaming the contrary.

Fighting back tears, I rest my forehead against the cool of the mirror. "I tried inhaling your sonnet, Karina," I whisper, "but only dirt came back out again. Help me. Please help me... I can't do this anymore. I'm breaking into pieces. I need to put my faith in something other than hope for once."

"Why don't you start with me?"

Startled, I swing back around. I didn't lock the door apparently because Aiden's standing in the doorway, slouched against the frame—a tall drink of everything wicked and wanton, as usual.

Keeping ours gazes fixed, he loosens his top button, shrugs off his black suit jacket, and starts to roll up his sleeves. He switches on the faucet next to me and runs his bloody hands under the water. I watch the swirls of pink become weaker and weaker, and then he's taking a towel from the rail and running it under the water, too. Once he's done, he moves to stand in front of me.

"Sit up on the vanity. Let me take a look at you."

Trembling, I do as he says, trying not to flinch again as he turns my face toward the light. His five o'clock shadow mirrors the circles under his eyes. Beneath his tan, he's as tired as I am.

"How did it go with my father?" I whisper.

"It was...satisfying." He shoots me a look to gage my reaction.

"Is the Riviera deal still on?"

"Without a doubt. I just learned that Aleksandr Dubov will do anything to stop Zaccaria breathing flames up his arse." After a while, he hums his verdict on my face. "The good news is I've had worse fights with Frankie's Escalade." When I don't smile, he plants a shockingly tender kiss to my forehead. "Nothing's broken, you're just busted up a little."

Cut me open, Aiden, and you'll see the real damage.

"How far did he go?" He daubs the damp towel against my lip. His movements are jerky and stiff. There's anger in his touch, which makes me instantly wary.

"Not that far." I wince at the sting.

"Far enough."

"I've never seen you kill before."

"You better get used to it, princess. It's a regular occurrence." There's a pause. "How did you know he was Interpol?"

The lie is right there on my tongue, but it won't seem to leave my mouth. The truth is barging its way to front instead, with my lips negligent security guards.

Meanwhile there are noises in the cabin. I glance through the open doorway to see three tall men standing over the body with Frankie. One is holding a roll of plastic tarp, and the other a yellow bag of workman's tools.

"You don't need to see that shit." Aiden leans over and kicks the door shut. "Let's hang out on the same side of this en suite for once." Smoothing the mess of dark hair away from my face, he tosses the towel into the sink and rests his hands on either side of my legs, trapping me against the vanity.

"It seems a long time since that night," I say, smiling weakly.

"Time flies when you're having fun."

We stare at each other for a beat.

"So," he says, breaking the silence first. "There's this game I used to play with a woman I liked... I asked her a question, and then she'd do the same to me, after an agreeably informative answer, of course."

"*Liked?*" I search his face for the worst kind of confirmation.

"Like," he corrects. "Against my better judgement."

"What does the truth really mean to you, Aiden?" I whisper. "Was it lost in the woods fourteen years ago, or are you still searching for it?" I reach up and cup his jaw, feeling the weight, the power… "Will it set you free when you find it, or will it trap you inside a new cage?"

"I'm all for taking chances, Issa. I'm taking a goddamn chance just being in here with you after what your father shared with me over a glass of my two-thousand-euro-a-bottle whiskey."

"Even if it means you end up hating…"

Me.

He takes my face between his palms, making sure to avoid all the swollen parts. "You're a razorblade, princess," he states huskily. "I'm trying to drink it away rather than admit to it, but you've sliced down to parts of me I'd forgotten existed."

"I can feel your strength drilling down into my soul."

"That's not all I want to be drilling… Even when you're hurting. Even when I'm a selfish bastard for admitting it." He leans in to kiss me, and then seems to think better of it.

"Ask me that question again," I urge, feeling his hot breath on my face. There's whiskey there, and something else I don't want to admit to. "Before I get too scared to answer it."

He nods slowly, reluctantly, as if he knows the pin is about to be pulled on us.

"How did you know Felix was Interpol?"

"Because he had links to MI6."

There's a pause. "What's British Intelligence got to do with it?"

The hand grenade slips from my fingers. "Because I'm working with them, too."

He sucks in a sharp breath, but he doesn't move away. He absorbs my deception like a body blow. "How much have you told them?"

"Nothing." I shudder as the first of my many weights slips from my aching shoulders. "It was never about…" I grind to a halt, trying to organize my thoughts. There's so much to admit to. *There's so much to share.* "Felix was onto you for the money laundering through your casino. He was trying to link Zaccaria and my father, with you as the common denominator. The Riviera deal made that link possible. As for me—"

"Are you an agent?" His fingers tighten around my face.

"*No,*" I deny, imploring him to believe me with a single word. "I'm just a woman trying to save my sister. Maxim cut a deal with the British four weeks ago for their protection. We can't simply run away, Aiden. Not with Karina being so sick. It's too easy for Zaccaria to hunt us down… It's a miracle he hasn't found her already."

"What was the trade-off?" His voice is like stone.

"Insider intel on some secret society that Zaccaria's involved in." The words are flowing freely now, and I'm stumbling in my haste to explain everything. I want so desperately to bring him back to our lightness. "Whatever it is, it's big. They've been working on it for years, but they've never gotten close to him before, because Zaccaria doesn't trust anyone, and he never leaves Sicily. Then the Riviera deal happened. With Karina gone, I was all set to marry Luca in her place. I was told to infiltrate *La Famiglia* and find out all I could about—"

"*La Società Villefort,*" he says grimly.

"It was never meant to be you, Aiden." My voice falters. "I was supposed to marry a bad man with bad intentions, not a bad one with good."

"Interesting choice of words when you just watched me murder a man... Why the bruises? The branding? Your father told me you asked him to do it."

"I wanted to show Zaccaria I wasn't easily bullied. That they could beat me and torture me all they wanted, but I'd never crack. I also needed an exit strategy from Sicily. I figured it would take less than a couple of weeks for a proud and stupid man like Luca to reject his ruined wife."

"He wouldn't have let you go, Issa," he says angrily. "You would have been pushing up the sidewalks with all the other corpses."

"It was reckless and rash. I know that now. But people make desperate decisions for desperate reasons," I say, echoing my thoughts from the other day.

"Wait a minute." He finally drops his hands from my face, and the loss of his intimacy is a bitter chill. "You say that the British have been building a case against Zaccaria and *La Società Villefort* for years? That's impossible. Zaccaria was only accepted into the fold three months ago."

"I'm just going on what they told me."

He reels away with his hands in his hair. "Fuck!" he roars at the white and gray calacatta marble tiles.

"I'm so sorry—"

"Is that everything?" He advances on me again, looking like a man on the edge. "Are all your stones unturned, *halfway*? What about your dead sister? What about your grief-struck family? What about the fact that my own wife is a goddamn liar and a traitor?" He moves in closer and I refuse to look away, even when he pinches my chin between his fingers. "What about the fact that, despite all this, I can't stop thinking about how much I need to be inside her, or how much I want to pretend that this goddamn evening never happened?" He stops then, breathing harshly, looking as shocked as I am by his admittance. "Fuck this shit. I need a drink."

He walks out, slamming the door behind him.

Chapter Twenty-Five

AIDEN

I stalk through the cabin, past the blood-soaked carpet, and I don't stop until I hit the main saloon bar. I need more than a drink, I need a miracle, but a large bottle of Glenfiddich will have to suffice. Two betrayals in one evening is making everything hurt.

I don't bother with a glass. I take the whole bottle outside and I stand on the bow of my superyacht at midnight, swigging freely like that kid in the park again.

I'm trying my damnedest to hate Issa, but I can't. I imagine pulling the trigger on her like I did Felix, but the pain in indescribable. I consider asking her to leave like I've done to so many women in the past—I'd even get Frankie to drive her anywhere she wanted to go—but the thought of losing all that grace makes me want to pull the trigger on myself.

Beautiful, kind, selfless, mixed-up, deceitful Issa.

Everything she does is out of love for her sister. She channels all that pain and suffering and uncertainty for that single emotion. I channel mine for hate and revenge.

I take another swig and curse her name to the wind. This loose feeling in my chest is like a wound now. I can't shore it up. It keeps seeping things I don't recognize. I want to dive into the dark ocean to wash them away, but the ocean breeze keeps whispering hope, and the moon speaks of a faith I find myself daring to believe in.

I only realize how drunk I am when I go to put the empty bottle on the table and I miss the edge by a foot. Staggering backward, I curse as shards of broken glass go flying across the deck.

"Don't touch it, you'll cut yourself." Issa steps out of the saloon with a red blanket wrapped around her shoulders. Her hair is wild and unkempt and her lip is bleeding again, but she's the only woman I see...

She's the only one I ever will.

She takes me by the arm and leads me over to the line of cream couches. Once upon a time, Maxim Lebedev sat here and warned me that Ielena Dubova was so much more than she seemed.

No shit, Sherlock.

"How does it feel?" I slur, collapsing into one and pulling her down on top of me—feeling her fragility and tightening my arms to stop it from slipping away.

"How does what feel?"

"To be good? To be so fucking altruistic you bleed your precious colors." I swipe my finger across her lip, catching a bead of blood. I hold it up to the moon and it shimmers silver. "See?"

"Liars aren't altruistic, Aiden."

"They are when they're my wife."

Tell her.

She curls up like a kitten on my lap and we sit in the rocky stillness of *us* for a moment. People talk about the calm before the storm, but this is the calm before the epic twenty-eight-foot tsunami into monsoon season with no survivors.

"I thought you'd kill me when you found out."

Tell her.

"Doesn't work that way, sweetheart." There's a pause. "Your sister's going to be okay. She made it through her operation. Her team is one of the best."

Frowning, she sits up and my arm slithers from her shoulder. "H-how do you know that?"

"I tracked her down." I keep my gaze steady as I drop the H-bomb. "I pieced together the clues from our conversations. I found your drawings. I had you under constant surveillance... You married a real piece-of-shit, Issa," I add, shaking my head at her ruefully.

"My drawings? But why would you even...?"

Boom.

I see the shadow pass across her face. A second later, she's scrambling up from my arms. "Please, no," she whispers, casting the red blanket aside to reveal the remnants of her torn white and amber silk dress. "Aiden, not you. You—"

"Wed you for a reason," I say bleakly. "First name was for your hand. Second name was for your sister's head."

"What names? What are you talking about?"

"For every noble reason, there's a dissolute one."

"I-I don't believe you." Her face is as white as virgin snow. "If you've known about her, why haven't you told Zaccaria yet?"

"Don't go searching for foot holds when you're climbing a mountain of shit... It's only a matter of time, in that respect."

"No," she says again, shaking her head at me. "You wouldn't do that."

"Don't presume, and never assume." My own head is starting to spin. "I'm not the man you think I am, Issa. It would take six years, not six days, to understand my motives."

"I know that you're an even bigger liar than I am! Worse still, you lie to yourself. You fight it constantly, but you hear the cadence in this marriage just as much as I do. The moments that shine on us are so blinding. What could possibly be worth destroying—"

Us.

"Revenge," I say simply, staggering to my feet like a kid who can't hold his drink. "And don't talk crap about how special our marriage is. Thirty minutes ago, you told me you'd cut a deal with MI6 to disappear."

"I told you because I wanted more." She sucks in a ragged breath. "Don't sell out Karina. Come with us."

"No, thank you."

The tears are streaming down her face. I want to catch them and taste her pain.

"I'm serious—"

"So am I. This is my world. My kingdom. *My Riviera—*"

"Your vengeance," she adds bitterly.

"I need another drink."

"Fourteen years," she says, grabbing hold of my arm. Her face is a canvas of pain, but it's the agony in her soft brown eyes that's the hardest to look at. "Are *you* the Count of Monte Cristo, Aiden? Have you locked your pain away for all that time? You're rich beyond your wildest dreams—superyachts, black Maseratis, casinos—but you're still locked in a prison cell. Tell me, what did Zaccaria offer you in exchange for your soul?"

"You know nothing." I shrug her off easily.

"Then show me," she pleads, following me inside. "I cut myself open for you earlier. I bled every failing and every untruth. Now my sister's life is in your hands. You owe me an explanation if you're planning on destroying us."

"It's a *fait accompli*, Issa." I pause with my fingers on another Glenfiddich bottle, catching sight of the tattoo on my wrist.

"Not all ravens have their wings clipped, Aiden." She comes to stand next to me at the bar.

"You're right." I wrench the cap off and take a deep draft. "After I disclose your sister's location tomorrow, I'll be as free as the proverbial."

"Then I want you to fuck me."

"*What?*" I crash the bottle down in shock. Her chest is rising and falling to the rhythm of her fear, and I can't take my eyes off it.

"I want you to fuck me so hard that the truth has no choice but to come spilling from your lips."

"You've got your sex ed mixed up, sweetheart. That's not how it goes." Even so, my cock is as hard as stone.

She closes the gap between us until all I can smell is her new perfume. "If you can't say what you need to my face, say it to the space between us. Say it to my mouth, my hair, my pussy... Just *say it*." She tugs the remains of her silk dress over her head and stands there naked in just a pair of white lace panties and the small square dressing taped to her chest.

She's fucking perfect—tall, slender, elegant as hell. Her breasts are small and firm, and my mouth hungers for a taste.

"I'll hurt you."

"Not as much as you're hurting yourself."

"Jesus Christ, Issa," I curse. "Some bastard just tried to rape you." I turn back to the bar, curling my fist around the neck of the bottle. Temptation is as much of a bitch as regret.

The next thing I know, she's plastering her naked body to my back, her hands are slipping around my waist, and my lust is kicking up a gear into something savage and primal.

"This is the one time you don't need to do the right thing, Aiden."

"I never do the right thing."

"You'd be surprised."

"I fucking hate surprises. And you're only doing this to save your sister."

"No, Aiden," she says quietly. "I'm doing this to save you."

My self-control shatters. I turn so fast her lips are still making declarations at me.

Grabbing her by her waist, I slam her up against the nearest wall, sending pictures flying as she cries out in shock. I taste it like it's my last meal, driving my tongue so deep inside her mouth that she has no choice but to submit to me.

She's kissing me back just as hard, moaning into my heart and soul.

Dragging my lips away, savoring metal from her cut mouth, I whirl her around to grind my erection into her so violently her palms, breasts, and cheek are pressed flat against the wall.

"You really want my animal?" I snarl.

"Yes."

"You want me to lose it?"

"Yes."

She doesn't even whimper when I tear her panties from her body and kick her legs apart. Pushing my pants and boxers away, I stoop down to line up my cock with her slick entrance.

"Do it," she gasps out. "Take me. Use me."

"I'll fucking shatter you."

"I'll mend us both."

"You asked for this, *halfway*."

Grabbing her hips, I tug her back to give her balance, and then I'm driving into her so deep my balls are touching skin.

"Shit!" she screams as I close my eyes in ecstasy. She's so tight she's gripping every single part of me.

I circle my hips and open her up even wider, and she mewls into the wall. "You want me to stop?" I taunt, repeating the same action, feeling her body tremble and strain.

"No, Aiden. I want you to let go."

"Then brace yourself."

Withdrawing completely, I slam back into her, the air whooshing from her lungs and forming condensation on the picture frame glass next to her mouth. I do it again and again, watching the same mark darken as my soul lightens. Her wetness is spilling down her thighs. She comes once, twice…convulsing and milking me as I destroy her barely broken-in pussy.

Heat is pooling at the base of my spine. The final rush comes up so fast I'm groaning out her name before I'm emptying myself. I come so hard and for so long, it feels like I'm leaving a version of myself inside her.

Afterward, we collapse forward together as her strength gives out. I ram my fist into the wall to stop the collision, and then we're slithering to the floor in a chaotic heap. I cushion the fall, pulling her onto my lap and wrapping my arms around her as we ride out the rest of the storm together—racing to calm our madness.

I never knew you could feel this close to a woman. She's slipped inside my skin. She's making our hearts beat in sync.

We're not perfect. We're messy and dysfunctional, driven together by circumstance and linked by forces that ambushed us and caught us unawares. But we're us. *There's an us now.* And that knowledge is coercing words from my mouth that I never thought I'd speak again.

"My parents were murdered, Issa." That single sentence is like the long, slow walk to hell. So many memories come crashing down on me that I have to take a moment before continuing. "I was just a kid from a council estate in Brixton, South London. The mafia didn't exist. Money didn't exist. Until I came home one night to find my mother drowned in the kitchen sink and my father's decapitated body stinking up the hallway. There was a decade-old note from Zaccaria stuffed in his mouth, but nothing else to go on. When the police shut the case down citing some bullshit reason, I followed that note to Sicily."

"Do *La Famiglia* know who killed your parents?" she asks quietly.

"Zaccaria said he could track them down by joining *La Società Villefort*. Said he owed it to my father, but it was a fourteen-year waiting list and I'd need to work for *La Famiglia* in the interim. What kid questions a don like him?" I add dryly. "Rich, powerful bastards move in mysterious ways. I hate them all, except Rick Sanders. There's a kind of honor in his sin. A corrupt logic. He skims the top off life without damaging the reefs underneath. As for Zaccaria, I was aimless, so he rooted me to a cause. He taught me how to kill, to lie, to steal, greed… I fucking enjoyed it, too. It filled a hole where decency used to live."

She blinks at me slowly. "And you were willing to make this sacrifice?"

"My parents were good people. Better people than I'll ever

be. They didn't deserve what life threw at them. My father was a mechanic. My mother worked part time in the local library. They should be in London right now, laughing at the TV and drinking cheap wine on a Friday night."

"Did you get the first name from Zaccaria?"

"Yes."

She hesitates. "That's where you went on our wedding night?"

I nod.

"And the second is in exchange for my sister's whereabouts?"

"I need that name, Issa…"

"No matter the cost?"

I can't lose her. I can't fucking lose her. Not when it's taken me thirty years to find her.

That certainty brings everything into sharp focus.

"Not if we're clever about it," I say as an idea starts to form.

Chapter Twenty-Six

ISSA

"**Y**ou know you do this weird thing with your forehead when you're thinking."

"You can't think in your sleep," he replies huskily, keeping his eyes shut.

"You can't talk in your sleep either, so you must be awake." I trace my name into his hard bicep.

"Is this pillow talk?" He tuts in disgust. "I knew there was a good reason why I kicked women out once playtime was over."

"You can't kick me out. I'm your wife."

"You were asking me about a divorce yesterday."

"I've changed my mind. I think we should get a dog instead."

He chuckles and slings a heavy arm around my waist, enticing me into his warmth. We're lying side by side, naked in his bed. The blinds are open and dawn is setting the walls of his cabin alight. We tore down our own walls with bloodied hands last night and now our light is constant. Last night I forced him to become undone, and he fell apart in the most beautiful way. We talked about a better time to come, about the ruin of his past… About pooling all our skills and resources into deceiving one of the most powerful crime bosses in the world.

"And what would we call this dog?"

"Madonna."

"*Madonna*?" This prompts one heavy eyelid to open and unleash a laser beam of disapproval. "No."

"No?"

"Dogs should have proper dog names like Max and Rex. They *shouldn't* be called after a pop star with a Botox problem."

I gasp in mock horror. "That's blasphemy. And because you said no, I'm definitely going to call her that now."

"Defy me at your peril," he growls, tugging me closer.

"Gladly." My smile fades into his chest. "I'm so scared, Aiden."

"Stick to what we discussed and we'll be sailing out of this port tonight and never returning."

"But your casino…your bars…."

"I have money. I have you. I'll have that second name, and hopefully the name of the man who ordered the hits. The rest is just noise." Once he'd figured out a way to keep me *and* have his revenge, everything else fell by the wayside. "We need to keep MI6 on our side until your sister is transferred to a private facility. It shouldn't be too hard. All they care about is having enough evidence to bring down *La Società Villefort*, so let's give them what they want."

"And Interpol?"

"Let me to worry about them. I have strings I can pull to make the law dance and the bodies disappear." He drops a chaste kiss on the top of my head. "Are you going into Cannes today?"

"I want to say goodbye to Eloise."

He's silent for a moment. "Fine, but I want you back here by lunchtime. Zaccaria's called the meeting for seven, although we don't have the location yet. We need to get you wired up and ready."

I roll onto my front to watch him doze. "Tell me something, Aiden… Do you feel different this morning?"

"I feel hungover," he rumbles. "I missed dinner, and I drank a shedload."

"I'm serious."

There's a pause. "My chest feels looser."

"Mine, too."

"My knuckles hurt like a bitch from beating up a man."

He kills and maims to defend me, and I love him for it.

"And my back hurts from fucking a woman so hard I lost my damn mind."

"Is she pretty?" I inquire innocently.

"No, she's not pretty." He finally opens both eyes and blinds me with calm seas and clear horizons. "She's so beautiful she'll make a man forget why he was fighting so hard to push her away in the first place."

Our lips meet, and the next hour is a blur of skin and him.

Steeling myself, I step under the showerhead, breathing calmly through my surges of panic. I count off each second as a new milestone for success before I'm pulling away, gasping and spluttering.

Forty.

I'm elated. I've never managed more than thirty before.

Walking back into the cabin, I discover some of the dresses Aiden bought for me the other day laid out on the comforter, along with a selection of underwear and shoes. The man in question is standing over by the window with a panoramic view of Monaco as his backdrop.

It will never be as breathtaking as him, though.

He's barefoot and talking on his cell, dressed in blue jeans and a white V-neck T-shirt. He wears his Armani suits like black-plated armor, and he wears his casuals like a golden God.

I cast my mind back to the moment I first met him. Back then, he was all about the surface colors. This new range and depth are even more dazzling than Van Gogh's *The Red Vineyard*.

He's giving up his businesses for me.

He's not betraying me.

He's risking his life for me.

Somehow, he's come up with a plan that's going to free us all from the shackles of *La Famiglia*, appease MI6, and avenge his parents' murder—and it frightens me more than he'll ever know.

There isn't an option to fail.

Hanging up, he rakes a lazy, seductive stare over my body that has me instantly fidgeting.

"No time for that, sweetheart," he says, reading me like a book. "We've got a busy day ahead of us." He gestures to the clothes on his bed. "The clean-up crew have finished, but you're moving in here now. Your make-up and purses are next to the bed... Get dressed," he orders, moving toward the door. "Frankie's giving you a lift in today. He's waiting on the top deck for you."

"Aiden?"

"Yeah?" He pauses in the doorway, and I want to Polaroid

the moment so I can shake it and stare at it over and over again.

"Can I get that number for Nina Sanders? I was hoping to send her some of my artwork."

"Sure. I'll forward it on."

I fashion a smile for him, but it's one of relief, too.

That's something else I haven't shared with Aiden yet… I always have a backup plan.

———

I don't have time to finish my make-up before we leave, so I'm sitting in the back of Frankie's Escalade with a mascara wand in one hand and a mirror in the other. He's a good driver, but the twists and turns of the mountainous *Moyenne Corniche* are making me curse at him under my breath. Fortunately, the swelling on my cheek and upper lip has gone down loads and my foundation is covering up the rest of it.

I'm trying not to think about the man who did this to me, or what my husband did to him. Life in the underworld desensitizes you to the worst of crimes and plays havoc with your morals. It's a constant switch to survival mode, where sin is the ultimate weapon.

"I'll try this again when we arrive," I tell Frankie as we hit a dip in the road and a black streak goes shooting up into my hairline. Rubbing it away, I catch his eye in the rearview mirror. "Thanks so much for driving me today."

He grunts and blasts me with a hostile missile of a glare.

Have I driven a wedge between him and Aiden? The Riviera has been Frankie's home as much as his for the past four years. What happens tonight is going to impact Frankie's life as much as our own.

"Your husband asked me to hang around and drive you home again."

"I take it he told you about—"

"Yeah, he told me."

There's a pause. "Are you going to help us?"

"Does it sound like I have a choice?" He switches the radio to mute. "Listen, I've known him a long time, Issa, and I've seen him make a lot of crazy decisions. I've never seen him make ones like he's making today, though. He's out of his mind if he thinks he can pull it off."

I choose my next words carefully. "You sound like you disapprove."

"Aiden does whatever the fuck he wants to, lady, and for twenty years I've been okay with that. This plan, though…" He trails off with a shake of his head.

"I know how close you are. If you're not on board—"

"Oh, I'm on board," he snaps back. "Aiden's like a big brother to me. I'd never let him down, but that doesn't mean I have to like it."

"He'll find out who ordered the hits first," I say, rushing to reassure him. "He won't be leaving that meeting until he has answers."

"Yeah, we'll see."

There's a strange atmosphere in the car, like someone has sucked out all of the warm air and replaced it with chilly unease. Frankie shifts his massive frame and rakes his hand through his hair, and an involuntary shiver courses through me. The moment passes and he switches the radio back on. We don't speak again until we're pulling into the same side street where Aiden parked yesterday.

"Come and meet Eloise," I say as we make our way up *Rue*

Meynadier together.

He shakes his head. "I'm good."

More silence.

"Frankie, wait." We've reached her store now and I can't take the tension any longer. "Are you angry with me about this?"

"I told you not to go and buy a shovel, Issa... I said you wouldn't like what you dug up."

"I'm trying to use that shovel to help lay us a new foundation."

He hesitates. "You really mean that? Because Aiden deserves a shot at something better."

"We all do."

"Nah, not me." I watch him glance up and down the street. "You two were sparks from the beginning. It was always going to happen, no matter what he told himself. I'm a part of tonight because he's earned his happy ending. And so have you, by the sounds of it." He stops and runs his hand across his jaw. "Whatever goes down later, I want you to promise me something: be the family he's always wanted."

"Frankie, you're scaring me. Is something wrong?"

He blows out a heavy breath. "Secrets are like dogs," he mutters. "Some are predictable. Others bite hard when you least expect it." He swings back to find me staring. "Go." He motions at the shop. "Say your goodbyes. I'll be waiting here."

Giving him a worried look, I go to open the door but it doesn't budge.

Locked.

That's strange.

Peering through the glass, I see that all the lights are off as well.

"Everything okay?" he calls out.

I check my cell, but there's no message. "Opening time was half an hour ago… She should be here by now."

"Do you have a key?"

"Yes." I find the one that Eloise gave me yesterday at the bottom of my purse.

Clicking the lock and stepping into the shop, I'm greeted by a sickly, metallic odor that makes me glance back at Frankie in concern. He's by my side in an instant. I know he smells it, too, because he's already pulling out his gun.

"Get behind me," he orders as fear explodes in every chamber of my heart.

The place is dark and empty and bathed in shadow. All the vibrant colors have been stultified. The odor is growing stronger and stronger the more we move toward the back room.

"Stay here."

I hover by the counter as he slowly pushes open the door, an inch at a time. When I hear him cursing, I rush forward. He swings his arm out to try to block my view, but it's too late.

Red.

Why is everything red?

He's grabbing at my shoulders now and trying to push me backward, but I see everything: the twisted angle of her body, her glassy, unstaring eyes, the crimson wound where her elegant throat used to be.

On the wall above her brutal wreckage are the words *La Società Villefort*, painted in her blood.

"Eloise," I rasp.

"There's nothing more you can do for her," says Frankie. "She's gone, Issa."

"She can't be dead! Help her! Call an ambulance or something!" I'm hysterical as grief ties rocks around my heart and tosses me into a familiar pool of pain.

"We need to get out of here."

"I'm not leaving her! I'm waiting for the police!"

"You're Knight's wife," he snarls, shaking me hard. "That's not their favorite name around here. He has them in his pocket, but they're always looking for ways to make holes in it." Slamming the back room door, he drags me kicking and screaming to the front of the shop.

"Let me go!"

"Listen to me," he says, shaking me again. "If anything happens to you, Aiden will start shooting up the Riviera, and that's not going to help anyone. I'll call the teams on the way back to Monaco. They'll treat her body with respect."

Body.

Eloise is just a body.

All that color… *Gone.*

I choke on another suffocating wave of grief. Every way I look I see her designs, her creations, *her life.* I close my eyes and I see a gently lined face with laughter and patience in her eyes, sitting in a café in a jade dress with a thirteen-year-old child so lost in the world she needed a stranger to give her direction.

"Why would anyone want to kill her? She's the sweetest, kindest—"

"I don't—Issa, watch out!"

The first bullet passes so close to my face the breeze caresses my hair, and then I'm hitting the floor and coldness is slamming into my skin.

Five more rounds are fired into Eloise's shop after that. There's glass flying everywhere and it's anarchy on the narrow street outside. Everybody is screaming and running in different directions as chaos and fear spread Chinese whispers up and down the narrow street.

There's a charged pause, and then the sound of five more deafening rounds as Frankie rears up and retaliates.

"Is there a back way to this place?" he yells out, falling back to the floor.

"I don't think so."

"Then we're going to have to run."

I gape at him in horror. "But what if the shooter is still out there?"

"Let me get a closer look." He crawls across the bed of broken glass toward the remains of the front window. "I can't see him."

"What if he's waiting for us?"

"Nah, I don't think that's his game plan." He rises to his feet and rams a fresh magazine into his gun. "They had a clear shot. He missed us on purpose. It's a warning." He glances down at me. "Jesus, you're shaking."

"Please take me back to Aiden, Frankie." I'm trying hard not to fall apart. *I need his arms. I need his comfort.*

Cannes is a ghost town as we weave our way back to the Escalade. Bags of abandoned shopping litter the cobblestones and sidewalks like dead paper bodies bleeding their consumerism. The sound of sirens is bruising the summer air as we turn into the side street.

We're a hundred meters out when a black vehicle powers up the road alongside us and swerves to a halt in an ugly squeal of brakes.

"Get in!" yells Maxim, ripping his sunglasses from his scarred face.

"Fuck off, Lebedev." Frankie pushes in front of me and reaches for his gun.

"*Ublyudok!* Your car has been compromised. It's wired to blow in one minute, and I'm not hanging around to see the fireworks."

"Is this your *Pakhan's* payback for last night? Is he feeling sore this morning?"

"Frankie? What—?"

"Just get in," Maxim roars. "I'll tell you once we're out of here, and not when I'm picking shrapnel out of my hair."

With a frustrated growl, Frankie wrenches open the back door and pushes me inside before jumping in next to Maxim.

I fumble for the seat, colliding with another hard body sat there. By the time I realize who it is, Maxim is screeching away from the curb and I'm flying forward into the empty space next to him.

"You," I cry in horror, seizing the grab rail.

"Hello, *kotyono*," says my father dryly, taking in my wild state and the cuts on my arms and face. "What trouble have you found yourself in now?"

Chapter Twenty-Seven

ISSA

"I have nothing to say to you!" I cry, pouring all of this morning's pain, shock, and anger into my rebuke. "And don't you dare call me that name. I haven't been your kitten since I was six years old."

Hearing the emotion in my voice, Frankie whips round and his expression blackens. "What the hell are you doing here, Dubov?" He pulls out his gun, and then braces himself against the door as Maxim takes another corner at top speed.

"I needed to see you, *kotyono*," my father says, ignoring my request.

"Is there even a car bomb?" I say, glaring at him. It's easier than looking at Maxim. He doesn't know that Aiden holds the keys to the treasure trove as well now. He doesn't know that all of our plans have changed. He'll be angry with me. He'll accuse me of putting Karina's life in jeopardy, and that's an unforgivable act in his eyes.

Instead of answering, my father flicks his hand at Frankie's gun. "Put that thing away."

"You're not the one who gives me orders, Dubov… I'm keeping it right here where we can all see it."

My father grimaces, and I notice the tight, pale pallor beneath his tan.

"Well?" I demand.

He shakes his head. "You're right. There is no bomb. But you wouldn't have spoken with me any other way."

"My God, it's always the same with you," I exclaim. "If you're not selling deceit, you're bartering with excuses. Please pull over when you can," I call out to Maxim as though he is a taxi driver.

"There's no need," says my father swiftly. "I only need five minutes of your time. Maxim is already circling back to your vehicle." He shifts in his seat and winces.

"What's wrong with you?" I ask, noticing his reaction.

"Your husband was free to show his displeasure with me last night. Didn't he tell you?"

"Tell me what?" I glance at Frankie, but he's not giving a damn thing away.

My father unbuttons the top of his shirt and pulls the left flap down. There, in exactly the same place where his insignia blemishes my skin is a black raven burned into his.

Regret bubbles up to my surface as he re-buttons his shirt. If I hadn't begged my father for his pain, Aiden wouldn't have given him his anger.

"Don't go to the meeting tonight," he says gruffly. "Put all of your hate for me aside and do this one thing." He pauses as another volley of police cars overtakes us. "I want you to know that I wish things had been different between us. As I explained to Aiden, I made a decision many years ago that I will always regret." He tries to take my hand, but I move it out of reach. "Money... Power... None of it matters without family."

"*Family?*" I can't believe what I'm hearing. "You acted like we didn't exist, Papa. You pushed us away and ignored us constantly. You made us feel like we were nothing. That our lives didn't count. That our problems didn't count. That our health..." I stop and force the tears from my eyes. How different our lives would have been if he'd been the father we deserved. Annika would still be alive. Karina wouldn't be recovering from a kidney transplant in a foreign hospital a million miles away.

"I'm concerned that your husband will make the same choice as me, *kotyono*. I don't want your life to be mired in more misery. I saw it in his eyes, whatever he says to you in the privacy of your bedroom, if it comes down to money and power or family, I am certain that he will make the same choice I did. That's just the type of man he is."

"None of this is making sense," I say wearily. "But I can assure you that Aiden is a far, far better man that you will ever be."

We're back in the side street again. No one speaks as Maxim pulls up to the curb in front of Frankie's Escalade.

"Wait," says my father as I reach for the door handle. "I've risked my life to say these words to you, Issa. You must promise me that you'll consider them."

"You're talking in riddles, Papa, and being tricked into this car and forced to see you again has only compounded an already painful morning. My friend—" A surge of emotion robs my next words from my mouth.

"Which friend?" he demands. "What has happened?"

"My friend who has the clothing store here in Cannes.

She—"

"Tell me, *kotyono*," he says, grabbing my arm and looking distraught.

"Let her go, Dubov," warns Frankie from the passenger seat.

"What has happened to Eloise Dubois?" He does as Frankie requests, but he still has the same wild look on his face. As for me, I'm shocked that he would remember her name from a single afternoon eleven years ago, and that his recollection would produce such a response.

"She's dead, Papa." I glance away so he can't see my tears.

"How?" he says gruffly.

"She was murdered."

What's left of his color drain from his cheeks, and then I'm watching my father—one of the most feared Bratva *Pakhans* in the whole of France—collapse to his knees, keening like an animal and crushed beneath an avalanche of grief.

Chapter Twenty-Eight

AIDEN

We all have flaws. Admittedly, I have more than most. Stick a vampire in front of a mirror and you won't see his reflection. Stick me in a courtroom and I'll vanish behind a stack of charges and indictments so tall, the judge will need a ladder to reach them.

Tonight, I need to take these flaws and build a goddamn army out of them.

It's five p.m., and I'm armed and ready. Sharp suit. Fitted shirt. A pocketful of fortitude and a trigger-happy smile. I check myself in the mirror and see a savage façade that only she can soften.

Striding back into the cabin, I slide my gun into my holster and grab my cell from my nightstand. The location for this evening's meeting has just come through. It's a medieval fortress on the outskirts of Monaco, toward the Italian boarder. Once the property of a media tycoon, it's now the temporary residence for the bad and the ugly, or whoever can stomach the eighty-million-euro price tag.

Issa mutters in her sleep suddenly, thrashing out with her arms, laying waste to the sheets as she tosses and turns. She's fighting demons that I want to slay for her. That I'm *planning* on slaying for her. She's meeting me in the middle, as usual.

Crouching down by the bed, I smooth away a strand of dark hair that's fallen across her forehead. It's damp with tears and grief, and I hate that I have to wake her so soon for more of the same.

"Is she really gone?" Her soft, broken lilt invades the quiet, and she lifts her hand to mine, holding it prisoner against her temple.

"Want me to spin it for you?" I say, frowning down at her.

"No, Aiden. No more lies. No more spinning." She lets go and rolls onto her back, blinking up at the ceiling. "When I was thirteen, I used to pretend that Eloise was our mother. We'd all live together in the small apartment above her store and we'd sketch dreams and designs on the kitchen table after school." She shakes her head, dislodging the memory from its dusty resting place. "God, I was so stupid... Idealism is such a flavorsome word."

"It tastes like black cherries to me." Sitting down on the bed next to her, I trace her swollen lips with a finger.

"Or chili chocolate?" She smiles weakly. "It's a sweet first bite before reality kicks in."

The corners of my mouth twitch. "That sounds like one of my lines."

"I like it when all of our lines blur."

Me, too.

I trace my finger downward to this beautiful, beating heart of hers. "You ready to go nuclear tonight?"

Issa nods. "I have more incentive than ever to destroy whatever this secret society is. I want answers just as much as you do." She falls into a troubled silence, and I know where her mind is wandering. "Do you think she suffered?"

"No."

One more white lie won't hurt.

She's been through enough, and I'll do anything to stop the pain flaring in those soft brown eyes. I've seen the unofficial forensics report. Eloise Dubois was a nighttime curio for a couple of ruthless bastards. Once playtime was over, they slit her throat with a blunt knife and watched her bleed out for twenty minutes.

It wasn't pretty.

It wasn't pleasant.

La Società Villefort are leaving a mess all over my town, and it's time to start issuing penalties.

Are you involved too, Zaccaria?

Have you ascended the ranks?

Are you pulling the strings like the wily old bastard I know you are?

She rolls onto her side to face me. "Do you think they were having an affair?"

Yes. But I'm not going to admit it. Why? Because she hates her father and she loved Eloise. No one wants to be haunted by images of a gazelle fucking a shark.

"You should have asked him outright."

"I never had the chance to. The wall rebuilt as quickly as it crumbled, and then he was ordering me and Frankie out of the car." She sits up, and draws her slim knees to her chest. "I've never seen him show emotion before, not even when Annika died. I never thought he was capable of it."

I make a note to tell Frankie to ditch the store footage as I stroke her head again, savoring her smallness, her vulnerability—all the more precious after someone took five shots at her this morning. Warning or not, that's a red card in my book.

"You never know what anyone's capable of until their world implodes." I chuck MI6's listening device onto the mattress. "Father Intelligence has been by and he didn't get stuck in the chimney. Time to mic up."

I catch the nervous glide in her throat, but she smiles like the bravest woman on earth. She shines like an angel and she fucks like a queen, and I want to fall to the ground and worship her.

"All the colors tonight," I tell her, glancing at the walk-in closet. "Blind him good, baby. Be the shining distraction we both need."

Her eyes are like glass. "For Eloise."

For her, for me, for all of us…

Château de Morcerf's driveway is lined with cypress trees, casting an arc of crossed shadow swords as we pass by underneath. The stone-gray château itself is perched on the side of a mountain, with the sky above a dusty blur of pinks, blues, and grays. True to her word, Issa is a blinding vision in the gold satin halter-neck slashed high to her thigh. Her real treasure lies just beyond that, and my hand is resting tantalizing close to it.

Frankie's driving—it's just us three musketeers—but he's been acting very un-Frankie-like throughout the journey. He keeps adjusting the rearview mirror, then toying with the half-opened packet of cigarettes in the change pocket next to the handbrake.

"If you light up one of those fuckers, you're walking home," I warn him as we approach the château's entrance.

"Always the big brother, huh?"

"I'm big in every sense of the word."

Still, I'm aware that I've made this decision without him: a decision that changes the course of all our lives. Ever since our parents died, he's followed me, supported me, *killed* for me...

He parks the Escalade by the sweeping front steps. Twilight has spawned outdoor lights, and the château is illuminated in the same vivid crimson as the writing on the business card that Rocco Rossi gave me. Black-suited security greet us, and it's only when we reach the raised portcullis that I notice the small, crimson key pins on their lapels.

La Società Villefort

I stop dead, and pull Issa closer to me. "Sweetheart?" I lean in with the pretense of kissing the side of her head. "That feeling of Frankie's is catching. I'm getting a bad case of it, too. If we get separated, make your way back to *The Cristo*. I've told the captain we sail at ten, no delays. Interpol are closing in on us and I can't hold them off. A search warrant is going to be issued at six a.m. tomorrow, and a warrant for my arrest is imminent."

I see the quick-fire panic in her eyes. "Aiden..."

"Shh," I soothe, projecting all the calm I don't feel into a crooked smile. I'm not even giving shit to Frankie, who is now openly chain-smoking. "Now walk and talk like the fucking promise that you are, and I'll follow you all the way.

"They're waiting, *monsieur*."

The security guys are looking antsy as they guide us through a main lobby that's all high arches and renaissance artwork. They pause by a set of huge, twelve-foot wooden doors with black iron pintles set into the stonework.

"Your weapons please, gentlemen," one says briskly.

"Aren't you going to ask her?" I nod at Issa. "She's more deadly than all of us."

With her shocked gasp ringing in my ears, I drop the clip from my Glock and hand it over. Reluctantly, Frankie does the same.

"Welcome to Château de Morcerf," one announces with a smirk as the doors swing open with ancient groans. "*La Società is expecting you.*"

Well, they could have invested in some fucking lights.

That's my first thought as we're led into a long, dark room that's bathed in the same sinister crimson as everything else. A large mahogany dining table sits dead center, set with twenty-four chairs, and finished with more gloss than a teenage girl's lips. All are occupied except for the one closest to us. Black suits. Black masquerade masks on their faces. There's a whole load of sinister in this room that instantly gets my back up.

"What the hell is this?" I say loudly, and all heads turn to me with a rustling of fabric and a squeaking of leather. "Don't tell me this is some kinky *Eyes Wide Shut* shit. If so, please point us straight to the orgy room and we'll be on our way."

There's a long pause, and then the man at the head of the table starts laughing—a rich and toxic sound that make the hairs on the back of my neck scream "danger."

I know that laugh.

It's a brown room with peeling paint. It's warm Limoncello. It's a faded 1994 World Cup Soccer Squad picture on the wall that played witness to a deal I never should have made.

Slowly, he unmasks himself, but I know his name already.

"Take a seat, friend." Tommaso Zaccaria's harsh accent slithers down the dining table toward me. "It is time for enlightenment."

Issa is squeezing my hand so tightly she's going to crack bones in a minute. Frankie's a mute statue. I'm as curious as I am guarded.

"I came here to agree terms to a Riviera deal between *La Famiglia* and Dubov's *Semion*, Zaccaria." I glance around at the other men in the room. "Looks like a couple more crashed the party." I swing my gaze back to him. "For someone who purportedly just joined this cult of weird, old man, you appear to be calling a lot of the shots."

"There is no Riviera deal, Aiden," he says silkily, his composure making the blowback of truth extra bitter. "It was a fabrication to get you right where I wanted you."

Not a muscle on my face betrays my shock. "I'm not a fan of manipulation, Zaccaria," I warn. "From my wife, or otherwise."

"Ah yes... The delectable Ielena Dubova." He cocks his head for a better view of Issa. "Step closer, *dolcezza*. I wish to see your tragic beauty for myself."

"*Mrs. Knight* is feeling a little shy this evening," I clip back, moving in front of her. "She'd prefer a sweet sherry, if you have it. Maybe even a vodka Red Bull to give her wings so she can escape this horror show through a turret window." Keeping Issa tucked behind me, I saunter forward a few steps. "Is Dubov even here?"

"Pietro," he calls out, ignoring my question. "Please escort Mr. Adams and Mrs. Knight away. This business is not theirs, but they can watch from the sidelines if they so desire."

"They're not going anywhere." I yank Issa even closer.

"Then we'll have to do it *La Società's* way."

On cue, there's a chorus of cocking guns from the security guards behind us.

Fuck.

"Go," I urge her as one of the guards approaches, but when I drop her hand it's like I'm carving out my own heart.

I then watch, scowling, as Frankie and Issa are escorted at gunpoint to the corner of the room.

"Take a seat, Aiden," says the *Capo Dei Capi*. "The truth has been a long time coming."

"You're telling me." I yank the chair out and glare at my neighbor. "This rolling stone is mostly moss after fourteen years of this shit... I want that name."

"Do you have my caveat?"

"Yes." I seek out Issa's face. She's a shivering vision in gold and courage: a lioness who doesn't know how sharp her claws really are. "My wife was most accommodating in that respect."

Her shocked gasp is a nice touch. Her Russian curses are even better.

"Where is the sister?" I can feel the Italian's cold, dead eyes mocking me from twenty meters away.

"The Royal London Hospital," I say without hesitating. "Bonus points if you can guess the location."

There's another pause, so long this time I can feel my foot tapping out a rhythm of unease. My attentions turn to a large, square box that's sitting right in front of me. It's the old-fashioned kind—some kind of expensive wood with shiny metal hinges. Engraved into the top is the outline of an ornate key, with the words *La Società Villefort* stamped underneath it in my least favorite color.

"What's in there?" I ask.

"Something that will set you free." Zaccaria clears his throat. "Gentlemen, if you would be so kind…"

Hands drift toward faces as, one by one, the black masquerade masks fall away.

Ho-ly.

Shit.

Heads of state and formidable leaders, both underworld and overworld… The kind of power that only dissolution and dirty money can buy.

"I didn't realize I was in such esteemed company," I drawl, catching sight of Dubov's face opposite. "Except for my father-in-law, of course. How's the chest? I hear it's burning on the inside now, as well as the out."

Dubov doesn't react, but he's staring straight at me, bludgeoning me with an unspoken message. His words from last night filter into my head.

"Tomorrow, there will be a choice for you. I fear that you will choose poorly and destroy my daughter's heart, as I did to my own wife's heart when the same choice was mine."

Never going to happen. Issa's heart is locked in a vault deep inside my casino, and not even Danny Ocean can crack it open.

"Shall we get this party started?" I make a big show of stifling a fake yawn. "Most of you look like acid jazz aficionados. As for me, I'm more of a…" I trail off when I realize half the men here are younger than Zaccaria, some by a decade or two.

"Villefort is a retirement insurance policy for a particular… generation. As corrupt men grow older, they grow weaker. They make mistakes—mistakes that can cost them a life's work, reputation, and fortune. There are no wrongs that Villefort cannot put right. Murders go unsolved. Illegal bank accounts remain

hidden. Tax evasion becomes a game."

It's a hard moment when you realize that the better player has outplayed you.

Fuck.

Without asking for permission, I flick up the lid of the wooden box. There, lying on a plush crimson cushion, is a black metal key that matches the design of everything else around here.

"We've been expecting you, Aiden. For a long time now."

"Fourteen years," I mutter.

"Indeed." Zaccaria flashes his white teeth at me. *He must brush them at least five times a day to remove the bloodstains.* "I became a member of *Villefort* thirty years ago."

"From three months to thirty years… That's quite a leap. Any more lies you'd like to confess to?"

"We are more than just a protection service," he continues tersely. "The earth spins on a clap of our command. Every country is our playground. Every government is under our auspices. If we want power, we take it. If we desire money, we kill for it. We are the people behind the headlines and the whispers in dark corners. There is nothing we can't steal, no mountain we can't conquer. We take societal justice and we make it our own. Put simply, we *are* the world, Aiden."

"You're making me feel like a bad date," I joke, forcing myself to inhale and exhale and hold my shit together. "If you were a member all this time, why string me along under the hoax of my parents' justice?"

"The fourteen-year membership application period is real. But it was never for me, Aiden… The application period was for *you*."

"Me?"

"You need this, Aiden. It's in your blood."

"My blood is mostly sponsored by Glenfiddich these days." *And the only thing I need is black and gold and trembling.* "Thanks for the offer, but I decline. Ergo, you have my permission to take my membership application, make a paper airplane out of it, and fly yourself back to Sicily…" I make to stand up. "After I have that name you owe me, of course."

"By the end of this evening you will be gorging on the answers to every secret," the Italian retorts, his composure finally slipping. "I suggest you take your seat again and stop holding up the proceedings."

There's a plan… I came here with a plan

Casting my gaze around the room again, I tick off the names in my head. It's all the heavy hitters and the pro players, the drug lords and the arms dealers—all except for one.

"Do you wish to know why the application process is a period of fourteen years, Aiden?"

"No, but I have a feeling it's going to be rammed down my throat anyway." I turn to seek out Issa's reassurance again and discover her mask of shock. Frankie's face doesn't fare much better. If it gets any whiter, they'll be performing an autopsy on him.

"We give people a taste of our power and a sip of our wealth. If you offer a dog the tastiest morsel of meat, it learns to crave it above everything. We turn our applicants into slavering beasts." He concludes this with a cold smile. "We socially isolate, we taper their emotions until all they feel is avarice, revenge, and gratitude. Everything else is an unwanted distraction. We alter their psychological maquillage by offering them something that becomes their obsession."

My parents. He's talking about my parents.

"And then we make them pass the test."

My head jerks up from the box in front of me. "What test?"

"We rip it all away from them," he says, his dark eyes gleaming. "We sink them like a ship. If they swim, we offer them a choice—full membership of *La Società Villefort*—or nothing. A life of destitution. No money. No friends. No family. You will be cast from this château with nothing but the clothes you are wearing."

"Tomorrow, there will be a choice for you."

I laser beam in on Dubov again, but he's staring straight at the table.

"And what did *you* sacrifice, Zaccaria?"

There's a pause. "I gave up my firstborn son. I gave him to a man in London, a distant associate who promised to care for him until I gained sufficient leverage to ascend the ranks of *La Società Villefort* and rescind my sacrifice in exchange for his inclusion."

I always hated surprises.

"Surely you're not suggesting—?"

"It is an agony of no comparison… To have your flesh and blood raised in squalor by another man. Your son. Your heir. To never watch him make the vows of *Omertà*. To have a Zaccaria denied his made man status."

"To be a *father* is a gift, not a right," I grit out. "Jacob Knight will always hold that title for me. The best thing you ever did was to give me away to that family. Their deaths will still be avenged… I'm disowning you, Zaccaria, at the same time you're supposedly fucking claiming me."

"You have no choice in the matter." He turns to one of the men next to Issa. "Pietro."

A beat later, my wife is being strong armed up to the table with a gun to her back.

"Let her go, Zaccaria!"

"So now it begins." He slowly rises to his feet. "This is the initiation process where we systematically destroy your life for the ultimate gain. Are you there, Stefano?"

A loud voice comes booming into the room via a sound system.

"Yes, Signor Zaccaria."

"Is it done?"

"His five bank accounts have been frozen, all fourteen properties in his portfolio have been signed over to you. Nineteen bars, clubs, hotels, and other legitimate establishments are now in the possession of *La Famiglia*, and all other assets have been seized, including *The Cristo*."

They better not take—

"One black Maserati has been seized, as well."

Motherfuckers.

Zaccaria tilts his thin lips at me, the grooves in his face swallowing me whole like a sea creature. "And the casino?"

"Is now in the name of your second son, Luca Zaccaria. I believe he's there as we speak, making the necessary changes and arrangements."

I catch Issa's eye for a third time. *It's only money, sweetheart.* I grew up poor. I can make it again. Fuck it, I'll sell my suit, make a grand, and rent an apartment in the arse-end of Marseille if needs be. I don't care, as long as I have her.

She smiles, and I feel a rush of emotion that no mafioso could ever take away from me.

"Excellent work, Stefano."

"My pleasure, Signor Zaccaria."

But not mine.

I watch his gaze slither back to Issa and my stomach sinks

like a stone.

"Leave her out of this!" I roar. But I'm cruising a fucking avalanche here, and the only way to stop is to hit rock bottom.

"Play the tape," he orders.

More voices filter into the room, ones that I recognize from twenty-four hours ago in my casino office. *What used to be my casino office...*

Mine.

Her father's.

"I am not in love with your daughter, Dubov, but neither do I think of her as damaged goods. I fuck her out of duty. I fuck her to keep my end of the bargain."

"Wait!" I slam my fist down on the table. "There's a goddamn context here." I swing round, but all that greets me is pain.

"I am not in love with your daughter, Dubov."

"I am not in love with your daughter, Dubov."

"I am not in love with your daughter, Dubov."

Some sick fuck has put my words on a loop, drilling my lie into every person here, including the one who I'm lying directly to.

"Issa." I stand to go to her and find a gun jabbed against the side of my head. "This was before…" *Before we laid our souls bare. Before our two halves of a heart became a whole.*

When she doesn't respond, I feel like I'm drowning.

"What about Eloise Dubois?" growls Dubov suddenly.

"What about her?"

"Why don't you tell my daughter how you threatened her life last night."

"Bullshit!"

"You played me a tape of us together," he accuses. "Footage

that you stole from her store security cameras. The threat was clear: If I didn't leave Eloise alone for Ielena's sake, the consequences for her would be dire."

"You had footage of them?" Issa looks even more devastated by this. "You promised me no more lies, Aiden."

"Again, context!" I feel like I've taken bad coke—I'm talking, but acting too shit-faced to hold anyone's attention. "I know what she meant to you. I wouldn't jeopardize us like that." But she's already backing away from the table and Pietro's letting her leave with a big fat smile on his face.

The click of her departing heels is the worst sound in the world. The slam of the door plunges me into darkness. I try to follow and get pushed down into my seat again.

"I never expected your wife to be such a thrilling part of this evening," crows Zaccaria, clearly delighted by the turn of events. "She was supposed to be a pawn in this game, not a queen."

"Then why the hell was she?" I say harshly. "You said it yourself. There *is* no Riviera deal. There was never any need for an arranged marriage—"

"She isn't just your sacrifice, Knight," says Dubov slowly. "She is mine as well. Sixteen years ago, I gave up the chance of a relationship with my daughters. A female sacrifice is valued less in *La Società Villefort*. I was required to lose all three."

"Regret it much?" I snarl. "And by the way, I didn't kill Eloise Dubois."

"No, we did," admits Zaccaria. "*La Società Villefort* has a strict code that we must abide by." I watch him pin Dubov with an icy glare, before giving the man sitting next to him the same—a man who looks unnervingly like his oldest son before he was gunned down in front of me a couple of days ago. "Occasionally, certain members need to be reminded of our rules."

"Are you done yet?" I say idly. "Can I get that drink now?"

"On the contrary." Zaccaria smirks. "Pietro!"

I'm starting to associate that man's name with a gong chiming at the gates of hell.

The ground tips again when I see Frankie being pushed toward the table.

"You let very few into your world, Aiden. I take full credit for that. I taught you well. But we needed leverage for when the time came, so leverage was created."

I open my mouth to refute it, and then I see Frankie's face. Broken.

Guilty.

"Why don't you share Karina Dubova's true location with the room, Mr. Adams?" he says, slam-dunking me in a steaming vat of betrayal.

"Cambridge, Addenbrooke's Hospital," I hear Frankie mutter, and I know it's hurting him as much to say it as it is for me to hear it.

"Good. Very good. But let's not stop there. Please give my son the name he's been so avidly seeking."

His head drops, and the avalanche hits the ground. The impact steals my breath away and rocks me forward in my chair.

No.

"For fuck's sake, Frankie, *tell me it isn't true!*"

I never thought of myself as a desperate man. I've never pleaded for anything. I was planning to take and take until I ran out of wanting.

Until now.

I'd do anything to hear him refute Zaccaria's claim, and I'm prepared to get down on my knees and beg for it.

"Of course, at fifteen, he needed assistance in decapitating

Jacob's head." Zaccaria chuckles darkly. "Lorenzo Gambino was more than happy to lend a hand."

"Then I'm happy I repaid the gesture."

They're strong words for someone this weighted in misery. My elbows are driving crevasses into the mahogany table. My head hangs low between my shoulders.

"Raven," hisses Frankie. "Raven, look at me."

I hold up my hand to permanently silence him. *My parents took him in and he betrayed them worse than Judas.*

I don't even flinch as the security guards set upon him like a pack of wolves, smashing his bones into silence as the rest of the room watches, unmoved. I feel his pain, though. *I feel it like he's still my brother.* When they're done, they drag his limp body into the corner and throw him down like dead meat.

"You ordered the hit didn't you, Zaccaria?"

He nods. "The time was right to cut the old ties and begin the application process and your education."

That's one hell of a confirmation.

They didn't deserve it.

Dad's laugh—as carefree as the one I've always aspired to have.

Mum's kindness—as true as the one my wife throws to me in a perfect game of catch and release.

"I'm going to kill you for this," I say calmly.

"No, you won't. You'll make the right decision when I ask it of you, because you are my son."

Never.

"Why did you break in and leave the business card next to Gambino's head in Siena?"

"We always leave a tribute to those who have served us loyally."

"And Eloise Dubois? How did she serve you?"

His face darkens. "That was no tribute. She was a warning. Dubov made the grave mistake of requesting to leave the *La Società*. As a result, another female sacrifice was required from his family. Once you enter the brotherhood of *La Società Villefort*, you can never leave. Eloise was Dubov's sister... Mattia Rossi required the same *incentive* this week, and so his son was terminated."

"And Karina Dubova?"

"She was to be another punishment for Dubov. Luca was planning to show her the color of our displeasure. But I've since learned that she's dying anyway."

There's a croak of pain from Dubov's direction.

Maybe he gives a damn about his daughters, after all.

"Enough!" booms Zaccaria suddenly. "The time has come."

There's movement from all around the room at this. Backs straighten as he rises stiffly from his chair once more, his expression fervent, like a priest who's about to issue me my last rights.

"Aiden Knight. Born Alessandro Tommaso Zaccaria. You are a man with nothing. We, the men of *La Società Villefort*, offer you everything. We offer you the opportunity to rule as you were born to. Do you accept, or do you choose a life of poverty, opacity, and solitude? Of dying like a dog, like the man who raised you?"

"Well, when you put it like that..." I glare at Pietro, who's moving up behind me again. "Can I get some fucking room here, please?"

All eyes are on me as I slide my hand into my jacket pocket and wrap my fingers around my father's old lighter. "I'm not going to lie, Zaccaria... If you'd asked me this six days ago, I would have accepted. No question. But you fucked up, old man. You sent sunshine into my Black Skies Riviera. You sent hope to a broken raven, and she unclipped his wings." Pulling out the lighter, I flick the hopeless flint wheel, and for the first time in years it produces a flame that's bright and solid. "You may have twisted me into your image for fourteen years," I continue, "but I had sixteen more with the man who really made me." At this, I reach into my other pocket to pull out the small black MI6 listening device that I had planted on me all along, and slide it across the table at him. "In conclusion, Zaccaria, I won't be joining you and your band of unmerry men. In the plainest way possible, I'm telling you to go fuck yourself, along with the twenty or so British Intelligence Agents listening in on this conversation in their Batmobiles outside… I also find it pretty poor form that everyone else in this fucking room has a drink except for me." Picking up my neighbor's full whiskey glass, I chuck the entire contents across the table. A split second later, my father's lighter follows suit and the whole thing erupts into red and amber hellfire.

"Burn with it, you bastards," I roar as pandemonium breaks out in shouts and cries, and bullets start whizzing past my ear. Dropping to the floor, I hear the sound of more gunfire outside, and then the doors are flying in on themselves.

Armed agents start pouring into the room to add their own brand of gasoline to the proceedings, but the thick smoke has turned their visibility to zero.

Keeping low and moving fast, I find Frankie's body and roll him over. To my relief, he's still breathing.

"Get up," I croak. "We need to move."

"Why?" he wheezes. "Finish it, Raven. For years you've lived and breathed for this moment. If I had a loaded gun, I'd hand it to you myself."

"Because my wife has a thing about forgiveness, and I need to get back in her good books."

"Don't deserve it." His words dissolve into an ugly coughing fit.

"The way I see it, we were both fucked over."

"I'm not going with you, Aiden. My leg is broken."

"Then hobble. Hop. Do the one-legged conga. I'm not leaving here without you."

He grabs my shirt, and I see the determination in his eyes. It's the kind that not even God himself could talk down. "Go."

There's a pause. "Why did you do it?"

His face crumbles in pain. "I have a sister. They threatened to kill her if I didn't. I wish—"

"There's a hell of a lot of regret going on in this room."

"Go," he repeats, his voice growing weaker. "The British won't let me die. I'm too good a witness for them."

"I'll get you out, brother. Wherever you end up."

"Did you hear what I said? GO!"

I can't see my hand in front of my face anymore. I start crawling where the air is cleanest, fumbling along walls for the outline of a side door.

I hear Zaccaria scream out a name through the smoke and the chaos, but I answer to Aiden, not Alessandro.

The next time he screams it, I'm already gone.

Despair is carved into my every step as I stumble back through the lobby and out under the portcullis, its sharp stakes now representing the ones piercing my heart.

We never expected all the members of *La Società Villefort* to be present.

I never expected a man like Aiden Knight to be capable of love.

I never expected his confirmation of that fact to hurt this badly.

And Eloise…

Did he really kill her?

My gut says no, but everything about tonight is proving unpredictable and cruel.

The security guards on the door jeer at me as I rush past them, with tears streaming down my face.

"Where are you going, *bebe*? We'll make you smile again."

Only Aiden has that power.

Night has fallen, changing soft shadows to dark wounds. The lines of cypress trees look more like enemy soldiers now. They're not the proud guards that greeted us when we first arrived.

The guards are still calling after me as I reach the end of the driveway. I veer left onto the main road and toward the two white vans parked up there.

The doors fly open as I approach. Maxim reaches me first and pulls me into his arms. I feel his reassurance bleeding into my skin and my tears increase. "Issa. Hush, *zvezda moya*," he croons. "It is nearly over. I received Aiden's message. We need to get back to *The Cristo* as soon as we can."

"We can't," I gasp out. "*La Società* has taken it away."

"Then we drive and drive until we figure out a new plan. He'll catch up with us, Issa. You know he will. Here," he shoves a burner cell into my trembling hand. "Read this."

A minute later, I catch Maxim's eye and the sweetest note of relief passes between us.

We don't need the British and their protection anymore. They never would have extended it to Aiden anyway, no matter what miracles he pulled off tonight. I made a judgment call earlier, and now Karina is safe and recovering in a new, top-secret location.

"I can't leave him behind, Maxim."

"He'd kill me if we didn't leave when we could. There isn't a place in this world where he won't find you, Issa."

"Ielena Dubova?" Maxim releases me as a smart lady in tight jeans and a blue shirt comes marching up to us.

No, it's Ielena Knight, now and forevermore… Even if my husband can't love me.

"Caroline Fletcher, Field Agent," she announces briskly.

"You did well in there. Your husband is doing even better."

"I'm taking her home," says Maxim.

Caroline sizes him up for a beat. "Fine. But stay in the harbor. We'll swing by once this operation is over."

"Fletcher," yells a voice from inside one of the white vans. "That's Knight's cue. We need to move."

Moments later, Maxim and I are speeding past the gates of Château de Morcerf, with heavy hearts and destinations unknown.

Chapter Thirty

AIDEN

I bring the stolen car to a screeching halt next to the quay. I can feel my heart pounding through the bloodstains on my shirt.

I have to get to Issa. I have to touch her, to taste her. To bring it all home to her. There's so much crap to sift through, so many revelations to come to terms with, and so many lies to dispel. I need her soft calm to help me unpack the chaos.

Am I too late?

I'm praying Zaccaria was lying about *The Cristo.* I'm imagining pushing open my cabin door and finding her lying there…

It's summertime, so *Port Hercule* is a hub of money and prestige. Every spare berth has been booked up for months, and at first glance it's impossible to distinguish *The Cristo* from all the other superyachts.

I break into a jog, checking the bow of each vessel in turn. When I reach the end of the dock, I jog back again to repeat the process.

Where the fuck are you, Issa?

Pulling out my cell, I hit her number but the call rings out. I try again, and the same thing happens. That's when I remember she never took the device with her to Château de Morcerf.

By now, I've completed a second lap and uneasiness is spiking the pit of my stomach with jagged thorns and barbed wire.

"Fuck!"

I sweep my gaze across the remainder of the harbor, but it's a pointless endeavor. My yacht is simply too big to berth anywhere else.

She wouldn't leave without me. Not after everything... Would she?

Exhausted, I fall to my knees by the edge of the water as the sounds from the nearby bars and cafes drift over me. It's the kind of mockery I used to deliver with relish.

She's gone.

It's all gone.

I roar her name at the empty horizon, but only a lifetime of lonely nights and barren days answer me back.

"When you're quite done howling your broken heart at the ocean, let me know," drawls an amused voice from behind me. "I have something that might interest you."

A man in a tailored, blue three-piece is standing ten meters away. Wide stance, hands in pockets, shrewd expression... His head is cocked slightly to the side, suggesting an air of amusement at my misfortune.

Prick.

"Who the fuck are you?"

"FBI special agent Roman Peters," he says, canceling out my roughness with his New York smooth.

"A little out of your jurisdiction, aren't you?" I say, groaning inwardly. "I take it you have an international warrant?" I hold my arms out, inviting him to cuff me. "Go on then. What are you waiting for? Whatever you're accusing me of, I've probably done it and worse."

He doesn't budge, though. He doesn't even glance down.

"I also go by another name, Mr. Knight," he says. "But only to close friends and acquaintances, of which you are neither. However, at my sister's request, I've chosen to make an exception."

"Let me guess... You're the Easter Bunny?"

"I'm afraid not." He laughs, but it's the stiff, scornful sound of a man who finds humor a challenge at the best of times.

"The Tooth Fairy?"

"Roman Petrov."

This makes me pause. "Petrov? As in Andrei Petrov's son? The Bratva boss?"

"*Former* Bratva boss," he corrects tersely. "He died several years ago. Nina Sanders is my half-sister. I also have the less agreeable honor of counting Senator Rick Sanders as my brother-in-law." His lips twist into a wry smile. "Unfortunately, he's starting to grow on me."

I drop my hands back down to my sides. "What are you doing here? Actually, don't answer that." I swing my gaze back to the ocean. "My life has just fucking imploded, so if you're not here to arrest me I'd like to get on with piecing it back together again." I pull out my cell to call Maxim, but he's not answering either.

"Perhaps we can help you with that." He takes a step closer until I'm glaring him back into submission. "I represent an organization that has developed an...interest in you, Mr. Knight."

"If it's a secret one with a pretentious name, it's a hard pass."

He laughs again, and this time it sounds almost genuine. "The man I work with has no need for such protection."

"What man?"

His eyes travel to a black Ferrari that's parked a little way along the dockside.

"This morning, Nina received a call from your wife requesting urgent assistance in transporting her sister to a private hospital facility. I was happy to oblige. I happened to be in Europe on business anyway."

"FBI business?"

"Santiago Cartel business," he says, casually dropping a bomb into the conversation, and then smirking when he sees my expression. "You've caught the attention of the really big players now, Aiden."

"I don't give a fuck how big the players are. I just want my wife back."

There's a noise behind us as the driver's door on the Ferrari swings open. I watch a tall beast of a man climb out under the white haze of a streetlight. When he moves in our direction, he's stealthy and uncompromising, like a tiger catching a scent. He's dressed in black jeans and a black T-shirt, and the sharp blades of a tribal tattoo stain his left arm.

"Aiden Knight," says Roman briskly. "I'd like to introduce you to—"

"Dante Santiago." He extends a hand to me, his deep growl wrapping around my throat like a fist. "Rick Sanders intimated that you might be in the market for some new business opportunities."

"Mr. Santiago," I greet, feeling the full force of his

intimidation. This man's Most Wanted image is as commonplace on the internet as Bob Marley posters on dorm room walls. "What opportunities are you referring to?" I ask, reclaiming my hand quickly.

"The mutually beneficial kind." His eyes drift toward the shadowed hills of Monte Carlo, flashing white and gold in the darkness. "I have a large amount of money that needs cleaning. I hear you're the man to talk to about that."

"Not anymore," I say ruefully. "From six a.m. tomorrow, I'll be a wanted criminal. The Monaco government will be revoking my *Carte de Resident, Ordinaire* status soon after that."

"What if I told you I could reinstate you in your casino... I could even get you your boat back." The corners of his mouth start to twitch. "I'm afraid you'll have to buy yourself a new Maserati, though."

"That's very generous of you, but the only thing I want is my wife."

"My own wife would call that an affliction of the heart... Eve has a way with words that spins darkness into light." His gaze starts to drift again. "What if I said I could help you with that as well?"

I stare at him for a moment, and then I'm holding out my hand again.

"If you help me find my wife, Mr. Santiago, we have ourselves a deal."

Epilogue

ISSA

Eight Weeks Later...

There's a café here that reminds me of him.

I find his past in the crimson awning and in the knives and forks on the white plastic tables. They glint like blades as the sun creeps around the pink-domed bell tower bordering the small bay. I find my future in the colors of the ocean: deep, cerulean-blue like his eyes. The lack of tide means that the hue is unflinching. Never wavering. Like the love I feel for him. Like the love I'm longing to make with him.

I miss those eyes.

We drove all the way to Marseille that night, catching snippets on the news about a huge fire on the outskirts of Cannes and the subsequent arrest of twelve fugitives. With my heart pounding, I listened to the list of names, but Aiden's was never mentioned, and neither was my father's.

Tommaso Zaccaria's was, though. There's a new caged bird on the Riviera, and this one will never be released.

To stop the British tracking us down, Maxim left his cell in Monaco. It meant that there was no way for Aiden to contact us, and for us to contact him. It still kills me to think he might have looked upon my sudden disappearance as my last act of betrayal.

After reaching Paris, we'd called Rick Sanders to make sure everything was okay with Karina at the private hospital he was funding for her, and to let him know that we'd be making our way to the UK as soon as the police heat had died down. I didn't ask him for the price of his compassion. Men like him never do anything for free. But however beholden we are to him now, having Karina safe and well was an easy trade-off to make.

I was hoping he'd crossed paths with Aiden, and I'd asked him as much. That's when he'd told me to go and live the dream that I'd shared with my husband one night in Cannes, when he'd bought me perfume and I'd fallen even more under his spell.

That's when I knew where Aiden would come for me.

We've been in Collioure ever since, that small picturesque seaside town of light and color on the *Côte Vermeille*. It's even more beautiful than I remembered, but it's also emptier somehow.

"Collioure has no shadows," or so the artist Andre Derain would like us to believe. In a way he's right, but for me there will always be one: the shadow of longing for better things to come.

Karina was finally well enough to travel here last week. As I sit in the café sketching fishing boats, I can see her and Maxim walking slowly, arm in arm, along the stone promenade. The transplant was a success and she grows stronger every day. We still have a long road ahead of us, but the loose grit in our lives is starting to level out into something smoother.

"Excuse me, *madame*?" A waitress appears at my table with a tray laden with goodies. Without further ado, she starts to unpack a bottle of red wine and two glasses in front of me.

"I'm sorry, you must be mistaken," I say quickly, as she reaches for her corkscrew. "I never ordered any—" That's when I catch sight of the label:

Saint-Émilion.

2001.

With a soft cry, I drop my sketchbook and rise to my feet, my eyes scanning frantically, but never daring myself to believe.

That's when I see him.

He's leaning against the sea wall about fifty meters away, wearing black like the free raven that he is now. He crooks his finger at me, and I smile despite the tears streaming down my cheeks. Instead of complying, I repeat his gesture, and then watch as he tips his head back and laughs.

That's where we meet again: halfway between his wall and my café; halfway between his desire and mine. When I feel his strong arms wrapping around me, I know there isn't a color in the world that could capture this moment.

Urbane.

Savage.

Beautiful.

And more. So much more.

"The 2015 is the better vintage," I blurt out.

"Bullshit... The 2001 is far more subtle, and it's less prone to being emptied over Armani suits."

"I've missed you."

"I love you."

I pull back to look at him, certain I've misheard.

"I wanted to tell you in that fucking château," he says, shooting me that crooked grin of his. "I wanted to scream it after you, but Pietro had other ideas."

"Where have you been, Aiden?"

"Busting Frankie out of jail, getting *The Cristo* back, establishing a couple of new businesses for a really dangerous criminal." His grin widens. "It's good to be bad, and I'm not planning on changing anytime soon... Your father sends his regards, by the way. He'd like to come and visit you and Karina. I said you might be washing your hair—permanently."

"I'll think about it."

"Think or drink? Speaking of which, let's crack on with that bottle." He turns to lead me back to the café, and then stops. "Wait, I have something for you first." He reaches into the pocket of his jeans and pulls out a folded packet of papers. "Here. It's a letter from my solicitor."

I open it up and the world stops turning. "You want a *divorce*? Aiden, I—"

He captures my face between his hands, the fierce love in his expression driving roots down deep into my soul. "We're doing this thing properly, Issa. The past isn't going to taint us any longer. I want to love you right. I want to marry you right. The minute you sign those papers, I'm down on one knee with a ring that'll dazzle fifty shades of purple, for all I care. Just as long as you want me back."

"Yes," I rasp, my eyes and my heart so blindingly full of him.

He lowers his gaze to my mouth. "Kiss me like you mean it."

"Is that a dare?"

"It's a request, embellished with a fair amount of begging and pleading. It's been a long eight weeks and I need to taste you again."

I close the distance between us to half... Always half. Because we're two parts of the same whole, and the child growing inside me is the perfect outline.

"Come and get me, Raven," I whisper.

Acknowledgments

To my husband and my two beautiful girls. So many sacrifices were made for me to be able to write this book. I sank, you rescued me. I cried, you hugged me. Cancer kicked me again, and we kicked back harder. I love you more than words can say.

To childhood summers spent in the South of France. To playing on the small beach in Collioure, and then running back to my parents who sat at the cafe with the red awning. To cheap meals, cheap hotels, but to memories as rich as Aiden Knight himself.

To Cora, Sammy, Sheri, Kathi, Sally and Julia. Thank you for cheering me on from the sidelines. This book was hard and I floundered more times than I care to admit, but you never let me flounder for long.

Amanda Marie and Sheri Glaesman. Thank you for your excellent last minute (because it's always last minute with me) proof-reading and editing skills.

To all the book bloggers and bookstagrammers who are still taking a chance on a sort-of rookie. Thank you. Thank you. *Thank you.*

To Jo and all the team at Give Me Books PR. Thank you for being so wonderful and supportive in every aspect of my life! #fuckcancer

To Maria at Steamy Designs. Thank you for taking on all my

demands, not disowning me, and for weaving your magic!

And finally to the readers. You make every invasive scan, test and operation worth it. I'll be writing these stories for you until they prise my laptop away from my lifeless fingers! Thank you for making all my dreams come true.

Catherine

P.S. Please consider leaving me a review on Goodreads and Amazon. I'd be so grateful.

Wiltcher

SINFULLY SEXY ROMANCE

About The Author

Catherine Wiltcher is an International Bestselling Author of ten dark romance novels, including the Santiago Trilogy. A stage 4 cancer thriver and a self-confessed alpha addict, her writing is best described as sinfully sexy and her characters always fall hard and deep for one another.

She lives in the UK with her husband and two young daughters. If she ever found herself stranded on a desert island, she'd like a large pink gin to keep her company... Cillian Murphy wouldn't be a bad shout, either.

For newsletter sign-ups and book updates, please visit
www.catherinewiltcher.com

Made in United States
Orlando, FL
07 September 2022

22061593R00217